HEAD GAMES

ESSENTIAL PROSE SERIES 98

Canada Council for the Arts
Conseil des Arts du Canada

ONTARIO ARTS COUNCIL
CONSEIL DES ARTS DE L'ONTARIO
50 YEARS OF ONTARIO GOVERNMENT SUPPORT OF THE ARTS
50 ANS DE SOUTIEN DU GOUVERNEMENT DE L'ONTARIO AUX ARTS

Guernica Editions Inc. acknowledges the support of the Canada Council for the Arts and the Ontario Arts Council. The Ontario Arts Council is an agency of the Government of Ontario. We acknowledge the financial support of the Government of Canada through the Canada Book Fund (CBF) for our publishing activities.

HEAD GAMES

Erika Rummel

GUERNICA

TORONTO – BUFFALO – LANCASTER (U.K.) 2013

Michael Mirolla, editor
Guernica Editions Inc.
P.O. Box 117, Station P, Toronto, ON, Canada M5S 2S6
2250 Military Road, Tonawanda, NY 14150-6000 U.S.A.

Distributors:
University of Toronto Press Distribution,
5201 Dufferin Street, Toronto, ON, Canada M3H 5T8
Gazelle Book Services, White Cross Mills,
High Town, Lancaster LA1 4XS U.K.

First edition.
Printed in Canada.

Legal Deposit – First Quarter
Library of Congress Catalog Card Number: 2012953447

Library and Archives Canada Cataloguing in Publication

Rummel, Erika, 1942-
Head games / Erika Rummel.

(Essential prose series ; 98)
Also issued in electronic format.
ISBN 978-1-55071-687-0

I. Title. II. Series: Essential prose series ; 98

PS8635.U56H42 2013 C813'.6 C2012-907657-0

ACKNOWLEDGEMENTS

I wish to thank my friends who read the manuscript in its various incarnations and gave me the benefit of their advice: Gisela Argyle, Antonio D'Alfonso, Karin MacHardy, Charlotte Morton, and my husband, Erwin. My special thanks go to Michael Mirolla, whose critical comments were invaluable in giving the novel its final shape.

THE SUMMER OF '78 WAS full of signs, but Lisa found them hard to read. The certificates on the wall of Dr. Lerner's office, for example. They looked reassuring, and turned out to be useless. Maybe they were too square, too black and white – like the office itself. Not a curve in sight, nothing to soften Lisa's longing for answers.

She tried to concentrate on what Dr. Lerner was saying, but the white walls were forbidding. She missed out on a question, something about personal space, and to cover up said: "I don't know."

The whiteness of the walls was spreading, settling in her brain like a blanket of snow, burying all thought, muting all sound. A string of words was coming out of Dr. Lerner's mouth, but Lisa was reduced to lip-reading and didn't catch the meaning.

She took a deep breath, and said: "I can't take any more of this crap." She exhaled, and "crap" rode the crest of the air, bounced against Dr. Lerner's cultured prose, and shattered like a cry.

"I'm sorry if my question made you uncomfortable," Dr. Lerner said in her even voice, the impenetrable armour of her profession, which no mild expletive of the "crap" kind could pierce. "Let's try a different approach." And she went on as if Lisa's cry hadn't happened.

Lisa didn't need more questions. She needed answers. Now. But Dr. Lerner insisted on the proper sequence, beginning with Lisa's childhood. They had to go from A to B to C, and through every letter of the alphabet. It slowed things down to a crawl. They were years behind Lisa's life. And even if she could talk about her present troubles, it wouldn't help. Dr. Lerner had no answers. She always sounded crisp and cheerful as if they were on the point of a break-through, but then she stalled and said, that's something we should explore further. Why didn't she just tell Lisa what was wrong? She had it figured out already. Why was she holding back? What good were the framed credentials on Dr. Lerner's wall if she refused to tell Lisa what to do? She always used the same old dodge: "I can't answer those questions for you."

Lisa waited until her fifty minutes were up. She didn't have to look at her watch. She could tell the time by the way Dr. Lerner rustled the papers and put down her pen. The session was over, and Lisa hadn't figured out a thing.

Dr. Lerner launched into her official last sentence. "I suggest we start at this point again when I see you next week," she said in her fluty, dictionary perfect voice.

Lisa left without saying good-bye. It wasn't a day for niceties. She had no intention of keeping the next appointment. The inside of her brain had faded to mushroom grey. It used to be Kodachrome in there. Something was blocking the spectrum. Lisa wanted the colours back, and Dr. Lerner's method wasn't working. She wanted someone to take her by the hand and say: This way, Lisa. But it was as if she had a contagious disease. Nobody wanted to touch her, get close to her, help her with her questions. Except Don Baker. He was the only one who really cared, who wasn't reluctant to give advice.

Okay, Don wasn't the ideal mentor. For one thing, he was old, forty-nine he said, although he looked older with those bruise-coloured bags under his eyes. He wasn't a man to fall in love with, more like a favourite uncle, old-fashioned and nice in a teddy bear-cuddly way. He didn't hold out on Lisa, didn't brush her off. He listened to her. If she asked him for advice, he told her what to do. She got together with Don at The Yellow Parrot every Monday after her session with the therapist – she needed a drink to rinse out her mouth and get rid of the bad taste Dr. Lerner's questions had left behind.

The patrons at the Parrot were mostly Latino, immigrants looking for a place where they could be themselves and forget Toronto the Good, where they could talk about the old country and swap stories about jobs, soccer, and family. Don wasn't Latino, but he'd spent years in Ecuador and Bolivia, in a jungle outpost with oil reserves, he said, and in a windblown town with silver mines. He always wore a blazer and striped tie. It was a holdover from the days when he was in the diplomatic service.

"Really?" Lisa said when he first told her. "You were in the diplomatic service?" She wasn't sure whether to believe him. Some people said Don was a liar. Maybe he was, but he wasn't out to cheat you. It was more like kidding you, trying on stuff to see your reaction. The stories he told weren't all that different from the games Lisa liked to play in her head, which sometimes became so real that they blended into her life and became indistinguishable from the truth. So she didn't mind Don fudging his life or lying about his career. She understood. His life wasn't anything to brag about. It wasn't a success story. He was in real estate now.

When he mentioned the diplomatic service, she only smiled and said: "Are you serious?"

"Well, it wasn't the champagne and caviar circuit," he said. "I was in trade law enforcement." Blazer and tie was the ceremonial garb of authority in places where life was cheap, where a man's signature meant nothing, he said. He was serious for once.

"So what happened?" Lisa said. "Did they fire you?"

"No," he said. "I left because they kept posting me to godforsaken places. I quit and got a job as a contract specialist with an engineering company in Argentina. In Catamarca.

"Catamarca!" Lisa said. "That's where my parents are from." Six degrees of separation, she thought. Or was it more than that, was it a sign? "How long were you there?" she asked.

"Five years. The job didn't work out in the end. But never mind my so-called career, Lisa. Let's not talk about me. Let's talk about you. Your parents are from Catamarca?"

Lisa almost came out to him then, almost told him her problem, the fact that her father wasn't her father and so, of course, she didn't know who she was herself, and that was probably why her life didn't come together and all she could do was try on different roles and look for a fit. She was about to tell Don of the scenes playing in her head, the different roles she had tried out, but she held back. She wasn't sure it was the right time to open up to him. Better wait for a definite sign, an omen, something to tell her it was okay to go ahead.

When Lisa walked out of Dr. Lerner's office that last time and stepped into the street, she was undecided: was this the right day to talk to Don? There was nothing to guide her, no signpost. Standing at the curb, watching the cars go by, she made a bet with herself: If I spot a Dodge Polara in the next five minutes, I'll go to the Parrot and talk to Don. If not, I'll skip the pub and go home.

She walked slowly around the block, turned into Balmuto Street, and saw that the Botanica was having a sidewalk sale. A bin sat outside the store, filled with a jumble of headbands, sticks of incense, bottles of shampoo and bath oil. Lisa still had four minutes left to spot a Polara. She watched the passing cars out of the corner of her eye and rummaged through the bin. The bottles of bath oil had strange labels: *Court Case, Money Bag, Peaceful Home, The Answer To Your Prayers*. Maybe an answer to her prayers was better than sighting a Polara. She picked up the bottle and went into the shop.

She knew the owner. He was a regular at the Parrot. Someone said he was from Bolivia. She had talked to him only once, but he was the type who took root under your skin.

Lisa put the bottle on the counter and smiled at him.

"How's it going, Santos?" she said.

"Ah, you remember name," he said. His skin was the colour of dusk. He blended in with the grimy inventory of his shop, odd pieces of furniture, mostly junk, cheap knick-knacks, and holistic stuff.

Santos looked at the label on the bottle: *The Answer To Your Prayers*. "You need answers?"

Lisa nodded.

"Bath oil no good for your problem," he said, turning the bottle over in his hand and back again, as if weighing it. "It make you feel good tonight. Tomorrow: same problem again. You need real answer."

"And where do I get real answers?"

"From the Saint."

"I'm not religious," Lisa said. "I don't believe in saints." But she began to waver when she looked into

Santos' dried-mud face. The whites of his eyes were glow-in-the-dark.

"You will believe, when you talk to the Saint," he said. "He come to me when I call him, but is much work, much trouble. For him and for me. He dead a long time, you know. Ten years."

She looked at Santos. He was leaning on the counter, fingers spread wide. His hands were like two palm leaves, a Palm Sunday promise of good things to come.

"You ask the Saint," he said. "We have séance when is full moon. On Friday."

"Not this Friday," she said. "That's my mother's birthday."

An hour before Lisa had been lost in a snow storm, a white-out, searching for directions. Now there were signs everywhere, but she decided to stick with the first one: *The Answer To Your Prayers.*

"Maybe we can do the séance another time," she said to Santos.

He shrugged and rang up her purchase.

Lisa put the bottle in her purse and stepped out into the street. *The Answer To Your Prayers.* It was the sign she had been waiting for. Now she could go to the Parrot and tell Don about her problems. Lisa's mood lifted. A drum roll went off in her head. The curtains parted. She was ready to play Queen of the Night. On second thought, no. Playing Queen was too demanding. She wanted someone to take care of her tonight. She was going to be Baby Love.

When she got to the Parrot, she ducked into the washroom and put on black mascara for doll eyes, pink lipstick for a rosebud mouth, and a cloud of hairspray for satin curls. *Ooh baby love, my baby love. Tell me: what did I do wrong to make you stay away so long?*

JIM'S ROOM AT THE PARK Plaza looked out on the leafy campus of the university and the carved gargoyles of the Royal Ontario Museum. It was a room with an executive view. It meant he was up for promotion. Unless he blew the presentation the following morning.

The thing was not to get uptight about it.

He switched on the TV and watched a sitcom, got restless, turned off the set, rifled through the pages of his presentation, realized he knew the words by heart and couldn't improve on them, kicked off his shoes and settled back on the sofa. Couldn't relax, sat up straight again, walked across the room and looked into the mini fridge. Nothing he wanted.

Maybe I should go downstairs and have a drink at the bar, he thought. Or call Don. There was no one like Don Baker for talking you down or easing you out of a snit. He was a man of epic stories and bottomless anecdotes. He was the world's greatest bullshitter. He and Don had met on the Catamarca project, two ex-pats reluctant to head home after work to a company-furnished apartment. Instead, they spent their evenings at a bar on Rivadavia. They sat at a sidewalk table, drinking brandy, talking, turning their faces to the pale winter sun. They watched the passersby, made scrappy comments on the men in Italian suits and spit-polished shoes and laughed at the women dressed up in fur jackets even though the subtropical wind had no bite. Happy hour on Rivadavia. It was a daily ritual, until Don resigned from the project. Some people said he left because of a scandal involving an under-age girl. Others said he had doctored his resume and was asked to leave. At Christmas he sent Jim a calendar with glossy pages depicting ranch bungalows and happy couples strolling on green, suburban lawns. Don's business card was stapled to one corner with a note: "Found my niche in real estate. Give me a shout when you're in Toronto, Jim."

He was in Toronto now, sitting in his hotel room, his head rustling with anxiety about tomorrow's presentation. So why not call Don Baker?

He dialed the real estate office, and Don answered on the second ring.

"Jim!" he said, instantly clicking on the name. "Good to hear from you." His voice wasn't as hearty as Jim remembered it. He sounded as if he was fielding a call from a client, but then he pumped up the register. "So how long are you in Toronto? Are you doing anything tonight? Let's go for a drink."

"Sure," Jim said. "Where?"

"Let's meet at the Parrot," he said and gave Jim directions. "You'll like the place. It's got a South American flavour."

The Parrot was in a neighbourhood of small shops and gabled Victorian houses, most of them in a state of neglect, crumbling brick walls and peeling paint. Jim noticed a few exceptions to the decay – white-washed porches and windows trimmed with macramé curtains, a blossoming of the whimsical, but the meeting place Don had suggested turned out to be an unregenerate old pub.

Jim pulled open the door and looked down into a long, narrow space. There was a noisy bar on one side and a row of booths on the other. The tables had chromium legs and scuffed Formica tops, and the benches were upholstered in orange leatherette. The only décor was a neon sign in the window: *Wouldn't A Dow Go Good Now?* From the stairs leading to the lower level came the sounds of a band playing funk vamp. Jim had expected something more glamorous, something to show that Don had "found his niche in real estate."

He spotted Don at a table in the back. He hadn't changed much, same big gut, same stiff neck, and a face running to lard.

They shook hands.

"How is Catamarca?" Don asked. "How's the project going?"

"Alright," Jim said. "Except for the usual problems. The corruption, the hassles with the junta, the red tape."

Don sipped his drink, listening to Jim with an air of distraction. He kept scanning the people at the bar and looking at the door as if he was expecting someone.

I'm boring him, Jim thought. He stopped talking about Catamarca. There was an awkward pause as their conversation dried up. The beat of the rock band in the cellar seeped through the taproom floor and played rim shot with Jim's head. He changed tack and asked Don about his new career. The question kindled a half-light in Don's eyes. He broke out the real estate anecdotes, a few warm-up jokes, then something with a little more jangle, but sadly below the old standard. It wasn't Happy Hour on Rivadavia – no fireworks, no exploding laughter.

"Last year I listed a property a couple of blocks from here," Don said. "A three-story Victorian with a shop on the main floor and two flats upstairs. They laughed at the office when I brought in the listing.

Nobody is going to buy that dump, they said. The owner lived on the second floor, with a dozen cats. Her bedroom was a feeding station. Litter boxes and cat food everywhere. The tenant on the third floor was a wino. The place smelled of piss. Next thing you know: the cat lady has a heart attack and ends up in hospital. The Humane Society carts away her pets. I visit the old woman in hospital and make her a bedside offer: I buy the house myself. Let me tell you, Jim: she was glad to get rid of it. It was nothing but a headache for her."

Jim grinned obligingly. "And so you bought the place? That was charitable of you." He noticed that he was humouring Don. Something had happened to the familiar landscape, a tectonic shift. The gap in their ages had widened. It was no longer the difference between thirty and fifty. It was something larger and unbridgeable. Don had turned into an old man who had to be humoured.

Don drained his Scotch. "Wait till you hear the rest," he said, signalling the waiter for a refill – his second refill. He was on a roll now. "So I get a new tenant for the shop and start renovating the old lady's apartment. I slap paint on the walls and have the floors sanded and refinished. The wino comes padding down from the third floor to see what's going on. 'How's life at the top?' I say. He breathes alcoholic fumes on me. 'Crappy,' he says. 'The whole city is crappy. A shit place to live in. You pass out on the sidewalk, and people step right over you, like you're a dog. Where I come from, they don't treat you like that.' He was from Sudbury, he told me. 'So why did you leave?' I said. 'Got fired from Inco,' he said. 'It's a company town. You work for Inco, or you don't work. I should've stayed up north and gone tree planting.' So I make him an offer. 'You want to go back to Sudbury, Frank?' I say. 'Sure,' he says, and starts reminiscing about family, classmates, neighbours. He goes all weepy on me. 'Jeez,' he says, 'we had a ball of a time. Jeez, I wish I could go back there now.' So I say: 'Tell you what, Frank, I'll buy you a ticket to Sudbury.' We drive to the bus terminal. I give him some pocket money and bundle him on the bus. You know the old Stompin' Tom Connors tune?

Well, the girls are out to bingo
And the boys are gettin' stinko

"Frank starts crowing, and half the bus joins in the Hallelujah chorus:

And we think no more of Inco
On a Sudbury Saturday Night!"

Don leaned back with a mission-accomplished grin. "So everyone's happy. I go back and tell the crew to paint the upstairs as well."

Jim tried to picture the wino in Sudbury, against a background of pine forests and granite boulders, pushing seedlings into the ground. "And Frank lived happily ever after?" he asked.

"Never heard of him again," Don said with a wide hand gesture. "Anyway, to come to the point of the story. A few months later I sold the place at a nice profit. The client fit the profile: upwardly mobile professional woman with an eye for interesting architectural detail. And really, in this kind of market, you are doing the client a favour. The house was a solid investment. The prices have nowhere to go but up. The signs of gentrification are everywhere. Take this street, for example. A year ago it was all rooming houses. Now there are three or four whitewashed façades and a boutique. In a couple of years the whole street will be chi-chi."

Don had developed a new spiel, with a real estate theme, but his voice had lost its upper range. It didn't reach the high C. He no longer knew how to command applause.

"This place, too," he said, waving at the bar. His movements were getting vague now that he had drained his third Scotch. "It could be a goldmine. If I owned the place, I'd get rid of the band in the cellar, set up a disco with strobe lights and a couple of go-go dancers in cages suspended from the ceiling. The place would be hopping, I guarantee you." He looked at Jim bleary-eyed. "You should think about investing, Jim."

Jim didn't reply. The real estate spiel didn't turn him on. He felt cheated of his expectations, like a kid discovering that the magician's trick was only a sleight of hand.

Don was cradling his empty glass and staring into space. The alcohol had started to immobilize him. His head looked like a piece of meat in cold storage. Suddenly something – the door opening, a draft of air – caught his attention. He sat up and looked past Jim, smiling.

Jim turned and saw that he had his eyes on a Latina. She waved at Don and made her way to their table, doing a kind of cha-cha, mouthing the lyrics to a pop song, snapping her fingers as if she wanted to wake up the whole place. She had Don's attention at any rate. He looked moon-struck.

"Lisa," he said when she arrived at their table. "You are late today."

"There was a sale on at the Botanica," she said. "I went in and talked to Santos."

Don's face dropped. "What's he selling?" he said. "Snake oil?"

Lisa patted his shoulders and said in a purry voice: "You're in a bad mood, Don. Want me to go away?"

"No, I don't want you to go away," Don said, and his body went into a praying curve. "Sit down. Have a drink." He patted the empty chair beside him.

Lisa sat down, letting her denim skirt ride up and flashing her pink tube top at Don. "Okay," she said. "I'll have a beer."

He ordered a Molson for her and did the introductions. "Lisa is working at a nursery school around the corner."

Jim could see her playing dress-up with the kids. There was something childishly impulsive about Lisa's motions. One moment she was patting her hair in a gesture of submissive grooming, the next she was popping her shoulders in little jerks. Jim couldn't take his eyes off her.

"You live around here?" Lisa asked.

"No, I'm in Toronto on business," he said.

"He's heading the project in Catamarca, the one I told you about, the one I did the contract for," Don said and started rolling out a long carpet of South American anecdotes, working his old magic for Lisa. Jim let him take over the conversation and gave his full attention to Lisa, opened a mental file on her, tracking her shenanigans: Bites nails. Licks fingers after eating chips from Don's plate. Traces figure eights into the spilled drink on the table. Picks label off beer bottle and makes little scrap heaps. Slurps the last of the suds and laughs hysterically. Can't stop laughing, inhales droplets of liquid, starts coughing, hiccups through tears. Jim gave her top marks for animation, but there was a flashing beacon at the end of his tip sheet: Danger. Do not cross the yellow line. Lisa had an unfiltered openness about her, a lack of reserve that unnerved him.

Don was still spinning anecdotes. Jim had heard them all before, but they seemed to have shifted shape and become a little more colourful in the telling. Maybe Lisa had heard them too. She got restless, wiggled her bum, cut in, and asked: "So how long are you staying in Toronto, Jim?"

"Until the end of the week," he said. There was something about Lisa, an uneasy longing in her eyes, a coded message that fuelled Jim's body heat, overriding the danger sign in his head.

"Lisa's folks are from Catamarca," Don said.

It was as if he had pressed a button at the back of Lisa's head. She opened her mouth and spilled the family history, pouring out a river of words, as if she had always wanted to tell Don and had just waited for him to give the signal and open the flood gates. She was a natural storyteller like Don, although she couldn't match his scope. She kept to one topic, went at it from different angles, but all points of departure led to the same dark corner: she didn't know who her father was. That was her leitmotif: she was searching for her father.

"Everyone needs a father, don't they?" she said. "You need to know your roots – right? Or else you don't know who you are." She had a fixation on the question of paternity. She told them the story piecemeal: a guilty affair in the old country between her mother and a married man, her mother's pregnancy, her shotgun wedding to another man who believed the child was his, who still believed he was Lisa's father. Those were the ingredients. Lisa mixed and stirred them into an embryonic broth of secret and forbidden things. "Really," she said. "How can you understand yourself, if you don't know your father?"

"One of these days I'll go to Argentina and look up my real father," she said, coming to the end of her story. "His name is Miguel Soriano." She mouthed the name with gusto, as if she couldn't wait to make him part of her family saga. She stopped and looked at them expectantly, waiting for their reaction.

"That's quite a story," Don said. He was ready to believe in Lisa's rogue father, but Jim had reservations. The Soriano character had a mythical sheen. Lisa laughed too much when she told the story. It was hard to say whether it was psycho-babble, or a soap opera dreamed up for their entertainment, or a fable with a moral he hadn't figured out yet.

Lisa saw the doubt in his eyes.

"You don't believe me, Jim?" she said and shot him a look, half pixie, half tortured soul. "Well, I can't prove it, but my mother was pregnant when she got married. And I know the man she married isn't my father."

She looked at her watch and was suddenly in a hurry. "My God, it's late," she said and got up from the table. "Thanks for the beer, Don. Nice meeting you, Jim." She waggled her fingertips at them.

Don tried to hold her back. "Can I give you a ride, Lisa?" he said.

He was puffy-faced with drink, in no condition to drive. Lisa saw it, too.

"That's okay, Don," she said. "I'll take the bus home."

WHEN SHE WAS GONE, DON said: "So what do you think of Lisa?" He was balancing his words carefully, trying not to lose his grip on the question.

"A little too intense for my taste," Jim said. He put resistance into his voice, the kind of resistance he meant to put up against Lisa's fatal attractions.

Don nodded, holding on to his empty glass, gathering strength for one last anecdote, one for the road. "She comes in here practically every day and chats up people. She has a tremendous need to vent. No one takes her seriously. They all think she's a little crazy. But I worry about Lisa, you know. She reminds me of my daughter, Asu."

Don had never mentioned a daughter before, but come to think of it, he'd never talked much about his private life, and what he told Jim was dated. He used to reminisce about his childhood, his mother's second marriage, the boarding school he attended, the dyed-in-the-wool British headmaster there. That's all he ever told Jim of his private life, and it sounded like an old spiel, a life condensed into a string of handcrafted anecdotes of the upbeat kind, stories he had told so often, they had turned into fossils.

"I didn't know you had a daughter," Jim said.

"I adopted her." Don shifted and stirred in his chair. "She was an orphan, but her grandfather treated her like chattel. If I wanted to adopt her, he said, I had to pay him compensation. That was his view of the matter. I had to buy her off the old man."

It was a new story, an exclusive that hadn't made the roster of Don's anecdotes. The Scotch had loosened his tongue, tricked him into telling what he maybe hadn't planned to let out.

"I was travelling in Northern Argentina at the time," Don said. There was a flush on his cheeks that drink alone could not explain – a confessional flush. "You've been to Jujuy, haven't you, Jim? The roads are like dry river beds. One of the tires on my car blew. Going on without a spare was risky. So I stopped at a *chacra*, a little farm, and asked them to fix the flat."

Don's voice was sodden. He seemed barely aware of Jim's presence. It was as if he was talking to himself.

"They were Quechua," he said. "I sat down on a bench and watched an old man vulcanizing the tire. He didn't talk much. Spanish was foreign currency to him, in short supply, tendered when needed. Apart from the old man, there were only women and children in the yard. You know, there is no employment in that part of the country. When the boys are old enough, they go to work in the mines of Bolivia. And the girls become maids in Salta or Tucuman. Or whores."

It sounded as if Don wanted to get the story off his chest, but was afraid to say too much. He stopped abruptly. There was a nervous furtiveness in his eyes.

"And Asu was one of the kids in the yard?" Jim said, winding him up again. The story was taking hold of him. Asu was still sketchy, but coming to life.

"She was a thin child, a little bird," Don said.

He gave Jim a one-cornered smile, a memorial smile for Asu. "They all looked malnourished," he said, "but she was more delicate than the rest. She was shy, hanging back at first. After a while she came and tried out a few words of Spanish on me. It broke my heart to think what was in store for her. I wanted to get her out of this hopeless situation. When the old man saw I took an interest in her, he said: 'You like the girl? She's ready to go to work.' 'I already have a maid,' I said. He smiled. He had a mouth full of stumpy teeth, yellow with decay. 'You tell her what to do,' he said. 'She's a very good girl. You take her for two hundred dollars.' I saw what he was getting at, what kind of work he had in mind for her. I played along. I made up my mind to rescue Asu. We started haggling. The women withdrew, discreetly left us to conduct the business by ourselves. I got him down to fifty dollars, which was all I had on me. It was a fortune for a man like him."

"And that was that?" Jim said. "Fifty dollars, and she was yours?"

Don shrugged his shoulders. "I paid up. He put the money into his back pocket and pushed Asu toward me. It was heart-breaking. The *chacra* was where she had lived all her life. It was the only place she knew, and he just pushed her away. 'Go, go,' he said and turned his back on her, didn't even wave good-bye when she got into my car."

Don stopped with a wriggle of unease. He was drawing back into his shell.

"And you adopted her?" Jim said. The question blocked Don's retreat, and he went on. It was a story that wanted out.

"Now here is the part that hurts," he said. "I took Asu back with me to Catamarca. I sent her to a convent school, gave her English lessons. I made sure she would have every chance to realize her dreams. But, no: just before graduation, she drops out and runs off with a gas station attendant." He paused, as if to reconsider his role in Asu's life, then shrugged his shoulders. "There was nothing I could have said or done to hold her back," he said. "She was in love. She left me a farewell note on the kitchen table, and that was the last I heard of her. She didn't bother to stay in touch with me. After all I did for her!"

"And Lisa reminds you of her?" Jim said.

"Well, I can't put my finger on it. There is no real resemblance, but Asu had the same craziness in her eyes."

The story had sobered Don up. He was returning to type, holding forth. "Those Indios live in a world of their own, a pre-rational world of magic and superstition," he said. "Lisa has the same take on things. She talks about signs – good signs, bad signs. She checks her horoscope. She jots down her dreams. She's looking for direction from above, the hidden meaning of things. 'Symbolic' is a favourite word of hers."

Was that the point of Don's story? That Lisa was superstitious? Was this about Lisa? Jim didn't think so. Don's sweaty excitement raised a flag. He was holding something in reserve.

"History has a way of repeating itself," he said grandly, starting to cover his tracks. "I am afraid Lisa will make the same mistake and fall for an unsuitable type. You heard her mention Santos?"

"He's an 'unsuitable type'?"

"A shady character. He called me up last year and said he was the nephew of someone I'd known in Catamarca. I showed him around town. I took him out for a drink. I shouldn't have brought him here. He kept coming back, sitting at my table, sponging drinks, asking me to help him get started in business. He was a pain in the ass. In the end, to get rid of him, I set him up in a shop on Balmuto Street, in the house I used to own, the one I told you about. I waived the first month's rent. It was an antique store, well, you know, second-hand stuff, knick-knacks. He could have made something of it. He promised to fix up the shop, but he didn't. It's in worse shape now than it was when I owned the house. And he sells weird stuff there: incense, bath oil, herbal medicine, and a whole lot he keeps under the counter. He's a dealer, you know. I've told Lisa to stay away from him, but I really shouldn't get involved. When it comes to women, I tell myself: Careful, old man, don't look, don't talk, don't listen."

Don was back to playing his cards close to his chest.

He can't fool me, Jim thought, I've seen the way he looks at Lisa. Let him pretend his feelings are dormant and his brain in hibernation. He is smelling spring time and coming up for air, sniffing. He's on a mission. He wants his daughter back, but he'll take Lisa in a pinch.

THE RECEPTIONIST AT HEAD OFFICE looked up and gave Jim a smile like a welcome poster. Her makeup was flawless, her beehive hairdo lacquered to shining perfection. Propped up on her desk was a small plaque saying: *Hi! My Name Is Claire.*

"Let me take you to the conference room, Mr. Brooks," Claire said in her Bell-trained voice. She got up, thrust out her pointy breasts and touched the single strand of cultured pearls around her neck to make sure they were still in place. "Everything is ready for your presentation," she said, heel-clicking on the terrazzo floor of the reception area. Her words were like little puffy clouds. "The caretaker has set up the slide projector, and I've mimeographed the statistics you sent us." She showed him into the board room, where the chairman was waiting to introduce him to the department heads.

Jim was ready for them. He looked at the men around the table and began his presentation with the good news: the project was on schedule. He used the right blend of words: The Catamarca team had met the challenge, fulfilled the mission, exceeded the expectations of the stakeholders. The visuals came next. Jim showed them slide after slide of the construction site, kept up the tempo, gave his audience no time to catch their breath. The solid wall of the dam cutting across the gorge was bound to exhilarate them. He knew exactly what they wanted, those earnest, square-jawed men around the table: proof of existence. They were in love with reality. Jim had them breathing in his words, but then something strange happened. It had happened a few times before. Halfway through the presentation, he began to despise his audience, dupes falling for his upbeat, celebratory voice. He felt a sudden disgust with his subject, with the sky-blued vision of the project, and a sharp discontent with himself, the way he had spiked his talk with mood-setting jargon. He was turning into a hack, giving a spiel, selling goods, selling himself. In spite of his self-reproaches, Jim's mouth kept going. He could hear himself talk; he could see himself reflected in the eyes of his audience. Jim Brooks, competent project director, effective speaker. He could see himself in their satisfied smiles, but really, he no longer knew what he was doing there, standing beside the slide projector. His voice suddenly sounded metallic, delivered by an operating system he was incapable of shutting off. He was tired of hearing himself talk, but the job had turned into an inescapable habit.

After the presentation, the VP took Jim out for dinner. They made pitch-perfect conversation. They were full of casual bonhomie as they toasted the success of the project, and Jim knew the meaning of the Masonic handshake sealing the evening. He had aced the presentation. He was up for a promotion.

Back at the hotel, he replayed the evening's conversation: snippets of the VP's praise, sales figures, contract clauses, a hint of opportunities opening up. He should have been pleased, but he felt only the familiar lowering of spirits in the aftermath of a command performance, the come-down-to-earth moment, the flattening out. Everything was predictable, a straight road from here to there, when what he wanted was a conga line, a snaking surprise performance, a fantastic journey, a new pop song in his head. Jim was afraid if he didn't change his life now, if he didn't find a cure for this flatness, his brain would seize and turn to concrete like the dam in Catamarca. That's why he ended up at the Parrot for the second night in a row. He wanted to see Lisa. She had the conga-line hips and the meandering mind that made all rational assumptions go away. Lisa was trouble, he knew, but he was desperate for her Barbie doll act, her psychic muck-raking storytelling act, and anything else she had in her repertoire that could take him out of his routine life.

When he got to the Parrot, he saw Lisa at the bar, talking to a short wiry fellow in jeans and faded T-shirt. The moment Jim saw him, he knew: this was the guy Don had mentioned, the unsuitable type, Santos.

Jim walked up to the bar. Lisa gave him a wave, but it wasn't a Barbie doll wave. She was on to a new act, something with a darker theme, a noir fantasy.

"Jim is working in Argentina," she said to Santos.

He gave Jim a nuclear smile and did a little on the spot jig, like Mohammad Ali limbering up for a fight. "Maybe Lisa go visit you," he said. The sweet smell of grass was on his breath and drifting into Jim's nostrils. "I tell her: she must go to old country."

Lisa swung her bouncy mane and gave Santos a starburst look. "I know I should go to Argentina," she said, "but it's too expensive."

"Is important you visit grave of fathers," Santos said to her. "The bones will speak." He waved his hands, as if he needed an updrift to keep the words afloat.

Lisa didn't bat an eyelid. Horoscopes, dreams, and voices from the grave all fitted perfectly into her grand narrative. Her problem was of a different kind. "It's not that simple," she said to Santos. "I don't know who my father is."

"Then you must look," Santos said. His hand went into a zigzag of encouragement.

"I am looking," Lisa said, and let out the story of her surrogate father. It was a variant on the one she had told Jim and Don the night before. This time she said her mother had been a nanny in the Soriano household.

"That's twenty-five years ago, and she still goes on about the girl she was looking after, Hetta – Soriano's daughter. You should hear my mother talk: Hetta was an absolute angel, Hetta was a darling, a princess."

Santos listened raptly. Weird radar waves were going between him and Lisa. They were feeding off each other's craziness.

"Such a talented child," Lisa said bitterly. "Everything that girl did was perfect, if you believe my mother."

"It mean: she want good daughter," Santos said with a gesture of exploding fingers.

"Right," Lisa said. "And I don't measure up to her idea of a good daughter. I don't measure up to Hetta Soriano." She started in on the story again, telling Santos of her mother's pregnancy and the shotgun marriage. Jim noticed, she didn't laugh as much as the day before. She became unmoored, slipped into a high pitch, smearing the words together. "But the man she married isn't my father. Of course I have nothing concrete to go on," she said to Santos, "except my uterine memory." She saw his puzzled look, and explained: "Before I was born."

"Uterine memory?" Jim said. "There's no scientific proof for that, is there?"

Lisa pulled down the corners of her mouth. "I don't care about scientific proof," she said. "I've got a definite feeling about it."

"Is important what you feel," Santos said, stirring Lisa's concoction and smiling into his inner mirror. "But is complicated. You need help of Saint. You come back to my shop, and we do séance. I call up Saint. He very wise man. He answer your question." The words tumbled out of his mouth, swept up and launched into the air by his spider fingers. Without warning, he bent forward, gripped Lisa's shoulders and pressed his nose against the side of her face as if he wanted to burrow into her head. "Like this," he said, lips moving against her cheek. "He enter. He look through your eyes. He see everything."

Lisa didn't move. She seemed stunned. Santos' sudden lunge forward had caught the attention of the other patrons. There was a stir of interest. The owner came over and said to Santos: "Can I have a word with you?"

Santos let go of Lisa, and the two men moved off to the end of the bar.

Lisa gave Jim an anxious look. The sound of rock seeping up from the cellar came to a thumping halt, and in the momentary silence they heard the owner say to Santos: "Get the fuck out of here and stay out, or I'll call the cops on you." He escorted him to the door, discreetly keeping in step with him. Santos tapped the wall on the way out like a blind man, or like someone putting a curse on the place. At the door he stopped and looked back, flashing Lisa a dead man's grin.

She gave him a distressed look. "I don't understand what's going on," she said to Jim. "He hasn't done anything wrong."

Except for the way he looks at you, Jim thought. With eyes that give you a sunburn. Santos was a storyteller like Don, like Lisa, but he didn't offer his fare with a take it or leave it shrug. He wasn't the kind who allowed doubt. He talked with the fervour of divine inspiration. He expected you to believe and never let go. But Jim knew that explanation wouldn't track with Lisa.

"He's a drug dealer," he said instead.

"That's what Don says, but it's not true," Lisa said.

"Maybe he bothers people in other ways," Jim said. The thumping from below resumed, and the din of conversation closed in on them. You had to raise your voice to be heard, but Lisa was whispering.

"Santos means 'holy'," she said, leaning in close. "He is a holy man." Jim was afraid of catching her mystic fever.

"Come on, Lisa," he said, fighting the contagion, the heat coming off her body. "That's crazy talk."

She teared up. "I thought you understood," she said. "But you're like the rest of them. You think anyone who is in touch with their feelings is weird." She wiped her tears and made mewling noises like a kitten wanting to be stroked by someone, anyone. Jim had no defence against Lisa's vulnerable promiscuity, her kitten noises. The blood rushed to his groin. He came close to surrender. He gripped the counter to keep his hands from straying in Lisa's direction.

"I have nothing against feelings," he said. "But there are limits."

Lisa didn't answer. She eased herself off the barstool.

"I'm going home," she said.

Jim watched her leave. He kept looking at the closed door as if he could follow her with his eyes and keep watch over her from a distance. A flower seller was making the rounds in the Parrot, holding out a bouquet to a couple in a booth. Jim waved him over and bought a bunch of roses. He needed something more than words to drive Santos out of Lisa's mind. For a moment he had doubts. It was Don who was supposed to rescue Lisa, who wanted to save her from unsuitable types. It was Don's job, not his. But the moment of doubt passed.

LISA WAS WAITING AT THE bus stop in the gauzy obscurity of the summer night. I don't stand a chance with Jim, she thought. I've ruined my chances the way I always ruin them when I like someone. I get too close, too fast. One moment, everything is super bright, saturated with colour, then bang. The lights go out. You need to respect people's personal space, Dr. Lerner said. Maybe that's what Jim meant when he said there are limits. But what limits? Santos, for example, didn't care about personal space. He put his mouth right up against her cheek when he said: *The Saint, he enter. Like this.* There were no limits for Santos. He didn't mind getting close, skin to skin.

Lisa tried to replay the scene in her head, and understand what was going on, with Santos, with Jim. It helped to replay a conversation, get everyone up on her mental stage, go through the dialogue or tweak it and try out a different version, to see which one worked best, but this time none of the scenarios gelled. Jim refused to play in her head and say the lines she had reserved for him. Santos kept interfering and taking centre stage. She could feel him moving in, fixing her with a stare, mesmerizing her. She was caught in his headlights. Their bodies collided violently, there was blood – no, not blood. Lisa came back to reality with a jolt and saw the roses, velvet crimson, wrapped in cellophane. Jim was standing beside her, holding out a bouquet to her.

"Why did you run out on me like that, Lisa?" he said. "I didn't mean to upset you."

She took the bouquet and started laughing.

"Red roses, Jim!"

It was a sign. She felt gales of laughter rising up, but she pressed her lips shut, and allowed only giggles to escape. It was bad luck to go too quickly from dreams to reality, from sadness to happiness.

When they took a taxi to her place, when Jim kissed her in the backseat, it was like a confirmation of the sign. The glow was back, surrounding them with rainbow colours. But, by the time they crossed the apartment lobby, Lisa's happiness was thinning. Going up in the elevator, she felt static in the air. Something was jamming the signals. Jim's voice had lost its elasticity. He was chewing his words like tough meat. Maybe the mess in the apartment turned him off. Pizza cartons and Mutt n' Jeff comics on the coffee table, unopened mail tossed on the carpet, an ashtray full of paper clips on the side table, an upside down hairbrush, a can of hairspray.

Lisa felt panicky. How to play a love scene against such a backdrop? She chose from the many roles in the hidden compartments of her brain one that was guaranteed to please: the belly dancer. Strip down to hot pink underwear, jiggle the midriff, keep in motion. It worked in any setting, but this time Lisa felt as if her mouth was filled with bubble gum. If I open my lips now, she thought, a pink bubble will blow out, so big that it will obscure my face. In her mind she could see the bubble burst and spew unopened mail, paper clips, assorted change, crumpled receipts, woolly lint. No, that was her purse sitting on the table, gaping open, contents spilling.

She was glad when Jim took the initiative and put his arms around her. She didn't object, but the belly dancing in her head came to a stop. She didn't know how to go on. What was the next scene after Lisa in hot pink underwear, chewing pink bubble gum? Lisa with big, bubbly lips? Jim's hands strayed up her legs, his tongue ran a bead on her neck, and she remembered the next move: supple, putty-pliable, pressing up against him. She was sure she could give a flawless performance, if only Jim did his job, the director's job, if he supplied the cues. She tried to get in tune with him, make his words part of the score in her head, but the music was garbled. Something was wrong. She stopped dead, and the scene fell apart.

"Maybe we shouldn't do this," she said into the silence that descended on them. "It works only when you are in love."

Jim didn't say: Then it should work for us because I'm in love with you. He cleared his throat and said nothing. Lisa could tell: it was stage fright, the fear of being caught up in the act. The fear was spreading like a nasty fog, making Jim hoarse. He wanted to break loose, slip out of Lisa's embrace.

He said: "Well, maybe I should go then." And under his breath he was saying: Ciao, Lisa, nice meeting you.

"No, don't go," she said quickly, holding him tight. "Let's just talk."

"Okay," he said. "About what?"

"Séances," she said. "Tell me what you think, Jim. Should I do a séance with Santos? I mean, would I get any answers?"

The sofa was too narrow for comfort. They were stuck in a semi-loving position, scrunched up against each other.

"You want my opinion?" Jim said. "Séances are a scam."

"But Santos has the right aura," Lisa said. "I sensed it the first time we met." She could feel Santos' presence that very moment. He was in the room with them, an invisible third body on the sofa. He had more emanations than the Holy Spirit.

"What aura?" Jim said. "He's a con man. You won't get any answers from him. What are you looking for anyway?"

"I want to find out about my father."

"Then talk to your mother. That's your best bet."

Jim's common-sense talk almost dissolved the Santos apparition hovering in the room.

"Ask her straight out," Jim said. "Maybe you'll get a straight answer."

"I can't talk to my mother," Lisa said. "It's no use. She won't tell me anything. I'm thinking of writing to Hetta Soriano instead."

Jim disentangled himself from her embrace. "The girl your mother looked after? What could she possibly tell you?"

"You mean I should write to Miguel Soriano directly?"

"I think you should forget the whole letter-writing business."

"Well, maybe you're right. Some things can't be said in a letter. I may have to talk to Miguel Soriano in person, go to Argentina and look him up."

"Or get a grip on your imagination," Jim said.

"What's wrong with imagination?" she said. "If I talk about what I've eaten for breakfast or what I've watched on TV – that's okay. If I talk about what's going on in my head and what's important to me, people think I'm crazy. Doesn't everyone have things going on in their heads?"

"Perhaps they do," he said. "But they keep them inside. It's the best place for them. Trust me on this, Lisa."

"I do trust you," she said, and melted into him with a puppy dog, lick-your-hand grateful move. "That's why I'm telling you what's in my head." She was looking for someone to let in on her dreams so they could watch them together in a complete network of the unconscious. She had been lonely for so long. "I want you to understand me, Jim," she said, and he kissed her.

"I understand you, Lisa," he said. "You think I don't want to escape from reality sometimes?"

Maybe he did understand, but something was lacking. Perhaps the belly dancer routine wasn't for Jim. Perhaps she should do the cabaret scene instead, a little number in net stockings and a corselet with a million sequins, shining and glittering. Or maybe she should dance the cancan for Jim, high-kicking it until her toes touched the stage lights and brought them down, one after another, until the stage went dark. Yes, it was working, the music started up. Lisa could feel the vibrations of her legs kicking the air, heard the swishing of her net stockings. The rustling got fainter and fainter until it was just a buzz in her ears, and then nothing at all, because they were kissing, she and Jim, and the action moved from the stage to her bed, from inside her head to her body, their bodies. For once she had read the signs correctly.

All next day Lisa felt warm with the promise of togetherness, the intimacy of shared dreams, but Jim didn't call. Not that day, not the next. On Friday, finally, he phoned. His voice sounded flat. He and Don were going to have a farewell dinner at the Park Plaza.

"Want to join us?" he said.

But Friday was her mother's birthday. And Santos was after her to do a séance because it was full moon. So she said to Jim:

"No, I can't make it for dinner. Maybe I'll drop in later, for a drink."

ON FRIDAY AFTER WORK, LISA took the bus to Willowdale, the suburban doldrums where fate was preordained and signs could never blossom. Everything was cast in concrete: the sidewalks, the front steps of her parents' house, the planter with the white geraniums. The tidiness turned Lisa into a zombie, force-marched her, one-two, up the path to the front door of the Martinez bungalow. The bells chimed a reveille. Her mother opened the door. She was wearing her navy blue suit with the gold buttons, which made her look like a stewardess. She was waiting for Lisa to give her a one-two kiss on each cheek.

One-two, Lisa handed over the flowers and the birthday cake she had bought at the delicatessen counter in Loblaws. The red and yellow icing on the cake twinkled through the see-through box top. Something was alive somewhere, specks of colour, rustling crinkly sounds, even if Lisa herself felt dead, even if this was going to be a one-two zombie dinner.

Her mother took the birthday cake and the flowers, one in each hand, no awkward juggling, she had perfect balance.

"You shouldn't have," she said to Lisa, meaning: *for once you did the right thing.* She was eyeing Lisa's pleather outfit. "Are you coming?" she said, meaning: *why didn't you change and wear something nice for my birthday?* She was good at saying one thing and meaning another, but Lisa could tell what's what. Her mother used a special pitch, a whining that alerted Lisa to the true meaning of her words. By now, she was an ace translator of her mother's whines.

"I didn't have time to change," Lisa said. She tried to manoeuvre by and escape into the living room, but her mother wouldn't let go.

"This outfit," she said and pinched Lisa's waist. "It's too tight on you."

Jorge – her mother called him "George" – came into the hall and said: "She's young, Maria. She can carry it off. Remember when you were twenty-two?"

She pursed her lips in reply, picked up the wrapping Lisa had left on the upholstered bench in the hall and went into the kitchen to put the flowers into a vase. "Don't forget to take off your shoes, Lisa," she said. "I just had the carpets cleaned."

Jorge put an arm around Lisa's shoulders and steered her to the pristine living room.

"How's life, *chica*?" he said with a conspiratorial grin and sat down in the recliner, keeping away from the freshly plumped sofa cushions. "Give your old father a kiss."

Jorge was okay. Lisa just couldn't think of him as her father.

They navigated the birthday dinner without running into any submerged icebergs. Lisa let Jorge do most of the talking. He handled her mother well, moved deftly between gallant and jocular, humoured her by eating voraciously. Maria took his show of appetite as an unspoken compliment to her cooking. She didn't mind cooking dinner on her own birthday as long as everyone ate heartily.

After dinner they moved back into the living room. Jorge lit a Derby and took the ashtray with him, holding it under his cigarette to avoid any accidental dropping of ashes on the carpet. He told his ancient after-dinner jokes to please Maria. In a *pas de deux* of mutual good will, she gave him a tinkling laugh of appreciation.

"You know about the Thousand Dollar cure they've come up with – guaranteed to get rid of your homesickness?" he said. "This is what you do: you sell your car and your appliances and buy a plane ticket. You get to Argentina. There are no jobs. The inflation is in the double digits. The government is as corrupt as ever. You return to Canada and buy a new car and new appliances. You lose a thousand dollars in the transaction, but you are cured of homesickness."

He laughed, hacking like a failing car engine.

"I don't know why you are so down on the old country, George," Lisa's mother said, smiling delicately.

Lisa ducked into the bathroom. Safely out of her mother's reach, she relaxed the smile muscles and exacted revenge for her unhappiness by dropping a sticky wad of chewing gum into the wicker basket. She tried a skit with her mother fighting off wads of gum sticking to her hands, webbing her fingers, but she didn't have enough time to develop the theme, and the bathroom was too glossy. It made her thoughts slip off the wall and crash on the tiled floor.

When Lisa returned to the living room with a fresh layer of camouflage smile on her face, she saw that Jorge was taking his *cafecito* over to the sofa.

Her mother said nervously: "George, please, don't. You'll spill coffee on the upholstery."

He looked at Lisa, and she gave him a secret smile. Her mother turned and caught her out. "Making fun of me?" she said. "You are just like your father."

"Like me?" Jorge said, with an exaggerated question mark, as if he, too, was questioning his paternity.

"You are both mockers. You can take that mocking smile off your face, Lisa. It doesn't look pretty, you know."

Lisa tucked in her smile and exchanged it for a pout.

Jorge studied her face. "Now she looks just like you, Maria," he said. "Like you on that photo I took of you at the beach, when you absolutely refused to smile." He did a perfect imitation of Maria's whine: "'I don't feel like smiling,' you said, 'and I'm not posing for the camera.' Where is the album? Lisa, bring the carton with the photo albums."

She knew they would get to that point sooner or later. Reminiscing about the old country was part of the ritual, a birthday present from Jorge to her mother, a special half hour of memories just for her, because Jorge wasn't a nostalgic man. For him the best part of life was now.

Lisa brought the carton.

Jorge picked out a photo of Lisa's mother in a one-piece bathing suit, blinking into the sun. "See?" he said. The large pores in his skin deepened and his little military moustache curved over his lips. "See? Same expression."

Lisa looked through the pile of loose photos at the bottom of the box and pulled out a group photo: two tiers of solemn men standing on rising bleachers, and a sprinkle of women in their Sunday best, sitting on a row of chairs in front, a precise configuration, a ziggurat pattern. Above the top tier, a blue and white banner, tacked to the wall: *Soriano Máquinas De Oficina*. And, in a bracket of golden laurels, the anniversary date: *50 años*. Fifty years of Soriano Office Equipment.

Jorge leaned over. "Haven't seen that one in a while." He pointed out a head in the front row: "That's the boss," he said to Lisa. "Soriano."

Miguel Soriano's face refused to come clear. He was stuck in the nebulous past of the group portrait, a tiny face, maddeningly unfocused but mysteriously illuminated in Lisa's mind.

"He was a clever fellow, Soriano," Jorge said. He pulled at his trouser leg. He had a habit of plucking at the crease of his right trouser leg, hitching it up and letting it go again. "*Sí, señor. Muy vivo.*"

"What do you mean, *vivo*?" Maria said. A frown appeared on her forehead. "He had brains, if that's what you mean."

"He was an operator."

There was a stand-off. Maria couldn't give full rein to her admiration for Miguel Soriano in Jorge's presence.

"I'm not sorry I quit that place," he said. "There was no future for me in Soriano's company. There was no future in Argentina. Period."

Jorge always said the same thing, used exactly the same words when he talked about that time in his life. And now it was Lisa's turn to say her lines. They each knew their part in the play, but today she couldn't be bothered with the chronology, going through one thing after another. She took a shortcut, impatient to get to the part that needed clarification. "So you came here," she said, speeding the narrative along. "And next thing, I am born."

Jorge winked. "Good things come from fast weddings, eh-he, young lady?"

"George," her mother said, "you are embarrassing Lisa."

"*Perdóneme*," he said. "I didn't mean to embarrass anyone." But there was a mischievous glint in his eye.

Lisa turned back to the group photo. The festive banner was a sign, beckoning her, pointing to something crucial. She bent forward and scrutinized the faces, one by one.

"Who is the kid in the front row?" she asked.

"That's Hetta Soriano," Jorge said. "And the woman beside her is Soriano's wife, Paula. She was a crazy bitch. Before she caught her golden boy, she was one of the girls in the typing pool. Not especially good-looking, not in my book anyway, but she strutted her stuff every chance she got. Large hips, fat ass." His hands moved in curves. "Well, everybody knew: she was crazy. They had to put her away. She's in a sanatorium now, Higinio says."

"Your cousin has the dirt on everyone," Maria said.

"He tells it like it is."

"I don't even want to read his letters," Maria said. "They are full of mean gossip. I never heard anything bad about the Sorianos when I worked for them. They were popular. "

"Oh, sure. Especially him. He was popular with the ladies. Half the women in the typing pool were in love with him. He knew how to lay it on. He was flashing money at them. That always impresses the girls."

Maria compressed her lips. She refused to be baited.

"He could afford to be generous with the ladies. He was filthy rich. Got rich on the backs of his workers, of course. Paid us minimum wage. But he didn't live to enjoy his money. He packed it in when he was what? Fifty-five? Stroke. Or was it a heart attack?"

He dropped the news on Lisa just like that, without warning. Miguel Soriano was dead. No discreet leading up. No black-rimmed announcement. It was another case of misleading signs, like the certificates in Dr. Lerner's office that left Lisa without counsel, like the red roses that left her without love. The golden laurels in the anniversary picture belied their promise. Miguel Soriano was dead. Lisa was lost in grief, and not allowed to show it. There were no condolences for the orphan.

"It was cancer," her mother said. "Hetta came back from Buenos Aires to take care of her father during the last year of his life. She was a devoted daughter." She looked in Lisa's direction, and Lisa knew what that look meant: *I wish you were like Hetta.*

"A devoted daughter maybe," Jorge said, "but what about her husband? She looks after her father in Catamarca. Great. Wonderful. Meanwhile her husband sits in Buenos Aires, in an empty house. So he finds himself another woman. Can you blame him? They should legalize divorce in Argentina, you know."

"The church will never permit it," Maria said primly.

It was too late for Lisa to go to Argentina and find Miguel Soriano, too late to ask him the crucial question and get – get what? His blessing? A biblical laying on of hands? No, just an answer to the question: "Who is my father?" Now there was only Hetta to ask, the angelic child, the last tenuous link to Miguel Soriano.

"I'd like to visit Catamarca someday," Lisa said, pushing down the choking sob, the trembling, cramp-inducing sorrow.

"You really should go," Jorge said. "I'll write to my cousin. Higinio will show you around Catamarca. Introduce you to the family."

No, Lisa wanted to meet the other side of the family. Hetta. She turned away from the photo, avoiding the child in the first row. She was afraid of giving away her itinerary by looking at Hetta.

"But it's an expensive trip," she said.

"If you want to go, Lisa, we'll chip in," Jorge said.

"How are the sessions with Dr. Lerner going?" Maria said. She meant: *We are already paying for your therapy, and now you talk about a trip to Argentina.*

Lisa wanted to say: But I didn't ask you to pay for my therapy, mother. It was your idea. You made the arrangements. You said I needed professional help, that there was something wrong with me, something I needed to get out of my system. You meant: *Let's sweep out your mind, Lisa, I want it suburban clean like this house.*

"The sessions are going okay," she said. "Maybe I won't need them much longer." She didn't want to get into an argument for which she had no come-back.

"A holiday in Argentina will do more for you than the sessions with the shrink," Jorge said. "They are a waste of time and money, if you ask me."

The anniversary photo was lying on the table. Lisa secretly put her finger on Soriano's face, bonding with the laminated surface of his skin. Afterwards when no one was watching, she held her hand up to the reading lamp and let the light play on the tip of her index finger to see whether Soriano's face had entered the grooves and taken hold, whether they were one in the flesh. She thought of Santos' offer to do a séance with her. It was the only way now to talk to Miguel Soriano, through the Saint.

She got up. "I have to go," she said.

"Already?" her mother said.

"I have to prepare things for tomorrow," she said.

She could feel the Saint rising up inside her, like a gathering storm, blowing away all doubts. *He will enter you. He will look through your eyes.*

IT STARTED WITH A SELF-CORRECTING shuffle, Jim thought, a conga line to escape the flatness of his life. That was the lead-in. Then came the build-up, Lisa's mewling kitten act. Then her apartment, like a Dixie whorehouse, dirty and exciting at the same time. He wanted to explore the dark corners, open drawers, and get into Lisa's secret places even though he was afraid of what he might find there – a fantasy life too rich for him, a cure for his ennui too strong to stomach. There was a moment when he hesitated, when he could have escaped and gone back to his straight and narrow life, but he lost his way in the chaos of Lisa's bedroom and couldn't find the exit. He stayed and played Lisa's game of make-belief. It was a mistake to get so close, to let her enter his bloodstream. It could take a lifetime to oust her, to filter her out of his system. The thought of Lisa's witchy black hair set a vein pulsing in his neck. The solution, he thought, was turning Lisa into a project. He could do anything with a project, shape it, handle it, turn it around, terminate it. He was an expert on project management. Let's define the scope: a make-over for Lisa. She wasn't a woman one could bring to a company dinner or brag about to friends. The light in her eyes was too crazy, her laughter had an airborne suggestiveness, her stories were too offbeat. Let's say the project was to shift Lisa from crazy to eccentric. With a few modifications she could be charming. All he had to do was develop a blueprint for a New Lisa and hire a crew to engineer the transformation. Or subcontract the job. To Don, for example, a man with proven skills in the makeover field. Don had transformed himself from contract man to real estate agent and converted a run-down house into an investor's dream. And he was willing to take on the job. He had said as much. So why not hand the project over to Don, or rather hand it back to him? The whole Rescue-Lisa mission was really Don's idea.

On Friday, Jim sloughed off invitations from colleagues at head office. He wanted to spend his last evening with Don and Lisa at the hotel, away from the Parrot, their smoky, down-at-heel home turf. The Park Plaza provided the right ambience to play genial host, show that he wasn't abandoning Lisa, that he had a therapeutic plan for her. He was putting her into good hands, and there was no reason why they couldn't remain friends.

Don said yes, he'd join Jim for dinner, but at the last moment he cancelled. He got an offer on a house, he said. He needed to shuffle back and forth between buyer and seller to clinch the deal. It could take all night. "That's the problem with being in real estate," he said. "You can't have a social life." Jim thought he detected an undercurrent of relief, as if Don was glad to escape the invitation, as if he had decided that their friendship had run its course, that they had exhausted all conversation topics. Everything that could be said had been said.

Lisa was apologetic. She couldn't make it for dinner. It was her mother's birthday. "She'll make a fuss if I don't stay for dinner," she said. "I'll join you for drinks afterwards, okay?"

So now Jim was stuck with Lisa, after-dinner, on her own. He consoled himself with the thought that she had made no cooing noises over the phone, had not even mentioned the night at her apartment. Perhaps he needn't worry about getting her out of his system. Perhaps Lisa had already demoted their affair to the level of just-friendship.

He had a moody dinner by himself, trying to figure out why he was in a funk. Was he in love with Lisa and not wanting to be in love with Lisa? Or was it the other way round? Was he upset because she had been cool on the phone, as if she didn't care for his company, as if he wasn't hot enough, didn't turn her on? That was probably it. Lisa had no time for his type, the uninspiring management type with an office-slackened physique, with a white smile and mousy brown hair – the hue peculiar to the once-blond. Jim's thoughts ran to seed after that. The Lisa-project was getting away from him.

He was left eating dinner with his morose self, eating too fast. He always ate too fast when he was on his own and had no conversation to slow down the chewing.

By nine, he felt like a zoo animal kept in lifelong confinement. Where was Lisa? What was he waiting for? He was wasting a perfect summer evening in a perfect romantic setting, the rooftop terrace of the Park Plaza. He looked at the stone balustrade surrounding the terrace, and thought bleakly: it's meant to keep suicidal people from jumping into the Bloor Street traffic below.

Nine-fifteen: no Lisa. He began to relax, hoping she wouldn't show. He would be off the hook. He could go and have a nightcap in the bar downstairs. Not a bad ending, he thought – when she arrived, wearing a faux-leather mini dress that jarred with the elegant surroundings of the terrace, the white tablecloths and the tuxedoed waiters.

"I can't stay, Jim," she said as soon as she was seated. She looked windblown, breathless, jumpy.

"What's the hurry?" he said, annoyed that she was jerking him around like that.

"I'm going to a séance with Santos. We need to do it tonight. Something about the moon phase and the fact that it's my mother's birthday."

When he didn't answer, she gave him a faint smile and said: "I was hoping you'd come along." Her eyes were wide, childlike. She had the jitters. She wanted to lay her head on someone's shoulder.

"Somebody has to protect you from yourself, Lisa," Jim said. "But I'm not the right man for the job."

Her expression changed, from nervous to helpless. "Please, Jim," she said. Her voice was a sugar-spun plea. "I'm scared to go on my own." She looked at him with moist Bambi eyes. Jim was afraid she'd start crying. To stop her he said: "Okay, I'll come along."

The Lisa-project was going badly. He was no longer in charge.

THEY MOVED FROM THE INCESSANT traffic of Bloor Street to the silence of Balmuto, where their footfall was audible. The block started out respectable with a small office building and a boutique, but after that it became seedy. The store fronts had a collective air of failure. They passed an unlit alley with discarded pieces of furniture looking like the flats of a forgotten stage production.

"That's the place," Lisa said and pointed at a shop window. "Botanica" was painted on the glass pane in a wavy line of red letters bordered by swirling leaves, a jungle suggesting hot stuff. The purple frame of the window was peeling. An old chocolate brown layer showed through the cracks.

Jim saw Santos in the neon-lit interior of the shop. His coarse black hair was dishevelled. He was sitting behind the counter, moving his shoulders to the sound of an inaudible beat, casting a brooding shadow like an apparition in a chaotic dream. He was looking out at Lisa and Jim, keeping them in his peripheral vision as they moved past the window and entered the shop.

"You bring him?" he said to Lisa in lieu of a greeting and without missing a beat of the music playing in his head.

She nodded. "I asked Jim to come along," she said. Her voice was thin with tension.

Santos looked at Jim darkly, considering the possibilities of reeling him in and landing him on the taboo coast. “I don’t know,” he said. “He don’t believe in the Saint.”

“Maybe you can make him believe,” Lisa said, shallow-breathing.

Santos looked unconvinced.

A wooden statue was sitting beside the cash register, a roughly hewn figure of a man dressed in black, face painted chocolate brown, with bushy eyebrows meeting in a V over the nose and a drooping moustache over a carmine red mouth.

“Is that the Saint you are talking about?” Jim asked to cut through Santos’ moody suspicion, to keep the possibilities alive for Lisa’s sake.

“No,” he said. “Is Jesus Malverde.”

“Jesus what?”

Santos looked past Jim disdainfully, contemplating the plate glass window. “Jesus Malverde. *Narco santo.* Executed 1909.”

He started drumming on the counter, patting it rhythmically with the palm of his left hand, doubling the beat with two fingers of his right, humming a low throaty tune.

Lisa looked dispirited. Her face was see-through. Her mood had faded to black.

“So are we going to have the séance or not?” Jim said.

Santos ran an eye over him as if to establish a pecking order. “We have séance,” he said, “but I don’t know if it work with you here.”

He led them past a row of dining room tables with upturned chairs piled on top, past worn chesterfields with scuffed armrests, to a moss-green felt curtain at the back of the shop. He parted the curtain and waved them through. The backroom was done up like a shrine, with a make-shift altar and flickering candles. The walls were hung with mirrors and plastic skulls wrapped in strings of beads – Halloween come early. There was a heady tang of incense in the air.

They picked their way through a delirious landscape, a parade of saints: Buddha statues, plastic Santa Clauses, a Christ child with outstretched arms, a gypsy woman with an apron of tinfoil. Jim looked at Lisa to see how she was taking it. She had an expectant smile on her lips. It was her kind of place, a little like her flat, messy and promising surprises. She looked at home with the puppet saints.

Santos left them standing among the paraphernalia and slipped a rumpled suit jacket over his T-shirt. He briskly moved a bucket with knives and scissors next to the altar. He rearranged the saints, paused, considered the effect, and added the bust of a wooden Indian. He mumbled a little, stopped again and fixed Jim with a mean look.

"He don't belong here," he said, talking to himself, shaking his head, sighing theatrically. "Sit on the floor." He took Jim's arm roughly, jostling him.

Jim settled on the floor. He wants to obscure my sightline, he thought, and keep me from calling his bluff. He expected some sort of knocking, spinning, exploding performance, a raid on the senses, something to slice through the nerve cable. He expected a hoax that depended on deep shadows, smoke and mirrors.

Santos motioned Lisa to go to the altar. He kept to gestures now, saving sounds for the main act. With articulate silence he crumbled incense in a tin can, lit it with a match, and spread the rising wisps of smoke in Lisa's direction. By the time he had pulled out a hand-rolled cigarette, the flame of the match was burning his fingertips. It looked as if he was lighting the joint with his fingers.

"Talk!" he said to Lisa. "Ask Saint!"

Lisa shivered as if she had been accepted into divine love and began the Soriano litany, doing an epic singsong of her family history. Her mood was solemn, overcome. Santos was riding her feelings. She was a natural medium, Jim thought. The perfect partner for Santos. A tight feeling caught in his throat, a surprise feeling of possessiveness and discovery. Lisa didn't need a makeover after all, and he was no longer ready to let her go, to hand her over. Not to Santos, not to Don. He was her watchman now.

Santos listened to Lisa with a smile like false teeth. His face was sharply divided, the lower half benevolent, the upper half brutal, menacing, incapable of being domesticated.

He pulled a pack of cards from his pocket and shuffled the deck.

"Pick card," he said to Lisa.

She pointed to a card. Her breath came in waves, crested and toppled.

He took the card, did a little mumbo jumbo prayer, and put on a pleased smile, as if Jesus had answered him in person. Jim was waiting for the fireworks to begin, preparing himself for exploding sounds, the flash of lightning, but Santos kept them waiting. He started moving around his saints again, brought out a bouquet of plastic flowers, set the pail of knives and scissors before himself, and finally got into the act.

He bent over the pail, hunchbacked and slack-jawed, making old man noises. The performance picked up speed. He gave a wolfish shudder, jumped up, and stamped his foot.

"Come back!" he shouted up to the ceiling. He shook his fist. He sucked on his joint and spit brown juice on the floor. "You ugly bastard," he screamed. He took off his shoes, rolled up his pant leg, and curled his foot into a painful arc. "I'll kick you – "

He stopped and said: "Ahh." His eyes had the look of junky satisfaction, a liquid rocking core. He took a last drag from the joint and stubbed it out on his tongue without wincing.

There was a shallow dish filled with green liquid on the altar. Santos took a gulp from it, swished it in his mouth, stepped up to Lisa, and with sudden fury spit it into her face. Jim started up. He wanted to protect her against Santos' wrath. "What the hell – " Santos spun around and screamed, not words, but a brutal and terrifying sound that travelled down Jim's ears whumping like a train.

Jim reeled, wire whipped by Santos' fury, his raw menacing stare. Santos moved his face closer to Jim until their noses almost touched. His breath fanned over Jim's face. It was acrid, an emanation of the netherworld. Jim could feel it seeping into his pores, dislocating his spirit, warping his skin.

Santos reached for the bunch of plastic flowers and began patting Jim's head and shoulders with it, working up a rapid rhythm. Afraid the rhythm would take hold, Jim moved his arm to fend off the magic, but Santos was already done with him. He jumped up, turned sharply, and dropped the bouquet into Lisa's lap. Her eyes were shut tight. Her face had the hard geometry of a marble bust. Green droplets were running down her cheeks like tears.

"Okay," Santos said with a smoky sigh, snapping his fingers at her. "Now pray."

Lisa opened her eyes and drew a deep breath. "What prayer?" she said. Her voice sounded tinny. She was dreaming with her eyes open. She had a concussed look.

Santos said nothing. He passed his hands over her face.

She closed her eyes again and began reciting *Our Father*. When she got to the end, she started over again, slurring the words. She slowed and trailed off. Her head hung back as if her spine was broken.

Jim could take no more. He scrambled up. "Enough," he said. "You've done enough damage." It came out hoarsely. His throat was parched.

Santos gave him a sightless look and slumped into a chair.

Jim went to Lisa and stroked her shoulders, ran a finger over her cheek, touched her lips, checking for signs of life. She came out of the trance, eyes heavy lidded, brimming with tears.

"Let's go, Lisa," Jim said softly. "Let's get out of here."

She made a feeble effort to get up from the chair and sank back again. She looked down on the bouquet of plastic flowers in her lap. "Oh," she said, "the flowers the old man gave me." The tears had left green streaks on her face.

Jim wiped her cheeks with the back of his hand.

Santos roused himself and took a few drunken steps toward them. "Go, go," he said to Jim. "Séance over. You drive Saint away. He back in Tilcara."

Jim pulled Lisa up and steered her toward the front of the store. She followed him like an obedient child.

Outside, the night sky was a dead colour, but the cool air was sweet. Lisa's arm was tucked under Jim's. She was leaning against him.

"I saw him," she said. "An old man wearing a black bowler hat."

"You mean Jesus Malverde?" Was she thinking of the statue on Santos' counter?

"No," she said. "The Saint. He was inside me, looking out. He didn't like what he saw."

Jim kissed her. "Lisa," he said. "Don't talk like that."

"The Saint wants me to visit him in Tilcara."

Jim held her close, wrapping his arms around her, tying her to himself as if he had to rescue her from drowning, or from the Saint of Tilcara.

ON THE WAY TO PEARSON airport next morning, Jim felt like a man turned inside out. He had given away all his secrets to Santos: that he was in love with Lisa; that he was no longer content with the dullness of his life. With the painful clarity of a morning-after sufferer, Jim realized that he had been wrong about Lisa. He didn't want her to change. She was the perfect partner on the dream stage, but recognizing her talent altered nothing. Jim wanted an exclusive engagement with Lisa. She knew no limits. She lent her soul to anyone: to Don, to Santos, to the Saint of Tilcara. It was all the same to her. She was willing to channel any man's fantasy. But Jim didn't want to share Lisa with anyone. The thought was unbearable to him. A new malaise had replaced the old soul sickness, and the only way to get over it was to swear off Lisa completely, to go back to the construction site in Catamarca and weigh his mind down with thoughts of heavy machinery, tether himself to the filing cabinets in his office, keep his eyes on the calming black and white lines of contracts. Forget Lisa, that was the solution. But Jim kept backsliding, skidding into Lisa thoughts – glimpsing her in the back of passing cars as the taxi cruised along the Gardiner Expressway to the airport. Every passenger was Lisa. The ghosts Santos had conjured up were in Jim's head, spinning a rolodex of images, a cluttering series of moving pictures of Don leaning into his drink at the Parrot, of Santos cursing, of Lisa at the séance with her eyes closed, and afterwards weeping green tears in his arms. Jim tried to stop the progression of images and train his eyes on the back of the driver's head. He studied the photo ID taped to the Plexiglas separating them, memorized the number of the taxi company, anything to move on and leave Lisa behind.

The taxi pulled up to the departure ramp, and now Jim's hands at least were busy. He wheeled his luggage to the check-in counter, put it on the conveyor belt, got his boarding pass, located his gate, and looked for Maureen McIntyre, who had been assigned to the Catamarca project for three months. She was scheduled to join his staff, do an end-run on the accounts and fine-tune the management contract for the transition period, from throwing the power switch to handing over the installation to the owners. Jim spotted Maureen in the departure lounge. Trim figure, Alaskan eyes, and ash-blonde hair that went well with the chrome plated chairs in the seating area and the serene grey and white colour scheme. She waved to him, and Jim realized: she was the antidote to Lisa. Why hadn't he seen it before, at the meeting yesterday when they discussed contracts? He felt a twinge of bad conscience as if he owed Lisa something, devotion or loyalty, but he walked up to Maureen, smiling.

Her eyes were not particularly welcoming. The message read: *I'm nobody's fool.* And that was fine with Jim. He had no intentions of going romantic on Maureen. He was grateful to her for changing the soundtrack in his mind, from *Rainy Day Monday* to *Crystal Blue Persuasion.* He needed the presence of a cool, rational woman, someone matching the glass and steel terminal, someone to cool the Lisa fever.

They chatted, waiting for the boarding call. Half an hour's conversation with Maureen told Jim he had come to a safe place. Maureen had no fantastic notions. She had no dream reservoir. She was in no way like Lisa. He was willing to plug Maureen into his brain, the business part at any rate, or even the part handling pleasure, because let's face it, the easiest way to deal with obsession was to override it and substitute one image for another. When they boarded, he kept his eyes on Maureen's shapely legs, her precision step, the sheer determination of her walk down the corridor to the plane.

It was a long haul to Buenos Aires, but Jim wasn't complaining about the togetherness forced on them by the fasten-your-seatbelt sign. He had no objection to their elbows touching on the armrest between the seats. Talking to Maureen was therapeutic, better than looking at project files or reading a mediocre spy novel or listening to the in-flight entertainment provided by Areolineas Argentinas. By the time they changed planes in Miami, he and Maureen had cleared a bit of common ground. Nothing personal, no family histories, just casual talk, a shorthand of looks and words that signalled cooperation, maybe even availability.

"You like going on foreign assignments?" he said to Maureen, as the stewardess served them dinner, sliding the tray onto their fold-down tables.

"Definitely," she said. She wanted the extra line on her CV and a chance to practise her Spanish. Is that all? he wanted to say, but Maureen left no room for questions. She talked with a set purpose, as if she was quoting an ancient authority or a principle too elementary to allow contradiction. Or admit questions. She knew she had the right approach to life.

Maureen had done her homework on Catamarca – number of inhabitants, average temperature, tourist sights. What worried her was the unknown: the hygiene at the hotel, the spicing of the restaurant food, the safety of the streets.

"I would have liked an apartment of my own," she said. "I prefer doing my own cooking and housekeeping. That way I know it's up to standard."

"We tried it," Jim said. "It didn't work. TECO rented apartments for us the first few years, but it meant dealing with brown-outs, cracked appliances, and filth in the hallway. It's better to stay at a hotel. They take care of everything, and you can concentrate on the job. By the way, Maureen, let's go through Schedule C first thing tomorrow morning. I want to make sure they don't stick us with a penalty if we run over. The schedule for the last phase is very tight."

"You can't get rid of the penalty clause," Maureen said, "but I'll see that the loose ends are tied up. We can't be held responsible if their people cause a delay, if they change the specs, or if there's a problem with the delivery of parts. Leave it to me, Jim. I know the ropes."

"How long have you been in this job?" Jim said.

"I've handled the Mexican project for the last three years. When Don Baker quit, they added Catamarca to my portfolio. If you ask me, Don wasn't qualified for the job in the first place. You need someone with legal training. All he had to offer was a big mouth. What was your impression of him?"

"I thought he was okay," Jim said. He didn't want to say more. Don was in transit on his scale of merits.

"He's in real estate now," Maureen said. "He sent me a calendar last Christmas and a card that said he'd 'found his niche'."

"I got one of those, too," Jim said. "He must have done a mass mailing." He moved Don down another notch on his scale. He had been naïve to think that Don wanted to get together for old time's sake. He was just after client development.

"Everyone at the office got one of Don's Christmas calendars," Maureen said. "A few months later he followed up with a phone call and gave me a sales pitch. Now's the time to invest in real estate, he said. Prices are going up. The downtown is developing like crazy. Don has a motor mouth, but what he said actually made sense. I took a look at what he had to offer and ended up buying a house from him. So far so good. The rent covers the mortgage payments. I think Don was right: All I have to do is sit on the property for a few years to realize a profit."

She was all bustling practicality. Don had found himself a real estate disciple, someone willing to spread the word.

"Rumour has it that Don doctored his resume, and Head Office asked him to leave," Jim said. He no longer felt a need to hold back.

"That wouldn't surprise me at all," Maureen said, "but I heard a different story: something about Don being involved with a minor or with a porno ring. But I guess you'd know about that."

"I don't know any more than you do," Jim said. "I wasn't in charge of the project at that time."

"From what I hear, Don denied the charges. But a month later he resigned 'for health reasons'."

She smirked, waiting for Jim's response. He thought of the story Don had told him about his runaway daughter. Was she the "minor"? The nostalgic smile had seemed genuine, and the pain in his eyes real.

"Maybe the job got to him," he said.

"Burn-out, you mean?" Maureen said with the voice of an unbeliever and dropped the subject. "Anyway. Tell me about the Catamarca team."

Jim gave her the rundown, who was in charge of what. By the time the plane nosed down in a wide sweep over the Rio Plata, they had settled into a collegial mood. The landing gear extended with a light thump and locked in position. A little while later, the plane set down at Ezeiza, taxiing along the tarmac to the terminal.

ALL SUMMER LONG LISA HAD been hopeful, but nothing worked out. Her life was jinxed. The signs were more confusing than ever. Jim went back to Argentina and never even dropped her a line. Santos had promised her answers, but the séances didn't work. The Saint, who was supposed to show Lisa the way, stopped talking, gave up on her because she couldn't read his groaning, shuddering, kicking body language. And Don wasn't the rock she expected him to be. She should have known. He kept changing his life story. At one time, he said he went to a private school for three years but his father went bankrupt and could no longer afford the fees. Don had to leave and lost touch with his friends. He was very lonely after that, he said. Then he changed the story. His parents split up, and he was sent to a boarding school. He had no friends there. Everyone made fun of him because he was a fat kid.

"Don!" Lisa said. "You told me a different story earlier on."

"Maybe I put it a different way," he said. "But it comes out to the same thing. I had an unhappy childhood."

He was like that. Careless with the truth, but he was the only mentor Lisa had left now that she'd given up on Dr. Lerner and the Saint had deserted her. Don was the only one with whom she could talk about her difficulties.

"I can't go on," she said to him. "I can't concentrate on what I'm doing with the kids at the nursery school. I can't do my job. I need time out."

They were sitting in the Parrot, at Don's favourite table, the captain table, the one with the hurricane lamp. Lisa felt stormy weather coming on. The tide was surging in her blood, pounding the breakwater.

Don was on his second or third drink. Lisa wasn't sure she was getting through to him.

"I think I'll take a leave of absence," she said.

He made encouraging noises, snuffling his approval.

"I need to cut down on my expenses, though," she said.

His eyes were half closed. She was afraid he was nodding off. Don's problem was that he couldn't hold his drink. Three shots were his limit. After that, he became mushy.

"I could give up the apartment and move back in with my parents, but I don't get along with my mother," she said. "Maybe I'll rent a furnished room."

Don rallied. "You are welcome to move into my spare bedroom," he said. "No charge."

Lisa wasn't sure he was serious. "I was just brainstorming," she said, but he looked suddenly awake.

"No, really," he said. "You can move in with me."

"That's nice of you," Lisa said carefully, in case he was teasing her. His face had gone pink as if he was holding his breath or suppressing a grin, but he didn't retract the offer.

"I'm just trying to be helpful," he said.

"Maybe I could do some housekeeping for you in return," Lisa said, warming to the idea.

He reached across and patted her arm. "You don't have to do a thing, Lisa. It will be good for me to have company. I drink too much when I'm by myself."

It was probably a fair exchange, she thought. Don's spare bedroom for her company. Don needed an audience. He liked to hear himself talk. Some people at the Parrot kept out of his way because he wouldn't shut up. He told you a hundred anecdotes if you let him. Lisa didn't mind listening to his stories. The arrangement might work for them both.

COMING INTO THE LOBBY OF Don's apartment building was like entering a chapel. It was silent and shrouded in a mysterious half-light. There was a couch and a coffee table with a metal ashtray, and a fake rubber tree – a kind of celestial waiting room.

Upstairs, Don's living room had the same eternal quality. The scene never changed. Lisa came in, and there was Don in a button-down shirt and permanent-press pants, watching TV. His feet were up on a hassock; he was leaning back in his easy chair, balancing a beer bottle on his stomach. When she crossed the hall, he turned his head and finger-waved.

To be friendly, she stopped and said: "What's on TV?" And he said: "Nothing really," turned it off, and started watching Lisa instead. His eyes came unwrinkled. Curiosity pumped blood through his veins and made his pasty face pink. He looked for a tip-off on what she had been doing.

"Been to the travel agency?" he said.

"No. But I will. Soon." She was supposed to book her trip to Argentina. Going to Catamarca in person was the only way to find out about her father. She hadn't told anyone except Don that that was the reason, that's why she was going. Jorge still thought she wanted to see the old country and get acquainted with the family. "Go ahead and book the trip," he'd said. "We'll make it your Christmas present."

Lisa had plenty of spare time now that she was on leave of absence, but she couldn't get herself to do anything. Every day she made plans: I will book the flight; I will do the dishes; I will make my bed; I will balance my bankbook; I will sort out the tangled mess in my head. Only she didn't know where to begin, what to do first, what next. Her life had turned into an unmarked slab of time. She no longer had the work routine to guide her through the day. There was no set time to get up, go to work, mind the children, go home, eat dinner, watch TV, go to bed. The leave of absence made Lisa's days stretch to the horizon. They dropped into the night, and bobbed to the surface again with each sunrise, rolling on in a slip stream of time, slipping away from Lisa. She was caught in the one-two zombie step, which limited her reach, one-two barely marched her from the bed to the washroom, from the washroom to the hall. Reaching the elevator took a superhuman effort. No day stood out. Sunday was like any other day. Mondays with Dr. Lerner were gone. Talks with Don followed no fixed schedule. When she told him she wanted to go to Catamarca, look up Hetta Soriano and ask her the all-important question, he didn't say: "Get a grip on your imagination," the way Jim did that first night, when she thought she could trust him. Don was a liar, perhaps, but he never said anything to discourage her. He knew what she was going through. He understood that she needed to find out about Miguel Soriano.

"Get it out of your system," he said, "but don't expect too much, sweetie."

"I won't."

He was easy on her. He wanted to help.

"You know, Lisa," he said, "you don't have to go all the way to Catamarca, looking for a father. I'll take care of you if you'll let me."

"I know, Don."

Don didn't mind sharing the paternal heaven with Miguel Soriano. He didn't complain about Lisa's zombie state. He washed the dirty dishes she left in the sink and put them in the drip basket. He picked up the shoes she dropped upside down in the hall and put them beside her bedroom door, right side up. "I don't mind, sweetie," he said. "Picking up after you is like a treasure hunt. Who knows what I'll find next?"

Perhaps Don was easy on her because he sensed that she was living on the edge. It wouldn't take much to tip her over. So he took care of everything with a Buddha smile.

"You are a sweet girl, Lisa," he said. "But you are the exception. The others are harpies. They demand. They demand I don't know what. Some sort of performance, a high wire act."

"You're too hard on women."

"No, Lisa. Women are hard on me. I must be doing something wrong."

"Maybe you're too – " She didn't know what to call it. Too pudgy? Too soft? Too much like a toy that's lost its stuffing? " – too nice for your own good."

"Right. Women don't appreciate that. That's why I like children. I walk past the school on Davenport and watch the little girls playing in the yard and wish they'd never grow up, never turn into domineering shrews."

"They don't all turn out that way, Don."

"I know. You're proof, sweetie."

Lisa didn't like it when Don called her sweetie, but she said nothing. She couldn't be mean to Don when he gave her that pleading look. When he talked about children, she thought of the framed photo above the chest of drawers in her bedroom: the photo of a girl in a private-school uniform, smiling through braces.

WHEN DON FIRST SHOWED HER the spare bedroom, Lisa felt vibrations. She couldn't tell whether they were good or bad. They crisped the skin on her arms. The climbing-ivy wallpaper in the room looked tragic and forlorn. The light filtering through the ruffled curtains made the bedspread glow dusty rose. When Don opened the curtains, the daylight turned the bedspread Bepto Bismol pink and made the room look garish, like a stage set. The bed seemed enormous, jutting out: the dramatic centrepiece of the room.

"Make yourself comfortable," Don said, but Lisa was uneasy about unpacking her suitcase or opening drawers or even disturbing the covers of the bed. The room looked untouched. It wasn't meant for everyday use. It was reserved for a special occasion, for a special person, perhaps the girl in the photo with the funereal black frame. She was no innocent child. Her dark, feral eyes held the wisdom of the ages. Was she a spirit child, whose touch had left no trace?

"That's my daughter, Asu," Don said when Lisa asked him about the photo.

"You have a daughter?"

"I adopted her when I was on assignment in Argentina," he said.

"And how old is she now?" Lisa asked.

Don gave her a sad Daddy Warbucks look. "Don't ask me about her, Lisa. I can't bear it. It hurts too much."

Was the feral child dead? "You shouldn't repress memories, Don," Lisa said. "It's unhealthy. You'd feel better if you talked to someone."

"Maybe you are right, sweetheart," he said. They were sitting on the sofa in the living room, a sofa with a matchmaking sag, a dip in the middle that made you slide together. Don put his arm around Lisa and settled in, as if he was going to tell her a bedside story. "She ran off with a young punk," he said. "One day I came home to an empty house and a farewell note explaining nothing. I still have the note. You want to read it?"

He reached for his wallet and took out a piece of paper. It was a folded square, shaped like the wallet itself, slightly concave from resting against Don's buttocks. It was a relic from another time, discoloured, with brittle edges. Don unfolded the letter and held it out to Lisa. She was afraid of touching it. It was an ancient thing, a museum piece. It belonged behind glass. There were creases, dark crevices, where the folds had been.

"You read it to me," she said to Don.

He read through Asu's girlish excuses down to the last "*mil besos.*"

"It must have been hard on you," she said. "How old was she when she ran away?"

"Seventeen."

"And he?"

"Eighteen, maybe. I don't know where they are now, if she's still with him. She never bothered to write, to tell me how she is getting on. I can't understand it. Why would she do that to me? Where did I go wrong?"

"Don't blame yourself, Don."

"No," he said. "It wasn't my fault. I am human, of course. I made mistakes, but I didn't deserve this. Wasn't I entitled to some gratitude? She lived in a slum when I adopted her. I got her out of that dump. I saw to it that she got a decent education. Was I not entitled to some love in return for offering her a good life?"

Lisa wanted to say: I'm not sure that's how life works. I'm not sure we always get what we deserve, but Don looked sad, and she didn't think she could argue with him.

"I was lonely after Asu left me. That's when I started drinking," he said and hugged Lisa's shoulders. "I'm glad you've moved in, Lisa. It's as if my girl had come back to me. You remind me of Asu, you know."

Lisa thought of the photo on the wall. Asu's eyes were motionless, like heavy water. Such eyes brought bad luck. "I don't look like her at all," she said.

"I wasn't talking about looks," Don said. "I meant: getting into trouble. Listen to me, Lisa: don't get involved with Santos." The guru light was shining in Don's eyes. "I'm warning you, Lisa. He's a drug dealer."

She lowered her eyes. "You always say that. Because you don't like Santos. Okay, so he smokes up once in a while, but he isn't a dealer."

"Don't go back to the Botanica," he said.

IN THE END LISA HAD to admit that Don was right. The Botanica was no refuge. The Saint had let her down, stopped speaking to her, refused to answer the quintessential father-question. Santos looked at her with cancelled eyes. Perhaps, he too had lost faith in the Saint. She wanted to tell him: it's over, I won't come back. But as soon as she opened her mouth, Santos shut down her breath, moved with flashbulb urgency and set off white explosions in her head.

"You wait," he said. "One day the Saint, he will speak."

Summer turned into fall, the leaden season. October pulled her down by the wrists. The rain-slicked leaves on the sidewalk got in Lisa's way. She had to fight the pulpy leaf mush, inch by inch. By the time she got to Balmuto Street, her will was drained. She no longer had the energy to tell Santos: I won't come back. The Saint will never speak to me again.

Santos was waiting for her, sprawled on a sofa he had set up near the shop window. The Botanica was his parlour, the place where he received Lisa with promises, promises.

He patted the seat beside him. "Come here, little sister," he said. He liked to call Lisa his little sister and treat her like his little whore. "Today we call the Saint." She swatted away his possessive hand, but the vapour of his breath stayed on her cheeks, like a tidemark.

There is no use calling the Saint, she wanted to say. He is balking, refusing to answer my questions. But the words wilted under his spectral look, a look made in the presence of lightning. She said: "I'm going to Argentina." There. She had told him. Going away was almost the same as not coming back, was it not?

"When you go away?" Santos asked.

"In December."

"You go visit Tilcara then," Santos said. Lisa wasn't sure: was it an invitation, a command, a prophecy?

"I thought Tilcara was in Bolivia," she said.

"Family is from Bolivia, *chacra* is across river. Argentina, Bolivia – is not important to Quechua. You take bus to Jujuy. I pick you up. Is not far."

"You mean you are going to be there in December? You never said a word to me about going away."

"The Saint tell me: go home," Santos said. "Here no good for me."

"And the Botanica?"

Santos shrugged his shoulders.

It was a twist in the plot line. So far there had been only one act in her Argentine play, and one set: Catamarca. And a cast of three: Lisa, Hetta Soriano, and Jim. She was counting on seeing Jim now that there was no one left to help her. After a year of signs promising a rich harvest, she was starving for love. That's why she had added Jim to the cast, to give her one-act play a happy ending. But now a second act was in development. Act II: Tilcara. Santos was writing himself into her play, and she didn't know how to stop him. She was stuck with him sitting by her side, staring through the rain-streaked shop window.

Santos raised an arm and waved it rhythmically, back and forth. "Need windshield wiper," he said. On the sidewalk, in front of the shop window, the SPECIAL sign was bleeding red and green all over the bottles of bath oil and shampoo, which Santos had abandoned to the weather. He stopped the wiping motion. "Ah," he said. "I see."

"What do you see?" Lisa said.

"I see empty frame of picture."

"What picture?"

"Picture of Asu in your room, the one you tell me about. She gone."

"I wish!" Lisa said. "Sometimes I want to turn that picture to the wall."

When she first told Santos about the black-rimmed photo, he nodded as if it was a well known story, as if Asu's name had already reached the Saint's ears.

"I've trouble sleeping with Asu's eyes watching me from across the room," Lisa said. The girl in the picture looked at her as if she wanted to read her entrails. "Her eyes are burning holes into my head."

"She gone," Santos said doggedly. "She missing. I see the Saint looking for Asu. I see him, all bones, no ass, no hip, just pant held together with leather belt. Roll up pant: stick legs, all dusty grey. He looking, but say nothing."

Santos pitched forward and dropped to his knees, raking the floor with his fingernails. "*Abuelo*!" he said with tears in his eyes. "*Abuelo*, don't be hard on Santos. You never want to visit, except I call you with many prayers, pulling, pulling, hard, hard. Wait, *abuelo*, I make you speak." He squeezed the bridge of his nose and kneaded his cheeks as if his hands could make words come out of his mouth.

A vast indigo blue silence descended on Lisa. She could see the old man, skin cracked and scarred with grimy wrinkles. She could see words drop out of the Saint's mouth, enter through Santos' eyes, swirl around in his brain, coming to rest there briefly, and spilling out. He was spitting, damning them.

"He say damn you, to hell with you, leave me alone," Santos said. He punched the wooden planks of the floor in angry despair. "But, *abuelo*, how I get hands on doughboy?"

Santos brought the palms of his hands close together and peered through the narrow gap. "I see you, cursing son of a bitch," he said. "I hear you yelling high and crazy, clear all the way up to the sun. He pay for Asu."

The old man faded from Lisa's vision. She grabbed Santos' arm. "Why is the Saint angry?" she asked him.

"He want to punch marshmallow face. He yelling: time to pay. He want to squeeze doughboy." Santos' hands were squeezing, strangling the air. "He angry at fat ass boy who talk like big boss and take girl, take Asu."

Lisa no longer saw the old man, she saw only Santos' chapped fist, his knuckles, bloodied from punching the floor. She searched his eyes in the semi-darkness. "Who is this doughboy you are talking about? You mean the guy Asu ran away with?"

Santos looked at her with dulled eyes. "You ask that question to *abuelo*," he said.

The old man who had all the answers, but refused to share them with Lisa. The séances no longer worked. The wooden saints in Santos' backroom remained unmoved by his chanting. The wisps of smoke from his clay pipe drifted up to the ceiling and thinned to an ineffectual breath of air.

"The Saint is tired of me," Lisa said. "He doesn't want to talk to me anymore."

"He talk to you tonight," Santos said. "Is All Saints' Day tomorrow, you know? Is holy night."

He took her hand and led her to the candle-lit backroom. In its womblike embrace her thoughts melted like wax.

"Come. You light candle for old man."

The altar was already crowded with candles. Lisa added the yellow taper Santos handed her, and lit the wick.

"You watch," Santos said to her. "I make sacrifice to *abuelo*." He pulled an envelope from his back pocket and opened the flap. "You see cheque?" he said. "Is rent cheque. Now look what I do." He held the envelope into the flame of the candle and let it burn, watching its edges curl until the charred remains reached his fingertips and turned them white with pain. "No more rent cheque," he said. "I use money to go home. I promise *abuelo*."

"But he is angry," Lisa said. "He is cursing us. He doesn't want to talk to us."

"He tired," Santos said. "He done all he can. We change method. We take elixir."

"No, I don't want your stuff," Lisa said. "It just messes me up."

"You want answers?" he said. "We find way. You take drop of elixir, is like mass, like sacrifice. Everything change."

He looked at her with his bird eyes, fixed her with a mesmerizing blackness. She was drowning in their unreflective pool.

"You try sugar cube," he said. "It open your eyes wide. You will see: the Saint talk to you, tell you all you want to know. You lie down on bed now."

Santos had cleared a space in the backroom between the wooden saints, the crucifixes and the bouquets of plastic flowers, and put down two mattresses, one on top of the other, a rival altar, softer and darker than the candle-lit table. The top mattress was covered with a satin sheet, a shimmering sea of black.

Lisa stretched out on the silky expanse and looked up into the sky above, a sagging baldachin of yellow damask Santos had nailed to the ceiling, an artificial sky with golden tassels.

"Open mouth," he said with tantric certainty, and dropped an amber cube on her tongue.

It melted and tickled the roof of her mouth. Santos laid his hands on her shoulders and began kneading them, a pulsating massage, push and let go. Lisa closed her eyes.

"Next time, you bring along Don," he said. His voice came from somewhere close, Lisa thought, perhaps from inside her ear. The sound ruffled her hair.

"Don? Why?" she said. "Why do you want me to bring him along?" She felt the words slipping out of her mouth, brushing her lips.

"He need talk to *abuelo*."

The words were pounding her, Don-Don, or was that part of the massage? Don-dough. A marshmallowing massage. She wanted to cover her face, protect herself against the murmuring bongo-play, but her hands multiplied. She looked at her twenty hands, black and white like the stills of an old movie, flickering clones of hands. Santos bent over her. His face was flat. There was a halo of sunshine around his head. He took Lisa's face into his hands and forced her to look into his eyes, an eddy spinning her around.

"Listen to me," he said. "We have ceremony with Don."

Lisa was gasping, straining to come to the surface, but he flashed her a red-lipped smile, drawing her back into the spinning galaxy of his black eyes and the golden sky above. Welcome back, girl. Welcome back to Santos' fantastic world. The folds of the baldachin above billowed.

Lisa was looking up into the cupola of a dome. Santos was conducting a liturgy, a rhythmic ceremony, soothing and caressing.

"Why you afraid?" he asked. It was impossible to pull away from his fingers. Such fingers! They took on the contours of Lisa's cheeks, the shape of her neck, her breast, her belly. Santos was protean. He changed from masseur to nimble-fingered thief of thoughts, from medicine man to lover, and back again. Lisa was in need of touch, and here was Santos with his voodoo charms and cure-all instincts and his long fingers sparking fire, ready to beat the drums and start the primordial rites.

The bed was no longer an altar. It was a sacrificial stone, on which to enact the holy rite of love- making with sacred fervour and burning tongues and grinding bodies, a rip and tug lovemaking. His words were a blinding red and gold shower scorching Lisa's eyeballs. She surrendered to the blast.

When she came to, Santos was Santos again. He looked intriguing, draped in black satin, like a medieval martyr, handsomely emaciated. Wisps of incense clung to him. He was lying on his back, breathing deeply. His open mouth was like a gaping wound. He looked suffering, as if he had made a great sacrifice for Lisa.

"Listen," he said, turning to her. "You hear what the Saint say about Asu? She my sister. He want her come back to Tilcara."

"What do you mean – your sister?"

He ignored Lisa's question, leaned over and took her hand. "You know Bible, Lisa? Bible say: An eye for an eye. A tooth for a tooth. The Saint want revenge."

Yes, but what does that have to do with me? Lisa thought. She wanted out. The old radiators in the backroom were crackling the truth, a wake-up call. The nirvana Santos was offering her was a mattress under a tasselled pseudo heaven. The sugar cube incense was in her eyes, and she had no magic to ward off Santos. She could not keep him from seeping into her pores. She wanted to take inventory of her brain, but Santos was crowding in, using up space with his Bible stories, jostling her, grappling, holding on tight with never-let-go strength. She thought: Didn't I tell Dr. Lerner once that I wanted someone to hold me, skin touching, heart pulsing? That I wanted to be close? And here is Santos. Only, wouldn't you know, he wants something in return: my soul.

DON WAS WAITING FOR LISA when she came home. The peaceful tableau of armchair and hassock had folded. The television was ominously silent. He pulled Lisa into the living room. He was soft-breathing on her.

"You've been to the Botanica again," he said.

She looked at Don glassy-eyed. Her fingers and toes were tingling. The walls of the living room were unbearably bright. The TV and the coffee table were rimmed in black. She put her hand on the table to steady it, but it kept pulsating.

"Lisa," he said. "You're playing with madness."

There were no certificates on the wall of Don's living room, but he was wiser than Dr. Lerner. He spoke with the voice of authority. His baritone came through the fog swirling in Lisa's head.

"I know," she said, contrite.

"Don't do it, sweetheart. It's not worth it."

He put his arm around Lisa, and she leaned into his soft pillow body, sank into the bolster of his arms. Her head was resting on his padded chest. She had never noticed his marshmallow face before. She was very sleepy.

He stroked Lisa's hair. "You want me to put you to bed?"

"Yes," she said, and let him take care of her.

He led her to the bedroom. He laid her down. He pulled up a chair and sat at her bedside, like a good physician. His hand was feeling her pulse.

"You are just like Asu," he said.

"N-N-N," she said. She meant "no." She had only first letters. The rest of the word was floating up to the ceiling, out of reach, a cloud broadening and dissolving. She opened her eyes with difficulty and looked at the photo above the dresser. Asu looked back at her, sombre, possessive, an iron maiden with braced teeth.

"Same almond eyes, same dark shiny hair," Don said.

Perhaps there had been an exchange of eyes and hair. Lisa suddenly noticed that there was a cut-out where Asu's face had been. Did Don expect her to step into the picture and fill the void left by the missing girl?

"S-S-S," she said. She meant to say, "stop talking."

She must gather those letters into words. She had a whole story to tell Don, a bible story, but the parts were stuck to the ceiling, hanging there like icicles.

"Tired," she said with a great effort.

"Okay, sweetie," Don said and pulled the covers over her shoulders, blacking out the view of Asu's photo and the icicle words hanging from the ceiling. "I'll let you sleep." He kissed her good night and softly closed the door.

At dawn Lisa opened her eyes. Don was in the room, an apparition. He wore a pair of grey and white striped pyjamas. He moved noiselessly like a sleepwalker, a grey and white striped shadow. He stood at the edge of the bed, looking at Lisa, taking her in. He walked around the bed and lay down beside her. She could feel the motion of the mattress like a wave disturbing the sea. She held her breath and waited. Perhaps Don held his breath, too. She could not hear him breathe. He lay motionless. There was a space between them, the breadth of a hand. She thought about him lying there on the other side of the no man's land and opened her eyes. He was a mountain silhouetted against the window, a lumpish hillside in the dark bedroom landscape. She thought about Jim who had fought free of her embrace, who had gone away, and she touched Don by mistake. The hair on his arm was warm and fuzzy. He took her hand and held it in his.

"My sweet little girl," he said. "My lamb."

In the morning, he was gone. A memory washed up in Lisa's tired brain, of Don beside her on the bed, but Asu looked at her accusingly. Liar, her braced mouth was saying. You are making it up. You were dreaming.

The thrum of radio news came from the kitchen, and the smell of coffee and buttered toast and bacon. Lisa got up and crossed the corridor in her rumpled yesterday's clothes, wanting to walk deeper into the room, but afraid of meeting Dr. Don in the kitchen jungle.

"Ready for breakfast, sweetie?" he said when he saw her standing at the door.

His cheeks were freshly-washed pink. The breakfast smell rose up, a nauseating bung in Lisa's black-coffee-only nostrils.

"Just coffee," she said faintly and took a tiny corner of a chair, as tiny as she could manage without slipping off. Don poured her coffee.

"Let's go to the travel agency and book your ticket," he said. "Today. We need to get you away from here."

"I wish you could come along to Argentina," Lisa said. The words came without premeditation, slipping out on the memory of Don's pillowy body, the restful downy hair on his arms.

"No reason why I can't," he said. His arm stiffened as if he had just made a resolution and was preparing to act on it. "Let's make plans, sweetie. Let's start with a beach holiday in Mar del Plata. My treat."

"I couldn't accept that," Lisa said.

"It's really a birthday present to myself. I'm turning fifty on the ninth of December. The big Five-0."

He looked at Lisa expectantly. Maybe she was supposed to say "You don't look fifty," Lisa thought, but she couldn't get herself to lie. She said nothing.

"After that we'll go to Catamarca. You talk to Hetta Soriano if you think that's what you should do. Then we do a tour of the North. It's picturesque country up there. What do you think, sweetheart?"

"You are putting yourself out for me," Lisa said. She didn't want Don trailing along to Catamarca. Hetta Soriano was private business. And she wanted to look up Jim and spend time with him. Don would only be in the way. On the other hand, she might never make it to Catamarca on her own. A great languor overcame her, just thinking of making the travel arrangements.

"The sooner you get away from Santos, the better," Don said.

"It's not that easy," she said. Last night's sinister, chaotic, black-magic rite was drifting back into her mind, seeping into her body, settling somewhere between her thighs and her heart, a trickbagful of menacing, garbled memories. "Santos said he'd be looking for me in Argentina."

Don raised his eyebrows. "What?" he said. "That's outrageous. Don't believe a word of it, Lisa. He's bluffing. He doesn't have the money to go to Argentina. And how would he track you down?"

"I told him I was going to Catamarca," she said.

"And how is he going to find you in Catamarca? He's stringing you along. Tell him you won't see him anymore."

Santos' face was like a ragged scar in Lisa's memory, a raw pitiless scar.

"There's something I need to tell you, Don," she said. "He is from up north, from a place called Tilcara. He says Asu is his sister. It's all very confusing. Perhaps it's just a phrase. Perhaps he means she's one of his people."

She stopped. Don looked like a man who'd heard an alarm and couldn't turn it off.

"He told you about Asu?" Don said. "Well, let me bring you up to date, sweetie. There is a whole subterranean story here."

Don's face had reached a crossroad. A collision was about to happen. Lisa had no idea the words Tilcara and Asu had such punch.

"Santos said to bring you along," she said. "He wants to talk to you."

"I'll come along alright," Don said. "But first let me tell you what's going on. After I adopted Asu, her grandfather found out where I lived and sent someone to harass me. He wanted Asu back. I made the mistake of offering him money to leave us alone. I thought I could buy peace of mind. But it was a mistake. Giving in to his demands only encouraged him. He tried to squeeze me for more money. When Asu ran away, I was devastated. I quit my job, I quit Catamarca, and moved here. I thought that was the end of the affair, but then Santos shows up and continues the game. He wants his sister back, he says. I told him, it's out of my hands. She's run away. I don't even know where she is, but he won't let go. He puts the blame on me. He says I owe him compensation. The blackmailing bastard! He wants me to come to the Botanica with you? Okay. I'll come and read him the riot act."

Here was something Lisa hadn't seen before: Don was suddenly brassy. He had turned into a man, grown out of doughboyhood in a hurry. But perhaps it was nothing new and Don was just unearthing old skills, diplomatic service skills, mixing and matching them up with white knight bravura.

THE AFTERNOON WAS A BLUR. They walked to the travel agency, hand in hand. Lisa would not have found her way otherwise. She followed Don's lead, sat down at a desk, looked obediently at the brochures the travel agent unfolded, couldn't think of dates because the days had lost their distinguishing marks, looked up at Don who stood behind her chair, kneading her shoulders, and said: "You choose."

"Okay," Don said and booked their flights to Buenos Aires, a week-long stay at a luxury resort in Mar del Plata, and a "discovery" tour of northern Argentina.

From the travel agency, he marched Lisa to the Botanica. Their parka-clad twin silhouettes were bobbing along, reflected in the shop windows as they passed. Don pushed open the door of the Botanica and went straight to the counter over which Santos presided, listless and indifferent to this customer.

Don looked him in the eye and said: "*Cómo te va*, Santos?" using Americano Spanish to hit him between the eyes and stun him.

Santos' forehead corrugated as Don's hand closed over his, held it fast, pressed his fingers down flat on the counter.

Lisa felt guilty about the lock-in greeting.

"You asked me to bring Don," she said to Santos apologetically and hung back.

Santos' eyes sideswiped her. She could see he wasn't accepting apologies. He twitched his fingers, trying to escape Don's grasp. His body was coiled. He was looking for a chance to spring an escape.

"So you told Lisa about Asu?" Don said. "Did you tell her about the blackmailing, too? About your people harassing me in Catamarca?"

Santos stared at the statuette of Jesus Malverde on the counter. He seemed to pray, to ask for Malverde's patronage.

"And the time you came to the Parrot last year and asked for help, and I set you up here, but that wasn't good enough, was it?" Don's back was rigid, his arm bent over the counter, holding down Santos' hand.

Santos raised his eyes and lowered them again, as if the blue light of Don's eyes hurt him. He wriggled out of Don's grasp finally, and pulled away from his touch.

"What you do with Asu?" he said.

"You know very well what I did. I paid the old man, your grandfather, to let Asu go. I ransomed her. I saved her from the usual fate of the girls in your compound. You think I don't know what happens to those girls?"

"What happen?"

"They end up on the street."

"If they go with man like you, yes. But no important where they are, they belong to Tilcara."

"Tilcara was a prison for Asu," Don said. "I took her out of a repressive environment and gave her an education. I was a father to her."

"Father!" Santos flicked the tips of his fingers in contempt.

"A good father. And if you think you can continue to blackmail me, think again. I report you to the police. They'll put an end to your business. I'll make sure they deport you."

"I don't want your money. I want you explain: Where is Asu?"

"I told you already: she ran away."

"Ah, run away from good father? Why she run away?"

"Hormones, Santos. You know the word? She ran away with a teenage punk when she was seventeen. There is nothing a father can do when a girl falls in love. I lost her. That's all I can tell you, I'm sorry to say."

"Then I tell you. She work streets in Catamarca. I see her. 'What you do here?' I ask. 'Go back to Tilcara,' I tell her. 'I hate Tilcara,' she say. That is what you do for her. 'Go away,' she tell me. 'To hell with Tilcara.' That is the good education you give her. I weep. I beg the Saint forgive her. Perhaps he forgive her, but you – ." He shook his head. "You pay," he said. "The Saint make you pay." He spit out Don's name. "You pay, Don Baker."

Don looked around the store, his mouth twisted in disgust. "I don't care about your saints," he said. "Go hide behind your saints all you like. I don't buy that nonsense, you know. And another thing – "

Don turned and looked at Lisa. She shrank back, but he took her by the arm and pulled her forward to the counter, making her stand between him and Santos. She went limp, but Don wouldn't allow her to slump. He put one arm around Lisa's shoulder to prop her up and shot the other across the counter, pointing a finger at Santos. His finger was an inch from Santos' sallow face, barring any objections he might have.

"And another thing: keep away from Lisa."

Santos refused to look at her. He pretended she wasn't there. He narrowed his eyes, shutting her out, shutting out Don's warning finger.

"You pay, Mister," he said.

"I'll call the police on you, boy. I'll put an end to your scam here. They'll close down your business and turf you out, you hear?"

"I hear," Santos said calmly, smiling, baring his teeth in an idiot grin, as if he had settled the matter and Don's presence was superfluous.

"So we understand each other," Don said. He let Lisa go, dismissed her from his prop-up embrace, put both hands on the counter and scowled.

Santos stopped grinning and nodded slowly. His eyes were opaque. His face was immobile, a mask, shadowed by black hair hanging down on either side, lifeless like a wig. He was inscrutable, a man without edge or definition.

Lisa saw the worry in Don's eyes and knew the reason. He had failed to make his mark. He had drawn no blood, but she could also tell that he was determined to see this through at any cost, to him or to her.

They stepped out into the street. The sidewalk was slick with melting snow and soggy leaves. The weather was tailor-made for hiding. No excuse was needed for Lisa to burrow down into her coat and avoid looking at Don. The fashions conspired. Lisa pulled her woollen tuque over her ears and made sure her scarf covered her mouth. No need to speak. No need to listen. She shuffled along beside Don, in her insulating layer of clothes, frosty breath veiling her face. But the tuque didn't shut out Don's words. The law was on his side, he said, he was going to get a deportation order. Then you and me, you and me, you and me – the same words over and over again, like a chugging locomotive. Lisa was afraid of being run over. She was looking for cover, a place where she could spill her thoughts without fear of leaving a mess on the floor and be told to put them back into the box. That's what Jim once said: keep your thoughts inside. Best place for them. But Jim looked like a man who needed to spill thoughts, too. She had seen them pressing against his temples, ready to burst out. Maybe Jim could manage his thoughts and keep them in. When I get to Catamarca, she thought, I must ask him how it's done, but it was probably too late to learn the lesson. She had lost control long ago. She was on a roller-coaster ride, and there was going to be spillage at the end of the ride, a skin-soaking deluge of sorrow.

THE HOTEL CONTINENTAL WAS IN the old part of Catamarca, on a street lined with fine colonial buildings. It looked like an urban palazzo with pilasters and friezes, rows of French windows and ornamental balconies. The entrance, manned by a liveried doorman, was regal. A sweeping staircase led up to the conference room on the mezzanine, but the splendour extended no further. The rest of the building was utilitarian. The rooms had been cut down to size. You could tell by the broken pattern in the ceiling frieze and the mangled corner mouldings where the dividing walls had been put up. The cavernous old rooms had been turned into suites with living and sleeping quarters and kitchenettes. The windows of Jim's living room looked out on a tranquil courtyard with potted orange trees, a reminder of calmer times and far from the angry traffic in the streets. It was a good hotel. The staff spoke English passably well, and the management stayed on top of things. Catamarca kept to the southern custom of late dining, which meant that no decent restaurant served meals before nine o'clock, but the Continental catered to a North American clientele and opened its dining room early. That is where the ex-pats ended up most evenings, trouping in and taking their seats at the reserved tables, like pupils at a boarding school. Jim longed to get away and live the indigenous life, but his stomach rarely held out long enough to go to a restaurant in town.

The hotel dinners became livelier after Maureen joined the team. Jim measured her success by the reaction of his staff: the enthusiastic sounds coming out of Kevin Anderson, who was a va-va-voom kind of guy. Even Stephane Millet, who had a philosophical bent, sucked his cigarette with increased vigour. The rest – married men – were discreet and watched Maureen with silent hunger. A spirit of competition took hold of Jim. He had a loopy dream in which he challenged Stephane to an arm-wrestling match. It was a Montreal dream, with French background noises, although the pub looked suspiciously like the Parrot. The air was thick with cigarette smoke. Stephane was wearing a black turtle neck sweater, Jean-Paul Sartre style, and holding a Gaulois between two straightened fingers, waving it like a wand. Then the arm-wrestling started. Stephane was sweating profusely. Or maybe it was Jim himself who was sweating. He felt hot because of the Zorro mask he was wearing, and he couldn't see clearly because the slits for the eyes were too narrow. He and Stephane had their elbows on the table and were gripping each other's hands. Stephane tried a hook, forcing a brief blast, but Jim out-powered him. He was hanging off the end of the table, putting pressure on Stephane's fingers. He leaned in and forced his arm down on the table with a thud. Stephane slumped. Maureen – where did she come from? – Maureen raised Jim's arm reluctantly. The applause was petering out when Stephane jumped up like a Jack in the box, and the match started over again. There was no end in sight to the contest. Jim wanted to argue that he had won, permanently. *Pourquois avez-vous* – he said, but that's as far as the dialogue went, because he ran out of

French words and woke up. Jim didn't need an analyst to interpret the dream for him. Stephane and Maureen popping up like that meant he was in the race. He was competing for her attention.

The company was leasing office space on the second floor of a building which had been a government complex until recently when the junta centralized the administration and moved their staff to Buenos Aires. The building retained an air of authority, but the ceremonial rooms with their high ceilings, crown mouldings, and inlaid parquet floors contrasted sadly with the shabby office furniture and dim lighting. Jim's office, which came with a gate-keeping secretary, was the exception. It was furnished with a pompous mahogany desk on bowed legs ending in brass lion claws and a glass fronted book case of baroque proportions, disturbingly empty until Jim draped a few files over its shelves. A deep leather sofa and a built-in bar allowed Jim to entertain government visitors. Appeasing them occupied a significant part of his time. The lingering *fin de siècle* atmosphere of his office invited romantic feelings, but when Jim walked down the corridor to the office Maureen was sharing with Stephane, when he saw her files neatly squared and paralleling the edges of her desk, he was back in the here and now, sucked into the undertow of Maureen's present-day efficiency. She was a woman of purpose, and now that she had turned into a trophy woman, the first prize in the inter-office tournament, she had become somehow more desirable. Jim was falling in love with Maureen's hands. They were strong firm hands. It was remarkable how robust they looked, how capable of performing well, whatever the task. But Lisa kept ghosting around in his mind, flashing her pink tank top, wiggling her bum in the tight fake leather dress she had worn on their last evening together in Toronto. And he knew why Lisa stayed on top and kept overlaying the Maureen images. She was the superior flirt. Maureen had no come-on. A little smile, a little batting of the eyelashes would have helped, but Maureen wasn't into that sort of thing. She gave no preferential treatment to anyone at the office. She was still at the choosing stage, playing the field. She didn't encourage Jim. She didn't retreat either. She just looked at him, blowing hot and cold, perhaps waiting for a mental click to settle her mind. There was no front runner as yet. Unless it was Stephane. Sharing an office with Maureen gave him the inside track. He had nothing to recommend him. He was a middle-aged divorcee from Quebec, thin-haired, with narrow shoulders and a pronounced Adam's apple, but he seemed to register on Maureen's scale of desirable men.

Jim hungered for success. He became Pavlovian about Maureen. Every time she passed him in the hall, in the breakfast room, at the office, the glandular response kicked in. He had to make a move. It became imperative. He asked Maureen out for dinner and took her to the Jardin del Rey, an old conservatory reborn as an eatery. The dining room was a vaulted glass pavilion offering magic-hour dishes: quail flambé lit with a torch, cakes in the shape of a chess board with figures of chocolate and marzipan, sushi served in a black lacquered box wrapped in an obi.

Their waiter, one hand studiously behind his back, listened to Maureen's order with deference, but at the first breath of hesitation, he butted in and started explaining the menu in English.

Maureen ignored him and continued in Spanish, soldiering on through the names of the exotic dishes on the menu.

"I'm trying to practise my Spanish, and they won't let me," she said after the waiter had left their table. She was annoyed. "It's the same thing at the hotel. Even the maid wants to palm off her ten words of English on me."

The hors d'oeuvres arrived. The platter was set atop a fishbowl with live minnows, their sucking mouths pressed against the glass. One of the little suckers went belly up as the waiter was serving them.

Maureen lowered her eyes for a moment, then looked up and willed herself to smile. She was determined to fight the minnow ghost, wasn't going to let a fish death cast a pall over their dinner. She did her part to make the evening a success, met Jim halfway in the rhetorical foreplay, told him, more or less, that she liked him, said nice things and made approving noises, but there was no carnality in her compliments. Jim tried to edge the conversation into the sensual sphere, but Maureen spoiled it all by bringing up real estate.

"Remember I told you about the house I bought from Don?" she said, putting out their spluttering romance. "Last week I got a letter from the bank. One of the cheques bounced, the rent for the shop on the ground floor." Her nostrils flared. She became animated. "So I phoned Don and asked him, as a favour, to look into the matter for me. I take back everything I said about him, that he's just a bigmouth. He really came through for me. The tenant is gone, he says. All he had to do was threaten to call immigration. It turned out the guy was in Canada illegally." She pursed her lips and looked moody for a moment, but her irritation cleared. "Well, Don has already lined up another tenant. He'll hire someone to clean and paint the place and cart away the left-over merchandise. It's trash really. On the specs, Don called it an antique store, but that was just real estate blarney. It was nothing of the kind. It was full of odd merchandise, voodoo stuff if you ask me."

Voodoo. A connection clicked in Jim's mind, but he couldn't close the loop because Maureen kept talking.

"The first time I went to collect the rent from the tenant, he asked me to come into his 'office' – the storage room at the back. It was piled with the oddest gothic junk – a collection of plaster saints, swords, crosses, candles – and reeking of incense. I almost choked on the smell. He gave me a lot of garbled talk about holding a séance and consulting the saints on my behalf."

Was it possible, Jim thought, was she talking about Santos, about the shop on Balmuto Street?

"Did you go for it?" he asked. "Did you have a séance with him?"

"Of course not," Maureen said and rolled her shoulders as if to shake off the idea. "Don says the guy was a drug dealer. Now he tells me! But I'm not complaining. He did a super job, getting me a new tenant."

"That shop," Jim said. "Is it called the Botanica?"

"That's the name. Don't tell me you know the place!"

"A friend once took me along to a séance there. When you described the backroom, I connected the dots."

The whole picture came into focus. So this was the house Don bought from the cat lady, fixed up and sold at a profit to an unnamed young professional – Maureen, as it turned out. Jim wanted to ask Maureen: did Frank ever make it back from Sudbury? He wondered how many other colleagues Don had tapped successfully.

"So you went to a séance?" Maureen said. "I didn't think you were the type to go to séances." Jim was glad she didn't say: "I always thought there was something odd about you." He was afraid that Lisa's craziness had rubbed off on him somehow and was showing in his face, that he had been infected and that's why he couldn't oust Lisa from his mind.

"I was just curious," he said. "I don't believe in the stuff, but Santos gave a first-rate performance."

"By the way," Maureen said, "Don sends his greetings. He and his wife will be coming down in December, for a holiday. He said something about looking you up."

"Don is married?" Jim said.

"Maybe I got that wrong. He just said 'Lisa and me'. They are planning to spend a week in Mar del Plata, then tour Northern Argentina."

Jim went on automatic pilot, trying to keep his brain from crash-landing after "Lisa and me" hit the side of his head.

"Everybody is raving about Mar del Plata," Maureen was saying. "I'm thinking of going there on one of my remaining weekends." Her three-month stint was coming to an end.

"If you like a packed beach, overflowing garbage cans, and blaring transistor radios," Jim said, trying to keep his thoughts on the level, or at least keep Lisa out of them.

"You mean it's just hype? In that case, maybe I should go to Bariloche instead," Maureen said. "Except it's a long drive. Not much fun doing it on my own." She let the suggestion dangle, but Jim was too distracted to take her up on it and offer to go with her. A broken record of Lisa and Don, Lisa and Don, Lisa and Don was playing in his head, the needle popping over the grooves of his soul. It took all his strength to wrangle the Lisa thoughts to the ground and raise his arm to signal the waiter for the bill.

BY THE TIME THEY LEFT the restaurant, the heavy weather had passed, and Jim's head was out of the clouds. He remembered: he had wanted to hand Lisa over to Don for the rescue operation. It was all turning out as planned, really. Don was taking care of her. That's what he wanted him to do, right? He worked himself around to that comforting version and stayed close to Maureen's side to keep away any more Lisa thoughts. He casually brushed against her in a move that made it natural to put his arm around her shoulder. She didn't discourage him. He was back on track, chasing the right woman: the prize woman, the one everybody was after.

In the hotel lobby they separated for appearance's sake and came together again in the elevator, in a natural fit of curves and angles, so natural there was no need to pause at Jim's door and pretend to say goodnight. They walked straight on to Maureen's room. He was kissing her even before she took out the key. The waltz from the door to the bedroom went off like a choreographed piece, except at the very end, when Maureen sank onto the bed like someone losing balance. It couldn't be the effect of the two glasses of wine she had with her dinner, Jim thought. He didn't worry too much about her wobbly descent. His neediness made everything seem alright, the yanking of Maureen's clothes, her wordless acceptance of his demands. Jim had expected hesitation, but Maureen was breathing tenderness. She didn't refuse him anything. Jim responded to the touch of her fingertips on his chest, the gentle heaviness of her closed eyelids. The sight of his tanned body so close to her pale skin put him in a trance. Her long silky legs make his heart stop, then go into a rolling beat. The rising heat was turning into a neural storm. He heard her faint cry of pleasure, and let himself go, sinking into a liquefied moment of oblivion. Satisfaction washed over Jim, and he floated weightlessly in the darkness of his closed eyes.

Maureen was silent. Jim gratefully stroked the curve of her cheek, and was startled when his fingertips came away wet. He opened his eyes and looked at Maureen's face in the light coming through the open door of her living room. He had expected a smile of exhaustion, but there were tears, making her cheeks gelid and shiny. A bluesy voice turned on in Jim's head, *falling like raindrops, falling like raindrops from the sky*.

"Sorry, Jim," Maureen moaned, struggling free of his embrace and rolling off the bed. He heard the click of the bathroom door. When she didn't come back to bed and went out into the living room instead, he knew the affair wouldn't survive the night.

He got dressed and joined Maureen on the sofa. She had slipped into white silk pyjamas, presenting him with a shimmering vision of light. The tears had melted the blue of her eyes to a soft dove grey. She looked innocent, virginal, in spite of what had gone before, and she kept saying sorry and apologizing, Jim wasn't sure for what – the tears, the sex, the whole affair manqué.

"I don't know why I'm so stupid," she said. "I shouldn't have had wine with dinner. Wine always makes me cry. Or maybe it was the Pear Hélène. I'm allergic to alcohol, I think."

Jim patted her arm. "It's okay," he said lamely.

He was desperate for a cigarette. He'd stopped smoking in June – his third attempt at breaking the habit, and his mouth was going dry every time he smelled smoke, even smoked meat or exhaust fumes. He was sure it was the exhaust fumes coming through the open window that were making him antsy. Or the memory of all the post-coital cigarettes he'd enjoyed.

Maureen's room looked out on the street, and the whoosh of tires, the whine of engines, the low rumble of trucks over the pavement was unceasing, even though it was now early morning. The craving became unbearable. Jim was desperate to get back to his room. He had one cigarette left, shoved to the back of his medicine cabinet, wedged against the first-aid kit the hotel provided, one cigarette in case of emergency.

Maureen walked to the bar fridge. "Can I get you some orange juice?" she said.

She was standing by the open fridge door, silky limbed, playing hostess. Jim could see the sparse contents of her fridge: an apple, a couple of cans of pop, bottles of orange juice.

It would have been bad form to get up and leave at that point. Jim sipped the proffered orange juice. It made his stomach roil. He noticed that the furniture of Maureen's room was exactly like his own, even the prints on the wall were the same. It was an immaculately tidy room. Jim was full of cravings: for Lisa's messy flat, for a smoke.

"I hate it when I fall apart like that," Maureen was saying. "The last time that happened – don't laugh – was when I collected the rent cheque from Santos, my ex-tenant. I didn't tell you the whole story."

Jim wasn't sure he could last through a whole story, but Maureen's hand was on his thigh, holding him down on the sofa. She needed to shed words to stop shedding tears.

"At first he was on his best behaviour," she said. "He brought out a plate of home-baked biscuits and offered them to me. They were probably hash cookies, but courtesy got in the way of my better judgment. I ate one of the cookies and started feeling wobbly. 'What's in those biscuits?' I asked him. 'It has many ingredients,' he said in his pidgin English. 'It bring you excellent mate.' After that we had a strange conversation about perfect mates and perfect children. God knows what I said to him. I was in a fog. He took me to the backroom, his warehouse of religious kitsch, and lit incense before the plaster bust of a gypsy." Maureen fluted her mouth in imitation of Santos: "'We ask gypsy woman to look for good man,' he said, and started putting questions to the plaster gypsy and pretending she was giving him answers. He kept talking in falsetto, moaning like a ventriloquist. It was eerie. I started crying. I couldn't stop myself. The tears were running down my face, and he kept saying: 'You need healing, Miss McIntyre, you need listen to your feelings.'"

She stopped. They were both exhausted, she from telling the story, Jim from listening.

"Well, maybe he has a point," he said gently. "About feelings, I mean."

"I think he's nuts," Maureen said. "I should have kept off the cookies."

Jim got up. They both saw the story had come to an end. At the door they kissed perfunctorily. They didn't turn away fast enough to conceal the shadow of relief passing over their faces simultaneously. It was embarrassing. To compensate, they held hands a little longer. Jim thought of the farewell scene in *Casablanca*, the bit about a beautiful friendship.

He was tempted to use the line on Maureen, as a nice comforting ending, but her eyes were brimming with tears again.

"I don't know what's the matter with me," she said. "I'm really sorry, Jim. I know I've spoiled the evening."

No beautiful friendship was possible after her admission of fault.

ON THE DAY OF MAUREEN'S departure, Jim kissed her on both cheeks, local style. They were standing on the sidewalk in front of the hotel. Stephane was putting Maureen's luggage into the trunk of his car. He had offered to take her to the airport, enough time to prepare the ground for further action, especially if he hung around in the departure lounge. Jim could see Stephane as Maureen's future rental agent. He could see him checking over her leases, making little Xs where the signatures should go, and Maureen bending over him, smiling approval. No, forget it. No more fantasies involving Maureen. That competition was over.

Jim watched Stephane's car turn the corner and walked down to the farmers' market. He went there every Saturday morning to buy fruit and be part of the native tableau. Three years in Argentina, and he was still an outsider. His Spanish was alright for everyday use, but he couldn't say anything profound or anything light, for that matter. That's what he missed most: kidding around. He couldn't develop the right pitch. He didn't pause in the right places, and the punch lines fell flat.

During his first year in Argentina, he had been keen on becoming part of the fabric. He read up on local history. He went on road trips every weekend. He watched the news on television, but after a while he got tired of the dreary talking heads and the clips of limousines driving up to official residences, chauffeurs opening car doors and standing at attention, men in uniform hurrying up marble steps. It seemed to be the same shot over and over, ending with doors being slammed shut and security guards waving away reporters, while a voiceover explained what was supposedly going on behind closed doors. Jim fell back on listening to the BBC on his short-wave radio. They accused the junta of violence and corruption, of the abduction and killing of dissidents, but the BBC wasn't a neutral source. A conflict was brewing between England and Argentina over the Falkland Islands, an English outpost to which the Argentines laid claim.

In Catamarca, information was hard to come by. When one of the Argentine engineers invited Jim to his house, there was a great deal of food and drink and good cheer, but no time for serious talk. The children were allowed to stay up until all hours. They climbed on Jim's lap and showed him their toys. They interrupted noisily whenever the conversation excluded them. When Jim asked the Argentines on the project about the junta, they said they had heard rumours of abductions, but only rumours. They didn't look at each other when they answered his questions, but it was as if they had agreed beforehand on what to say and had synchronized their accounts. The rumours were spread by leftists, they said. They knew no one who had actually been harassed. And what about the mothers on the Plaza del Mayo, who held candle-lit vigils for the *desaparecidos*, their missing sons and daughters? Manipulated by agitators, they said, incited by people who had their own agenda. They spoke with a finality that imposed silence. When Jim mentioned the Falklands, they turned into flag-waving patriots. They lectured him on the history of the

Islands. They had been Argentine since 1820. The English had muscled in and then abandoned the inhabitants. Life on the islands would be intolerable without Argentine transport ships, Argentine supplies, Argentine postal services.

In the city itself, there was no evidence of the generals' heavy hand, except for the military compound on the outskirts of town. It was guarded with machine guns and posted with signs that said "No stopping" and showed a soldier pointing at passersby with an Uncle Sam Wants You gesture, only he was pointing a rifle. Once Jim ran into a military roadblock. They checked his papers and tested the mandatory fire extinguisher in the trunk of his car. It wasn't working, and they slapped him with a fine, but they were perfectly courteous, and the whole incident was annoying rather than intimidating.

It was hard to know why Jim found himself on the sidelines: was it the air of denial that pervaded all conversations? Or his lack of language skills which drew a curtain around him? Or the fact that he was tall and sandy-haired, and so obviously a foreigner? It was this loneliness that made the noisy outdoor market with its crowded, happy life so attractive. It became his favourite place in town. It made him forget his isolation.

When Lisa comes to Catamarca, he thought, I'll show her the market. But reason kicked in with a pang. Lisa wasn't visiting *him*. She was looking for information on her father. And she wasn't coming alone. She already had a guide: Don. She didn't need Jim.

DON RENTED A MINT GREEN Ford Taunus at the airport in Buenos Aires, "because a compact doesn't get you respect," he said. He was fussing over the car. He was fussing over the route to Mar del Plata, checking maps, adding up mileage. Lisa was in no mood for a beach holiday. She wanted to go straight to Catamarca. She had urgent business there: see Jim, visit Hetta Soriano. The beach could wait.

"Why don't we go to Catamarca first?" she said.

Don folded up the map and hugged her. "Because it doesn't make sense to change all the arrangements. Wait until you see Mar del Plata, sweetheart. You'll love it."

They headed out on Route 2. *Any love is good love, baby*, was playing on the tape deck. Lisa turned up the volume, but she couldn't bob her head or snap her fingers to the tune. *Any love is good love* sounded wrong with Don in the driver's seat. She was impatient to get through the day and through all the other days that stood between her and Catamarca.

"Turn it down, sweetie," Don said, raising his voice over the quadraphonic pounding. "I'm going deaf."

Lisa pressed the stop button and listened to the white noise of the engine instead. She needed some background music to conjure up the right kind of lover – tall, sandy-haired, with a laid-back smile. Jim. She rolled down the window to a rush of air, afraid of floating Jim's name inside the car, in case the memories made their way to her lips and caught Don's ear.

"We should have stayed overnight in Buenos Aires," he said. He was tired after the long flight. There were two hundred and fifty miles of pampas between them and Mar del Plata, a ribbon of asphalt under the glaring sun that made Don squint in spite of the sun visor.

"I tell you what, sweetheart," he said. "We'll take the next exit and look for a motel. I was hoping to cover at least half the distance, but I'm too tired to go on."

"Fine," Lisa said. She was tired, too. Tired of being close to Don. It was hard to spin dreams when he could reach across and pat her arm any time he wanted. They turned off the highway. As soon as she saw a vacancy sign, Lisa said: "How about that one?" The sign was hanging from the arched entrance to a villa with wrought iron balconies.

"A *residencial*?" Don said. "I don't know. It's probably sub-standard."

"Looks okay to me," Lisa said. She was impatient to put more than a car's width between them.

The room was dingy, but the single beds were on opposite walls. Lisa savoured the cool expanse of tiled floor between them.

She kicked off her sandals. "I'm going to take a shower," she said, and rummaged in her bag for her special shampoo: *Good Luck*. She tried to hide it from Don, but he had already caught sight of the label and frowned.

"Souvenir from the Botanica?" he asked.

"Don't bug me, Don," she said and deliberately upended her travel bag on the bed, rummaging for the conditioner: *Happiness*.

She disappeared into the bathroom.

Don sighed. "You are a messy little girl," he called after her.

She knew he would fold her clothes, zip up the bag and put it away. She wished he'd say: "I've had it with picking up after you." Then she could say: "Okay, let's split." But Don was patient.

"There are no towels in here," she called from the bathroom. "Get me some towels, Don."

"You are treating me like a servant," he said, but she could tell he was smiling. He took his orders like a man in love with his servant job. Don had the kind of devotion no insult could kill. He was relentlessly nice. She shouldn't have said to Dr. Lerner: "What's the use of a relationship if I'm not allowed to get close." It was bad luck to say out loud what she wished for: "I want to get close, I want to be touched." The words hovered and gathered around her like an aura. They travelled with her, crossed lines with the words of others, and got entangled. She was enveloped in those words "I want to be touched" when she went to the Botanica. That is how she snagged Santos. That's when he started putting a tracer on her. She lugged those words with her to the Parrot and allowed them to drift across the table to Don. No wonder he was clinging to her. She should have reserved those words for someone else. Jim.

The so-called shower was a corner in the bathroom, marked off with a plastic curtain, a niche large enough to hide behind and squeeze in private thoughts. The water splashed against the curtain, pearled down, and ran in rivulets along the tiled floor to a drain in the centre of the room. Lisa let the water play a drum roll on her back, and thought of Catamarca, of seeing Jim again, but at the first twinge of longing, just as Jim's body was taking shape in her mind, the door of the bathroom opened, and Don came in with the towels. She had to put her thoughts on hold.

He was lurking on the other side of the shower curtain.

"I brought you the towels, sweetheart," he said.

"Drop them on the counter and leave me alone," Lisa said. She was cross at Don for not being someone else.

The bathroom floor was flooded when she stepped out from behind the shower curtain and wrapped herself in a towel. There was a squeegee leaning in the corner. "It's all wet in there," she said when she came out of the bathroom. "Go and mop up, Don." The effort of giving orders was draining her, and she had no sugar-cube supply from the Botanica to prop her up. She was impatient and listless, angry and sleepy at the same time. She couldn't concentrate long enough to give orders. The air was thick with shadows, dark beings floating in the room, refusing to take on recognizable shapes.

She lay down on the bed and flattened her spine against the mattress, trying to fly under the radar of the phantoms hovering in the air. She tried to conjure up a pleasant vision of herself and Jim in Catamarca, but Don's goodnight kiss strangled all dreams. She lay awake for a long time and dropped into a heavy sleep that brought no relief.

She woke at dawn, opened her eyes and saw the sign. Above her, on the ceiling, was a triangular shape, black against the white stucco. She broke out in cold sweat. Her skin puckered at the thought of the black thing swooping down, wings brushing against her forehead, hairy legs dancing down her arms, stinging her, tattooing an ominous message on her wrists. She felt the sting with prickling anticipation. She shrunk back, crawled under the blanket. "Don," she breathed, and wished she could recall the name as soon as it was out of her mouth. One bad omen after another.

Don stirred, sat up, and came to the edge of her bed, casting a shadow of body heat over her.

Lisa pointed to the ceiling. The triangle was expanding and contracting like a black heart.

Don picked up his shirt and slapped it against the ceiling. The triangle glided down silently and disappeared between the wall and the headboard of the bed. Lisa whimpered.

"Just a moth," Don said, and turned on the light.

The dusty corpse of the moth lying under the bed made Lisa's skin crawl.

"It's okay," Don said and opened his arms to her, but she refused to let Don comfort her. She pummelled his chest.

"Leave me alone," she said. "I need space. Tomorrow I want my own room."

"I thought you were afraid of sleeping alone, sweetheart," he said soothingly, and Lisa remembered why she had brought him along. She needed someone to fight the ghosts for her, the black moths hovering overhead, and Don had been the best man she could find for the job.

"I booked us into a super resort in Mar del Plata," he said. "You'll have all the space you want at the Villas del Mar. And you don't need to worry about *mariposas* there."

NO, THERE ISN'T ENOUGH SPACE here, Lisa thought. The porter carried their luggage to one of the bungalows set in a circle around a kidney shaped pool, a mock village with dwarf houses. Lisa inspected the bedroom. There was one king-size bed.

"You'll have to sleep on the sofa in the living room," she said to Don, and closed the door of the bedroom behind her. She stared at the pale green meadow of shag carpet. The bedspread and curtains were matching striped chintz. Moorish lamps dangled on chains to the left and right of the bed. Lisa wasn't in the mood for interior decorator nice. She was full of aching needs. She changed into her bikini and checked on Don.

He had taken the seat cushions off the sofa and was eyeing the fold-out mattress, testing its thickness. Lisa sidled around him and stepped through the glass doors out on the patio. She needed a sweep of air between them, but the patio was for lovers, secluded, screened from view by a lattice overgrown with wisteria.

Don came out after her. "Like it, baby?" he said and put his arms around Lisa, taking his cue from the honeymoon setup.

Lisa walked away from him and sat on the edge of the pool, letting her legs dangle in the glittering water. The patio was deserted in the early afternoon heat. The lovers were taking their siesta. It was a perfect setting for dreams, except for Don hunkering down beside her. Out of the corner of her eye, Lisa could see the spotted back of his hands. He was discreetly silent, but he was there, and she wanted to be alone. She drew circles in the water with her naked toes: outward bound, inward bound. She rubbed the palms of her hands against the concrete of the pool's edge. She needed a numbing exercise, a mesmerizing finger and toe exercise to block the murmurs of anxiety.

"I should have brought a hat," Don said. "I'll get sunburned."

Lisa had never seen Don so naked. He looked better in the guise of indoor living under low wattage, with a suit and tie camouflage, blue eyes melting, pudgy cheeks scented with Aqua Velva, Cupid mouth puckered for a kiss, lovable Daddy-Don. Here he was, a faded copy of himself, aged in the harsh light of the glaring sun, dressed too sparingly. His Bermuda shorts cut into the pink flesh of his belly. They exposed his dimpled knees, his soft-haired shins, his smooth, unmarked feet.

The next day and the day after that, Lisa lived in Babylonian captivity under Don's loving eyes, allowing the foray of his fingers over her arms and shoulders, his caressing words, Baby this, baby that. A suffocating breath of affection brushed Lisa's cheeks every time he spoke. She wilted under its heat. On the third day, she told him there was a change of plans. She didn't want him to come along to Catamarca.

"I need to sort out the Soriano question by myself," she told him. She was lying. She didn't want to be by herself. The ghosts were still hovering overhead. She hadn't managed to banish the *mariposas*. She still needed someone to guide her through the bestiary, but it wasn't Don.

"I wouldn't get in your way," he pleaded.

Lisa shook her head. She didn't want him around. She was planning to call Jim and ask him to pick her up at the airport in Catamarca.

"What about the trip up north?" Don said.

"I'll go on my own." Or perhaps she could persuade Jim to come along. "I'll meet you in Buenos Aires afterwards," she said. "We'll be together for three days in Buenos Aires before we go home." She sighed. Three days.

"I would have to change all the arrangements," Don said.

Lisa shrugged her shoulders. She was merciless. "I can't help it," she said.

Don looked beagle-eyed, but he trundled off to make the changes. "Whatever makes you happy, sweetheart," he said.

She still had Don's birthday to get through, Don's big 5-0 birthday. She had no present for him, and she couldn't get herself to leave the resort again. The last trip to the shopping plaza had brought on a streak of bad luck. She couldn't afford another misstep. She'd gone to the plaza to buy a package of tampons, and then she didn't need them. It was as if buying the package was keeping her period away. Or maybe it was the shock when she came out of the plaza and had a glimpse (or was it a flashback?) of Santos in a beat-up Fiat. It was hard to tell what was real and what wasn't. The air was filled with foreboding shadows. Santos had threatened to track her down, but there were so many brown-skinned gristle and bone men in Mar del Plata, mixing with the tourist crowd. There were so many young men wearing faded jeans and tight T-shirts and driving beat-up cars. It was hard to tell them apart. One of them may have been Santos. The worst of it was: while she was out shopping, Jim phoned back to say, yes, of course he'd pick her up in Catamarca. Don delivered the message quietly. He had his voice under control, but his eyes were loud with accusation: Why ask Jim? I would have done everything for you, baby.

Lisa took no more chances. She did not venture outside the resort. She stayed in the shadow of the walls, moved stealthily between the bungalow and the pool, hid behind Don's broad back when they walked to the dining room in the main building of the Villas del Mar.

One more evening to get through.

"I have no present for you," Lisa said on Don's birthday. "Sorry."

They were sitting on the patio after dinner. She was in no mood for the faux-romantic night sky.

"But I have a present," he said. "And it's big enough for both of us."

He handed Lisa a jewellery box. Inside, resting on blue velvet, was a diamond ring. There must be a mistake, she thought, and ripped open the envelope that came with it. Perhaps the card explained it all, but the message inside the envelope was even more mysterious. It was an application for a marriage licence, filled out, dated, and signed by Don. Only the Lisa Martinez signature was missing. She looked up and saw Don watching her face, expectant, hopeful of being kissed, embraced, thanked.

"Don!" she said. "This is a joke, right?"

His face fell. "I'm completely serious, sweetie. I wouldn't joke about a thing like that. I love you, baby. Don't you love me a little in return?" He hoisted his jowls up into a smile, but it was shot through with anxiety.

Lisa thought she had settled that question. She thought Don understood he was on sufferance.

"You've been very nice to me, Don," she said. So much was true. "But." The "but" was hard to spin into something definite. It made her squirm to think what came after "but". Lisa wasn't cut out for a message of that kind. It was too cruel to come from her mouth.

Don read her mind. He could tell that "but" would be followed by something devastating. He tried to ward it off.

"I'd do anything for you, Lisa," he said.

"I know, Don, but I never thought of you as a – ." She didn't say the word. It was bad luck to have Don and lover appear in the same thought.

"I'm too old, you mean."

"You are more of a father figure to me."

"That's saying the same thing."

"Don, please, let's not talk about it anymore."

Lisa held out the jewellery box to him. She wanted him to take the bad luck charm out of her hands, out of her sight.

"You're in love with someone else."

Lisa frantically tried to blot out all thoughts of Jim. She could feel her head going transparent and all her hidden thoughts being exposed to Don's probing eyes.

"There is someone else, right?" he said.

"Stop interrogating me, Don."

"I don't mean to 'interrogate' you, sweetheart. If you tell me there is no one else, I'll wait. I am a patient man, you know." He put his octopus arms around Lisa. "Please, give me a chance, baby."

She struggled against his embrace. She felt sorry for Don, but she wanted out.

"Wear the ring. Please," he said. "Wear it at least for the rest of the trip. That's all I'm asking for. Think about me while you're in Catamarca."

"I don't want to wear the ring. It makes no sense."

"I just want you to take my proposal seriously. I'm asking for a few days, sweetheart." He grasped Lisa's hand. He straightened her fingers. He slipped on the ring. Lisa's hand went into rigor mortis.

"And when I come back?" she said faintly. She felt tagged.

"When you come back, you give me your considered reply."

"And if I say no, you'll ruin the last few days in Buenos Aires for me. You'll bug me all the way home."

"I swear, baby, I'll accept whatever you say. I'll respect your decision. Cross my heart."

He picked up Lisa's hand and kissed it. The ring flashed a terrible warning. It predicted disaster. Lisa could see it coming.

She said: "It's crazy, you know, Don. I can tell you right now – "

He put a finger on her lips. "No, don't say it. I want to be hopeful for one short week. You'll do that much for me, won't you, ducky?"

Lisa made a mistake then. She lost sight of the flashing omen and looked into Don's pleading eyes. "Okay," she said, but she was thinking: I need to get away from Don and the easy comfort of his arms. I need to move out of his flat when I'm back in Toronto. I don't care if it makes a hole in my savings. I'll put someone else in charge of swatting the *mariposas* and clearing the air around me. Jim. She felt a sudden access of energy and confidence. The Don phase was over.

"I'm going to the beach," she said. His presence was clotting her life, turning it sour.

"Wait for me," he said.

"No, I need to be on my own."

"It's very late," he said. "It's not safe to go to the beach on your own."

"I can look out for myself."

"I'll wait up for you."

"Go to bed, Don. Leave me alone."

He looked hurt, but his hands made no more demands on her. He retreated. Even so he was taking up too much space, jutting into Lisa's life. She walked out into the night, past the bungalows, along the concrete path leading down to the beach. The fake gas lanterns made the concrete look an alarming yellow.

When she stepped out of the circle of light and on to the sand, a shadow unfolded into the silhouette of a man, an apparition: Santos. Was this the meaning of the flashing diamond and the alarming yellow path? A warning – watch out for Santos? This was a scene she was not prepared for, a play with no end in sight, a play with an indefinite run. On stage: Lisa in the spotlight. In the wings: men waiting their turn. Don goes off-stage. Enter Santos.

"What are you doing here?" she said to him.

"Looking for you," he said and fell in step with her, trotting along like a shaggy dog.

Lisa sat down on the sandy ridge above the sea. He sat down beside her. Together they watched the waves rolling in on a crest and falling back into glazed smoothness.

"So when will you come to Tilcara?" he said, switching to Spanish, speaking with new-found precision. Correct grammar made him both more commanding and less exotic.

Lisa ignored his question and asked one of her own. "How did you track me down?"

"I phoned your mother. I told her I was going to Argentina. I was a friend of yours and wanted to meet up with you. She gave me your itinerary." He looked at Lisa sideways. "You look annoyed. Why? I did nothing wrong. I asked a question, and I got an answer."

Naturally. Lisa's mother was a member of the crew that kept her on stage. She was the prompter. Go, go. Next scene: you're on again, Lisa.

"I'm annoyed at you for asking, and at my mother for giving out the information."

Santos picked up her hand, the one with Don's ring, looked at it, and put it down again gently.

"Your mother said nothing of this," he said and fell silent. The breakers were eating into the shore and etching white lines into the sand.

"She doesn't know," Lisa said. "Don sprang a proposal on me. I didn't say yes. I told him I would think about it when I'm on my own."

Santos curled his lip. "But you are never on your own. He is with you all the time."

"I'm going to Catamarca tomorrow," she said. "On my own. I don't want Don around. Or you. *Comprendes*?"

He nodded, but it wasn't a nod of approval. "When you are in Catamarca, go to the farmers' market and look for Asu," he said. "She works there." He said it as if he was recommending a tourist attraction.

"Asu? But you said she was – "

"I know what I said. But she is beginning to listen to the saints. One day they will show her the way home. You go to the market and look for Asu. Talk to her about Tilcara."

"Santos, listen to me. I hope Asu finds her way home, but I'm not going to look for her or talk to her. I have problems of my own."

"Then you must come to Tilcara." The promised land, the magical place to heal all sorrows. "Your mother told me you are booked on a bus tour to the

North. The bus stops in Jujuy, no? You wait for me at the hotel. I'll pick you up and drive you to Tilcara."

He said Tilcara so often, it was becoming a chant.

He pulled a flask out of his back pocket. "You want?" He showed Lisa the sepia label: *Dr. Brown's Magic.*

Lisa needed magic in her life now that she had to contend with two unwanted followers. Her resolve weakened. One more time: to lift the weight of life. She drank from the bottle. She kept taking sips as they sat in silence.

"What time are you leaving tomorrow?" Santos said. His voice was echoing in the vast chamber of the open air.

"At seven. I should pack my suitcase now," Lisa said. She tried to get up, but her legs were stuck in the sand. Santos hauled her up and frog-marched her to the bungalow. The concrete path had turned into a snaking ribbon. There was light in the living room. It came at Lisa through the shutters and slashed her face. Santos knocked on the door, and Don let them in. He didn't seem surprised. He waved them in, or perhaps it was Lisa's body that was waving. On the coffee table was a bottle of whiskey. Had everyone fallen off the wagon?

The floor was like jelly. Lisa avoided looking at the walls, she was afraid of getting lost in their crevices. She walked into the bedroom and dropped on the bed. It billowed like the sea. She balanced on the waves precariously, watching the two men through the open door. They were talking in the living room, one brown and skinny, the other white like the belly of a whale parting the waves, spurting water through his air hole, no, whiskey, no, blood through his nose. The colours were confusing. There was only red or green and nothing in between. Lisa closed her eyes.

A moment later, it seemed, Santos shook her awake. She was lost in the percussion of her heart, a gritty noise, then the noise flattened out, and she saw that it was morning. She squeezed her eyes shut, wanted to go back to the dark place inside, but Santos wouldn't let her, was standing over her, his voice grating on her ears.

"Time to go," he said. "Call a taxi."

She sat up, tried to move her legs, make contact with the floor. She felt hot and sweaty. Her slept-in clothes were clinging to her. She couldn't face the idea of washing up and changing, but she got out of bed, obedient to Santos' wake-up call. Holding on to the dresser, the back of a chair, the walls, she made it to the bathroom.

"Don will take me to the airport," she said, but she could see for herself. Don couldn't possibly take her. He had turned to stone. He was lying motionless on the sofa in the living room, buried under a blanket. The whiskey bottle on the coffee table was empty.

"Don't count on him" Santos said. "Call a taxi. And don't forget: look up Asu in Catamarca."

"I told you: I don't want to see her."

He looked at Lisa sadly. "But it's your last chance."

"Last chance for what?" she said impatiently.

"To talk to Asu."

"No. I said no."

"*Bueno*," he said. "I'll see you in Jujuy then."

By the time the porter came to pick up Lisa's suitcase, Santos was no longer in the room. She couldn't remember saying good-bye to him. She didn't know how to say good-bye to Don. The porter looked at the man stretched out on the sofa and at the empty bottle. Lisa tipped him generously to wipe the look of pity off his face.

IN THE ARRIVAL HALL AT the Catamarca Airport, a travel agent held up a hand-lettered BIENVENIDO sign. His welcome wasn't for Lisa but it set the mood. A sign is a sign. The air was thick with happy messages. And there was Jim.

"How was the flight?" he said and hugged her. Lisa burrowed into his chest, letting him stroke her hair and ease last night's delirium.

"Rough," she said. She reached up and touched her fingertips to his cheek. Dr. Brown's magic elixir was crowding her thoughts, but in the untidy pile of self-loathing nausea there was something new and crisp, the joy of touching Jim. She kissed him gently, afraid of disturbing the current of happiness flowing between them.

The road from the airport cut a swath through the middle of the city, and suddenly she realized that she was in another country. It had taken her that long to become sensible of the difference. She had brought Toronto along in her suitcase, unpacked it every night in Mar del Plata and surrounded herself with the familiar props of unhappiness. Now she was beginning to breathe the foreign air, to notice the foreign sky. The balconies of the high-rises to the left and right were hanging over the traffic like baffles over a blaring orchestra pit. And now, the noise was entering through the fissures of Lisa's soul, diluting and dissolving her euphoria. Or perhaps it was the effect of Jim's words.

"Too bad you didn't come last week," he was saying. "This week is crazy. I'm up against a deadline. In fact, I shouldn't even be here. I should be at the construction site. I'll get you settled in at the hotel, and give you a quick tour of the centre, but that's all the time I can spare today. Sorry. I have to drive out to the dam this afternoon. We'll get together later."

The disappointment was coming on so fast it fused Lisa's thoughts to the tune of *Alone again, naturally.*

Jim reached over and put a consoling hand on her arm. "I'll be back in town for the weekend."

"But I'm booked on a bus tour," she said, feeling the murmur of anxiety in her breast. "I'll be leaving tomorrow." She didn't say: I was hoping you'd come along. Jim didn't say: Why don't you cancel the trip? *Despite encouragement from me/No words were ever spoken.* The O'Sullivan tune was hovering, but there was no place for it to settle down. Everything was cluttered with impossibilities.

"I'm supposed to meet Santos in Jujuy," Lisa said. She might as well tell Jim the worst. Fate was against her. Nothing *could be mended / left unattended. What do we do? What do we do?* The signs were all wrong. Jim had withdrawn his hand. In the sky, a plane left a vapour trail, crossing out Lisa's plans. The traffic came to a stop as the lights ahead switched to red. The stop was meant for her.

"You are still in touch with Santos?" Jim said. "I wouldn't trust that man."

I know, she wanted to say, but no one can escape fate. "He said he'd drive me to Tilcara," she said instead. "He's invited me to spend a day at his *chacra.*"

"You'd be safer staying with your tour group."

"I don't want to hurt his feelings," Lisa said. She couldn't say: I may have to consult the Saint of Tilcara. She knew what Jim thought of saints and séances. Instead she said: "I'm going because I've promised myself to tie up the loose ends." *I've promised myself to treat myself –* . There was so much she had to do: find out about Miguel Soriano from his daughter and, if Hetta couldn't help her, she had to consult the Saint. He was her last resort. "When I come back, I'll start a new life."

"With Don?" Jim said. The car was inching forward toward the crossing. They were caught in the honking traffic of the city centre.

"No, no," Lisa said. The complications kept coming at her. She couldn't fight them off fast enough. *What do we do? What do we do?* "I swear there is nothing between me and Don," she said. "I had to cut down on my expenses, and Don offered me his spare bedroom, free. That's all."

"And he threw in a trip to Argentina? And a diamond ring?"

Jim had noticed the ring! His arm crept back to the passenger side. He took up Lisa's hand, feeling the ring, as if her story was etched on it in Braille and could be read by passing a fingertip over it.

"My parents paid for the trip," Lisa said, but she knew it was hopeless to defend herself. No words, no arguments could shield her from the coming evil. "The diamond ring – ." She took her hand out of Jim's grasp and pulled at the ring, the omen. It was stuck at the knuckle. "It's not what you think. It's a complicated story."

"You have a knack for complicating your life, Lisa."

"But it's all going to change," she said, desperately wanting to believe in the possibility of change, of overturning fate, but she could hear the hum of failure in her voice. She could smell failure seeping through the car windows, the fumes of disappointment. "I'll move out of Don's place once I get back to Toronto," she said. "And I'll settle the Soriano question this afternoon. I phoned Hetta from Mar del Plata. I'm going to see her at four. It's just a matter of confirming what I know already." She was talking fast. There was so much to explain.

Jim was shaking his head. Lisa realized just how crazy her story was: from chaos to order in half a day.

"Anyway," she said, winding up where she had begun, the trip up north. "I'm off tomorrow morning."

"When do you come back?" Jim asked.

"Sunday night," she said. "And I leave for Buenos Aires on Tuesday morning." Not much time to spend together.

"Okay," Jim said. "On Sunday evening, we'll celebrate the start of your new life." He was smiling. She couldn't make out what kind of smile it was, mocking or forgiving.

"But right now I'll give you a tour of the city centre," he said, "and then I'll take you to my favourite place."

A little happiness sneaked back inside her. Jim's favourite place. Something special to share with him. There was consolation in that.

"The market," he said, and Lisa's hope died, struck down by the fateful word, rubbed out by the force of a word said too often, first by Santos, now by Jim: the market. Where Asu was working. Lisa did not want to see her, was afraid of Asu's bad-luck eyes, but fate had run her to ground. The decision had been made without Lisa. Her will no longer mattered. Her whole self was suspended, kept at a distance from herself. Her arms and legs stopped obeying her mind and moved into the one-two zombie rhythm. She trailed after

Jim. She looked at the sights of Catamarca with one-two sightless eyes, as her mouth pushed out words to the one-two count of "nice" and "interesting." Plazas, quaint courts, the cathedral.

"I guess you aren't into history," Jim said, putting an arm around her drooping shoulders. "We'll go to the market. I think you'll like it."

It was a produce market, but at the far end there were stalls selling cooking utensils, clothes, and handicrafts. They walked through the aisles, Jim's arm keeping Lisa close, but not close enough to shield her eyes against the omen: Jesus Malverde. She stopped in her tracks. Jim stopped, too.

"Hey," he said. "That looks like the statue Santos had in his shop. Must be a new stall."

A young woman sat among the painted figures, crouching on an overturned crate. She had a child's body, skinny without being angular. Her brown face was framed by glossy black hair. And she looked at them with the bad-luck eyes Lisa knew by heart.

Jim picked up one of the wooden saints.

"*Es Jesus Malverde, no*?" he said.

The woman got up and answered in English: "You know about Jesus Malverde?" She spoke to Jim but she looked at Lisa. Her eyes were of a brooding blackness that swallowed the light.

"Just his name," Jim said.

"He is the Mexican Robin Hood," she said. "They call him the 'Angel of the Poor.'" She spoke English with the stiff correctness of someone who uses it infrequently. "And this is San Simón of Guatemala." She pointed to a seated figure with a wide-brimmed hat and a white shirt. "He is the trickster. People invoke him when they are in trouble with the law."

"Your English is very good," Jim said.

The woman gave him a tight smile.

Jim picked up San Simón. "How much?" he said.

"Depends," she said.

On what did it depend? Could San Simón the trickster be bought off?

It depended on the exchange rate. The woman quoted Jim a price in dollars, but that left the question of converting dollars into pesos. Was it to be the official bank rate or the *paralelo*, the higher rate paid on the street? Jim haggled without conviction and ended up paying the *paralelo*.

Lisa kept watching for a sign from the woman as she wrapped the statue in newspaper and tied it up with string, but she did not give her another glance.

"It's for you," Jim said to Lisa, as they walked back to the car. "A souvenir."

"No," she said, hiding her hands behind her back. "I don't want a trickster."

Jim laughed. "Oh, come on, Lisa," he said. "Don't be so superstitious."

But Lisa couldn't afford to be careless in the face of fate. She refused to touch San Simón, and Jim gave up.

"Okay," he said. "Forget it then."

He put the statue into the trunk of his car and drove Lisa to her hotel. *And as if to knock me down/ Reality came around.* The porter came out, opened the car door for her and took possession of her suitcase. Jim kissed her on the cheek.

The distance between them widened.

"I wish you'd come up north with me," she said.

"I wish I could," he said, "but I told you: this week is crazy. The head of the junta is scheduled to visit the site tomorrow. If I don't show my face, they'll interpret it as lack of respect. It might have serious repercussions for the project. They are boneheaded about that sort of thing. Otherwise I'd come along." He hugged her. "I wish you weren't going to Tilcara."

"Maybe I won't," Lisa said, but she knew she was fated to go. She had seen Asu at the market and looked into her eyes. San Simón the Trickster was in the trunk of Jim's car.

"I tell you what," Jim said. "Phone me on Friday night, and we'll arrange something. I'll drive up north and meet you halfway. We can take it from there, do our own tour."

"Okay," she said. "I'll phone you."

"Promise?" he said. She promised, but really it wasn't up to her. It depended on fate.

Her arms were around his neck. She couldn't let him go. "Jim," she said. "I have this tune going in my head: *Alone again, naturally.* If it's natural, I guess I'll have to get used to it."

"You think I don't feel lonely sometimes?" he said, holding her tight. "But we'll have a weekend of luxurious togetherness. Maybe I can take Monday off, too."

She couldn't ask for more. She had to let him go.

LISA'S HOTEL ROOM WAS CRUELLY neat. It was as if her mother was silently presiding over the scene, with her "don't touch" housekeeping. The dreary atmosphere of back home, the doldrums of suburbia, descended on Lisa. The covers on the bed were creaseless, the mahogany table by the window polished to a sheen, the chair pushed in tidily. There was something reproachful about the room, telling her: see how neat everything is? Keep it that way, Lisa.

"*Todo bien?*" the busboy asked. He was standing at the door, discreetly waiting for his tip. Lisa found a crumpled dollar bill in her wallet and gave it to him. His radiant smile made her suspect it was too much. *Si, todo bien*, she said. Everything was in order. There was a crisp clarity about the room. Not a setting in which to conjure up the ghost of Soriano *padre*. Hetta was her only hope. On the phone, her voice had sounded promising: a high, pure soprano inviting Lisa to tea – to read the tea leaves? She sounded like a woman who could channel a dead man's spirit.

In the afternoon Lisa took a taxi to the address Hetta had given her. The sky, lucid blue in the morning, was streaked with white clouds now, blurring the picture. The driver looked into the rear view mirror. "*Americano?*" he asked. His eyes were eager. His mouth and the little moustache above it were askew, a question mark. He seemed disappointed when Lisa said: *Canadiense*. Perhaps American tourists were better tippers.

He dropped her off at a fine old building not far from Parque Navarro. Lisa walked up to the second floor, the *belle étage*, and was shown into the living room by the maid.

A woman was standing by the glass doors leading to the balcony, petite, elegantly dressed, a slim silhouette against the afternoon light. She closed the balcony door, shutting out the windblown sound of traffic, and stepped into the room. The slanting rays of the sun left the room in semi-darkness and gave her a mysterious air.

"So you are Maria's daughter," she said, holding out her hand to Lisa. "Welcome to Catamarca." Her hair was a forced blonde, and some of the peroxide brittleness seeped into her speech. She had a small face and wide-set eyes like a Pekinese, delicate and purebred, showing traces of the perfect child Lisa's mother had adored.

A faint scent of lavender rose from the pair of cropped plush sofas facing each other. They had the withered look of pieces in an attic. The walls were hung with colonial portraits and classical landscapes. Yes, this was the place to meet the dead. Miguel Soriano's spirit was palpable.

Hetta sat down under the pensive portrait of a distinguished gentleman – Lisa's father? She sensed his aura, but his face remained flat, two-dimensional. She missed the softness, the warmth, the feel of skin against her fingertips.

Hetta crossed her legs decorously at the ankles. An elegant economy governed all her movements. Lisa was cowed, intimidated by her daintiness, embarrassed by her own crass fatherless past. She felt humble, an intruder in the Soriano noblesse, a bastard.

The maid reappeared with a silver tray of tea things and set it down on the table between them.

Lisa secretly touched the table's edge for luck and pointed to the portrait over the sofa.

"Is that your father?" she said. She would have liked to say "our" father, but so far no tokens of kinship had passed between them. There were no distinguishing marks, no subliminal signs as yet that they were half-sisters.

"That's my father," Hetta said. "But he was a father to everyone. People couldn't help loving him."

Lisa's mouth formed an O, perhaps she said Oh! She couldn't hear herself talk. Her ears were blocked. *A father to everyone, couldn't help loving him* was humming and vibrating in her head. Hetta was speaking to her in code, in signs, willing to share her father, willing to admit: Lisa's mother *couldn't help loving him.*

"He was a wonderful man," Hetta was saying, "warm, kind-hearted, generous – I wish you could have met him."

"He was generous to my mother," Lisa said.

A shadow passed over Hetta's face. Memories of the sins of her father? But the shadow cleared.

"I have very fond memories of your mother," she said. "She had a thousand ways of making a child happy."

All of them spent on Hetta, nothing left for Lisa. "But you didn't stay in touch with her," she said.

There was the shadow again. "It was an awkward situation," Hetta said.

"Awkward? You mean because – " Lisa let the words dangle. She wasn't sure whether to go on.

"Did your mother tell you – "

"She told me nothing," Lisa said quickly. "But I always had my suspicions. The way she talked of him – " Again, she wanted to say "my father" but perhaps this wasn't the right moment or the right order of things. To be on the safe side, she said "him" and pointed at the man in the painting. "The way she talked about him – I could tell she was head over heels in love."

"In love?" Hetta raised her eyebrows. "You mean to say, fond of him?"

"No, I mean in love. And he with her."

Hetta put her hand to her mouth. "*Dios mio*!" She leaned back in her chair to distance herself from such blasphemy. "I cannot imagine who put that idea into your head. No, no! My father was the most proper person in the world. He would never – " Her lips were a prim line of disapproval.

"But you said yourself that it was an awkward situation."

"Let me explain," she said. She paused, gathering up the threads of the story. Lisa had no desire to hear it. She could tell Hetta was no storyteller. The best she could expect from those prim lips was a sermon.

"My father treated everyone like family," Hetta said. "Your parents didn't have enough money to pay for the passage to Canada. They came to my father, and he helped them out with a loan."

"A loan?" Lisa said. "I was under the impression that he had made them a present of the money."

"There was a misunderstanding. Nothing was put in writing. My father was like that."

"You mean to say: he considered it a loan. My parents considered it a gift, and he was never repaid?"

"I don't like to put it that way, *querida*. Let's just say, they disagreed about the nature of the transaction. Your mother, who is a decent woman, was embarrassed and wanted to pay the money back, in instalments. But my father was too proud to accept it in the circumstances. If they were under the impression that it was a gift, he would leave it at that. He didn't want to hear anything more about the business. He wrote the money off. And that was the end of our correspondence. I didn't mean to tell you all this, but I couldn't leave you under the misapprehension that, that – ." She trailed off.

Lisa was unsure what to do with Hetta's explanation: Swallow it whole? Eat it piecemeal? Spew it out as a lie, a cover-up? There was nothing to guide her now. The aura around Soriano's portrait had vanished. His spirit had fled the room and left it slightly shabby. Lisa saw that the Persian carpet was faded and threadbare. The frame around the portrait was chipped and tarnished – she hadn't noticed it before.

"It happened so long ago," Hetta said. "It's time to forget."

Lisa looked into Hetta's melancholy eyes. They were both grieving for Miguel Soriano. She made faint excuses, about another appointment, about needing to be on time. Hetta walked with her to the door, put a limp hand in hers and wished her *Buen viaje.*

All the loose ends Lisa had hoped to tie up were still loose, trailing, entangling her, tripping her up.

At the corner of the street, Lisa stopped, looking for a taxi in the parade of cars going by, or else she was looking for the right father in the phalanx of ghostly images in her head, an unattractive line-up: Don in Mar del Plata, curled up on the sofa bed in a fetal position, moaning "baby, baby." Jorge Martinez, pouring over his accounts, refusing to pay back the loan. Soriano *padre,* his suit jacket ripped open, his hand pointing to a flaming heart. An electric storm was raging in Lisa's head. Who would make it up to the weeping orphan? She had to go to Tilcara. That was the meaning of Asu's words at the market stall: *Depends.* Depends on whether you believe Hetta's story. And that was the meaning of Jim buying the Trickster. Fate was against Lisa. She needed a saint's touch now.

AT THE BUS DEPOT THE next morning, the tour guide handed Lisa a nametag. She put it away and climbed on the bus incognito. Most of the seats in the front half of the bus were taken. She headed for an empty row near the back and put her bag down on the seat beside her to discourage anyone from joining her. She was practising loneliness. This was an educational tour for Lisa, an instruction in the art of being *Alone again naturally*. That's how it was going to be from now on. One more indulgence: the embrace of the Saint. After that, no more gurus. Lisa wanted to wean herself off fathers and mothers, off the advisors she had tried and found lacking: Don, Santos, Dr. Lerner. She would have liked to keep Jim, but she had a premonition that he wasn't in the cards.

A couple of pensioners, tagged Osvaldo and Felicia Guzman, settled heavily in the seats across the aisle from Lisa. Osvaldo eyed her, leaned over and asked about the missing nametag. His voice was full of paternal admonition. He would not accept anonymity.

"I don't speak Spanish," Lisa said in English. "I'm from Toronto." Her best defence was pleading ignorance of the language.

"*Ah, Canadiense*," Osvaldo said and lapsed into enforced silence. Felicia craned her neck and gave Lisa an uneasy smile. It wasn't fair, her crimped smile said. A whole bus of happy, chatting people, and they had ended up across the aisle from a silent foreigner.

The bus lumbered out of the terminal, burping a cloud of diesel fumes, clattered through the outskirts of Catamarca, and picked up speed on the open road. Dust curled up, seeped through the bus windows, and settled in Lisa's lungs. She felt parched and dry-mouthed, thirsting for an answer from the Saint of Tilcara. The Guzmans were watching the road in discontent. Osvaldo twisted restlessly. He half rose from his seat, waved to someone up front with come-back-here fervour, but they insisted on staying in their premium seats right behind the driver. He got up and made his way forward, swaying. He stood in the aisle beside his friends, gripping their headrests, gesticulating, joking, and returned with a fellow pensioner in tow.

"*Mi amigo,*" he said to Lisa, introducing him: Manuel Sanudo.

Manuel smiled broadly. "I speak the English," he announced.

Lisa lowered her eyes, too late to discourage him from giving her a demonstration.

"Has very cold in Canada, no?" he asked.

"During the winter, yes," Lisa said, and clamped her mouth shut again.

Sanudo wrinkled his brow trying to put together another sentence. "My friends," he said, pointing to the front of the bus. "You must come. I introduce you."

"Later," Lisa said tonelessly.

The two men exchanged looks of disappointment. They had hoped for more give and take. Manuel was running out of English. "*Hasta luego, entonces,*" he said, looking defeated. He shook hands with Felicia, exchanged perfunctory family news, and returned to the front.

The bus was rolling through a bare landscape of salt flats. Lisa closed her eyes and beckoned the dazzling white sheets into her mind, a vast tabula rasa, on which to design the rest of her life in clean, strong outlines which would not fade at the first sign of doubt. When she opened her eyes again, sugar cane had replaced the white desert, but the outlines of her life remained flat. The foreground refused to meet the background. A gap remained, and Tilcara was spreading its name like a mist over the tableau. Tilcara was on her mind all day, until the bus stopped under orange trees in San Miguel de Tucumán. Lisa suffered through lunch and a walking tour of the town, playing dumb, stuck with her lie. She had to remain Spanish-less and allow Manuel Sanudo to interpret her words. She was glad when they boarded the bus again and she could escape to the isolation of her seat. Was she falling in love with loneliness, or was it the dearth of single people on the bus? There were only *jubilados*, round matrons and their puffy-faced white haired husbands, and a few young couples freighted with children.

THE FULLNESS OF HIS DISCONTENT struck Jim later, when he was driving out to the construction site. He could have had a good time with Lisa, break out, escape to the jungle of Lisa's mind, to the pulsating wilderness of her life. But he had opted to stay in his prefab cell. Instead of spending the night in Lisa's tree house, he was staying on the ground. As he was driving, reality closed in on him. Go to the dam, sleep at a trailer camp, eat breakfast in a canteen from dishwasher-safe plates, use tinny cutlery, sit on wooden benches elbow to elbow with beefy men reeking of sweat and tobacco. There were no urban comforts at site, no refinements, no air-conditioned rooms, no movies, no gourmet food, nothing to please the eye or the mind. No Lisa. There were only deadlines. The men were gruff and foulmouthed, working under pressure. Jim suspected there was camaraderie under all the coarseness, under the brutish snarling and muscle flexing, but he was on the outside looking in. He was management, city bred, a man with a university degree – three strikes against him.

The site supervisor, Brian Cowley, was a sad-faced Irish bulldog, fluent in the poetry of Yeats and in the American vernacular. He and Jim were on hand when the General and his retinue came out for the "opening ceremony." They were more than a year away from handing over, but that timetable was at odds with the junta's scheme. They needed a photo op now. Some ribbon-cutting hoopla was called for. The General's handlers had scouted out a photogenic spot and instructed Brian to clear it of debris. They set up a carpeted dais and a microphone. The white and blue flag went up on the improvised flag pole to the melancholy strains of the Argentine anthem. The medals pinned to the General's chest glittered in the sun. His goons stood at attention. He gave his standard progress and prosperity speech, and shook hands with Jim, too briefly apparently for the cameras. They shook again, this time with the General's left paw resting firmly on top of their joined hands, locking in the success story. Jim looked into the mirror of the General's black sunshades and saw Lisa hog-tied in a concrete cell, kicking her legs to a chorus of women like the one who had sold him the statue of San Simón. What the hell was going on in his mind! It must be the Lisa-effect. She always put him into a fantasy spin.

The image of Lisa vanished as the General dropped Jim's hand and turned his spotlight eyes on a priest rustled up for the occasion. The junta ruled only over bodies and relied on the church to coerce people's minds. Together they kept an iron grip on the citizens. The priest, robed in a lacy alb, intoned a prayer and blessed the dam, flicking holy water over the rim. The ritual sprinkling set off a camera blitzkrieg among the journalists. And that was that. The General waved a dignified *adios* and climbed into his limousine. The motorcade blasted off, the journalists loaded their gear into a banged-up van, and the crane operator climbed back into his cab and started up the machine with a valedictorian shudder.

"Assholes," Brian Cowley said. "Gasbags."

Jim grinned. "Does Yeats have anything to say about that?"

"Sure," he said. "*Great black oxen tread upon the world* – but forget Yeats. Those bastards cost me three hours. That's two hundred and forty fucking man hours." All of Brian's will power was distilled into profanities now. "How the fuck do I explain that to accounting? Tell me, Jim. We are over budget, as is. That dame they sent you to negotiate Phase Two was a washout. You should have brought in what's his name, the jigging bugger: Don Baker. That guy was a first-rate bullshitter. What happened to him?"

"He was let go for padding his CV, or something like that," Jim said.

"Ah well," Brian said. "He was full of shit, but he got what he wanted."

He was in the mood to complain. He let go a profanity laced tirade against the junta and the "apaches" who were servicing the heavy machinery, the shit-holes who supplied the concrete, the men who thought of nothing except booze and whores. Jim nodded, waiting for a pause in Brian's rant. He wanted to get back to Catamarca.

"Well, I'm off," he said as Brian was catching his breath.

"You're off? What's the hurry?" Brian said. "You bloody office types are always in a hurry to get back to the city. You should spend a couple of days here, Jim, get a taste of what I'm up against."

"I don't want to take up your time," Jim said. "You are a busy man, Brian."

"I am a busy man, but don't take my word for it. Stick around. Watch me sweat."

There was no escape from another dreary day at site, and after work, to pacify Brian, Jim tagged along to the local night spot, a windowless pyramid made of concrete like the dam itself.

"They should serve us free drinks here," Brian said. "TECO paid for the place. It was built with material stolen from site, every bucket of concrete, every pipe, every sheet of metal. They got it from our depots."

The Disco Embalse sat in a cow pasture, at the end of a bulldozed road, an ugly surprise, a misshapen cocoon put up by an enterprising thug with connections to the underworld.

"They offer a full range of services," Brian said, "but they take only hard currency. No funny money, except for the local hooch. You can pay with pesos for that. It's high octane. One shot and you are joy-gushed. The girls are high octane too. You should try one."

The girls were recruited from the slums of Catamarca, Brian said. "Complexion too dark to make it in the marriage market, but they've got the essential parts." The men were hungry for a touch of flesh to satisfy their cavernous wants. They didn't care about looks. The women looked passable under the strobe lights in their tight minis and halter tops, visible only for jerky seconds at a time under the pulsing white light. The music was a bass-heavy, pounding, demonic noise. By midnight, the dance floor was filled with spastic bodies, frenzied couples voraciously clawing at each other and strafed with catcalls and grunts by the lonely men seething around the bar. The dirty talk inspired Hustler capers in Jim's mind, with Lisa taking centre stage, but his desire remained unrelieved. The whores were too sweaty-dirty to suit his fantasy or to contemplate in reality. After midnight a screaming punching fistfight erupted. Brian waded in singlehandedly and separated the gamecocks from the victims. After that, the crowd thinned. They walked to the car in the cool night-air. Brian switched on the headlights and transformed the disco into a vision of dazzling white, a mirage in a desert landscape. At the edge of the parking lot, they saw a man lying in the ditch.

"Roy," Brian said. "He's pissed again."

"Let's haul him up," Jim said.

"No way," Brian said. "I don't want him puking over my backseat. Leave him alone. *Many times he died. Many times he lived again.*"

"Let me guess," Jim said. "Yeats?"

At noon next day, when he was driving back to Catamarca, he saw Roy trudging along the road to the dam. He stopped and offered him a ride.

"Don't take me back to the construction site," Roy said as he climbed into the car. "Just drop me off at the trailer camp." He was full of self-pity, reeking of vomit and bitterness. "Might as well take the day off," he said. "That fucker Brian plays hardball. If you haven't punched in by eight, he rips up your time card. No pay. He's a fucking slave driver, that man."

BACK IN CATAMARCA, JIM WENT for an after-dinner stroll. As he stepped out of the hotel lobby into the melancholy dusk, someone waved to him from across the street. He recognized the woman from the market stall, where he had bought the statue of San Simón. Jim waved back. The way she was dressed, in a tight skirt and stiletto-heels, the way she had her purse slung over her shoulder and was standing very close to the curb, hand on jutting hip, she looked like a hooker waiting for a customer. Too late Jim realized that she *was* a hooker, selling saints by day, and her body by night.

She crossed the street to where he was standing. Was it a chance meeting? No, it was not.

"I was looking for you," she said when she caught up with Jim. "I thought you might want to go for a drink."

"How did you know where I was staying?" he said, annoyed.

She smiled at him through painted lips. "Most foreign businessmen stay at the Continental," she said and took his arm familiarly. "I meant to look for you yesterday, but the boss came around. I have to humour him, or else."

"Or else what?"

"He'll beat me up," she said casually. "Luckily he comes only once a month, to collect his percentage.

He is the one who supplies me with those wooden statues. So you want to go for a drink?"

She was clinging to him. There was no way to get rid of her without attracting attention.

"Okay," Jim said reluctantly, walking away from the hotel. He didn't want to be seen with a cheap whore.

"Good," she said, "Let's go to the Luna."

They walked through side streets and stopped under a painted sign reading BAR LUNA.

"In here," she said.

The bar was no more than a hole in the wall, a counter with half a dozen stools in the semi-darkness of a single lamp. They were the only customers.

"You are early, *negrita*," the barman said.

She did have a dark complexion. *Indio*?

"I was afraid of missing my friend here," she said, and laughed coldly as if she was guarding against any joy. She ordered a gin and tonic and looked at Jim sideways. "Can you let me have a cigarette?" she said.

"I don't smoke," he said.

She rolled her eyes. "*Deme dos de los especiales*," she said to the barman, and he brought out two joints for her. She lit one, drew hard on it and tipped her head back to let the smoke sink into her lungs.

"I've been thinking about dyeing my hair," she said. "Do you like red hair?"

"I don't care," he said.

"Red doesn't turn you on?"

The fabric of her blouse was so thin that Jim could see the dark rosettas of her breasts. He felt guilty as if he had taken something from her without paying. He wanted to put an end to the scene.

She leaned forward on her bony elbows and looked into his eyes.

"Could you lend me twenty dollars?" she said.

"I don't carry dollars," Jim said, and asked the waiter for the bill. "Let's not waste any more time. I'm not interested in your services, okay?"

She smirked at the waiter. "*Gallina mojada, este,*" she said, and to Jim: "You are a wet chicken. You know that expression?"

"I know the expression," Jim said, "but it's not a matter of being chicken. I don't go in for hookers."

She shot him an angry glance. "That's alright," she said. "You aren't my type anyway."

Jim got up to go.

"Wait," she said and put her skinny hand on his arm. "I'll take pesos." There was a gleam of despair in her eyes. "I need the money."

"For drugs?"

"What's it to you? But if you want to know: I need the money to go to Buenos Aires. I've had it with this place. The old man treats me like shit."

Jim walked out of the bar, and she followed him.

"I have some information you'd be interested in," she said, lighting the second cigarette and pulling at it greedily. "If you don't want to fuck, just pay me for the information."

"I don't need your information," Jim said. "I'll pay you for leaving me alone." It was the only way of shaking her off. She had a wretched determination.

She grabbed at the money he offered her and counted it quickly.

"Not enough to go to Buenos Aires," she said.

"That's all you are going to get from me," Jim said.

She didn't budge. They walked silently back in the direction of the hotel.

"You don't deserve the information," she said. "You're a prick. But I pity that little bitch, your girlfriend."

"What are you talking about?" Jim said.

"You know what I'm talking about. The woman who was with you at the market. Keep an eye on her, or she'll disappear – poof!"

She threw her head back and laughed. There was a manic edge to her laugh. She stopped short and became serious again.

"They are after her," she said, and walked away quickly.

THE BUS WAS CROSSING THE sierras. Lisa kept a silent watch on the road, on the look-out for the inevitable. They stopped in Salta and trooped through an *artesanal*, fingering souvenirs. Felicia refused to believe that Lisa wanted nothing, absolutely nothing. Not even this? She held up a maté gourd. Lisa shook her head. Lack of English did not keep Felicia from talking to Lisa, or keeping up a dumb show. But you must have a souvenir to take back, she said, convinced that every memory needed tangible proof, convinced that the evident truth of her sentiments was getting through to Lisa. Truth conquers all, even language barriers.

The bus got on the road again. It was then that Lisa spotted a car on a switchback curve, a solid object against a wall of porous rock. She looked down on it and saw the sun's rays glinting off the car roof, flashing a message: Santos is on your track.

Jujuy came into view. The children had made the last row of the bus their jungle gym. They were tumbling on the seats, pulling at each other, squealing. Felicia looked back and gave them a distracted grandmotherly warning. "*Basta, Guille,*" someone called from up front. "*Cállate.*" The wrangling and squealing ebbed and rose again.

The bus lumbered into Jujuy and halted in front of the hotel El Halcón.

"*Bueno*," Manuel said, as they climbed out, "in the end here is the hotel. And it looks something nice, no?" A little girl in a frowzy pink dress came over and looked at him curiously, fascinated by the foreign sounds coming out of his mouth. She hugged her teddy bear and aped him: *Nais-no?Nais-no?*

Manuel beamed at her, pleased with his disciple. "*Muy bien*," he said to her, and to Lisa: "She already learns."

Lisa shrugged. Manuel was on his last leg of English, but unwilling to let go.

"You play the cards?" he asked apropos nothing.

Lisa shook her head.

"You must learn," he said urgently. He grabbed Osvaldo's arm, making him a conspirator. "She must learn to play cards, no?" he said to him in Spanish. "We'll teach her tonight."

"I don't like playing cards," Lisa said.

"How come?" Manuel said, but he could see he was fighting a lost cause.

At dinner he wouldn't leave her alone. The guide had handed out the Jujuy itinerary. Manuel made her go over the schedule with him. Friday, 9 am-noon: city tour. Afternoon and all of the next day: optional tours. Manuel ran his finger down the list and recommended Termas de Reyes.

"Or the cactus wood churches," he said with importance.

Lisa was planning two days of freedom from the pensioners.

"I'll decide tomorrow," she said and got up. Time to escape to her room.

The Guzmans looked at her in surprise. You can't go now, Osvaldo protested. There will be a fiesta. The band is setting up. Manuel translated dutifully, lending his support: "You cannot leave at this moment."

"I'm tired," Lisa said, and Manuel echoed: *Esta cansada.*

The Guzmans refused to believe it. How could she be tired after sitting in the bus all day, dozing? It was too early to go up to her room. Manuel was pleading with Lisa. "You must stay. It has dancing."

She shook her head, no.

In her room, she lay down on the bed and thought of Tilcara, seeing Tilcara rooflines, Tilcara silhouettes in the shadows cast on the ceiling by the streetlights.

In the morning, at breakfast, she broke the news to the pensioners: she did not want to go to Termas de Reyes. She would not even join them on the sightseeing tour of Jujuy.

"But it's included in the price!" Osvaldo said, and Manuel translated for him.

"I know," Lisa said, "but I'm not interested."

Manuel's eyebrows met in two perfect arcs of astonishment. "What will you do in Jujuy alone?"

"Meet up with a friend," Lisa said.

A look of disappointment came into Manuel's eyes. "You have friend? Here?" And he thought he had the English monopoly.

Lisa stayed behind in the breakfast room as the pensioners marched outside to the bus from Turismo Jujuy and joined the line-up waiting at the curb. From her table at the window, she watched the driver check off their names on his list when Santos pulled up in an old Fiat. He cut the engine and jumped out, lean and nimble like a race dog. Lisa picked up her canvas bag and met him at the entrance of the hotel.

"Ready?" he said.

They walked out, and Lisa stood beside him on the sidewalk, in full view of the group boarding the bus. She could see it in their eyes: she was a manifest sinner. Felicia was at the window, watching her, scandalized. Her eyes were blinking rapidly. Osvaldo's face appeared beside hers, eyes alive with suspicion. Lisa defied them with a negligent wave of good bye. Manuel Sanudo sitting in the row behind the pensioners, craned his neck to see what was going on. He cranked open a window, and shouted: "Is okay everything?"

Lisa nodded. In his amazed eyes she read the question he could not put into English. What was the *Canadiense* doing in the company of this shabby individual? Was this her friend? Manuel looked embarrassed. He had been duped into believing that Lisa was a nice young woman.

Santos opened the car door for her. It listed toward the sidewalk on weak hinges. The plastic cover of the seats was cracked. Lisa climbed into the car, and Santos started up the engine and drove off with a dust-raising shudder.

She was on her way to visit the Saint, but somehow the consultation seemed no longer as urgent as it was the day before yesterday, when the portrait of Miguel Soriano in Hetta's apartment had failed to give off encouraging rays. The quest for Soriano *padre* had lost something in the patriarchal climate of the bus. There was a surfeit of volunteer fathers all wanting to take care of her. The trip to Tilcara now looked more like an outing, a last fling with Santos and his spirit world. Would the Saint speak to Lisa? He had been silent for a long time. Perhaps he knew: there was nothing to say, and Hetta had spelled it out for her: it was all a misunderstanding. Lisa was stuck with Jorge. The Saint had known it all along and remained mute on the question of her missing father.

He will enter you, Santos had promised Lisa. He will speak to you. He will look out through your eyes and see all. And he did, but he had nothing to say about Lisa's missing father. He spoke only of the missing girl, Asu. He was searching for her. Lisa understood now why the Saint could be coaxed to put in an appearance at all. They had something in common: a familial absence, the need for someone to fill the void and complete the group portrait of smiling heads.

"Why didn't you talk to Asu when you were in Catamarca?" Santos said as they left the tree-lined streets of Jujuy behind and drove through a rocky desert pierced by giant cactus. "She told me you came to the market, but you did not talk."

"I couldn't open my mouth," Lisa said. "She has the kind of eyes that seal your lips. I don't know how Don could stand living with her. Is it true that he bought Asu from your *abuelo*?"

"He bought her body, not her soul," Santos said. "He had no right to her soul, but he opened it up as if it were his, cut out Tilcara, and put himself inside. He came like a robber and took away the love that was in her soul. When we get to the *chacra*, you'll see the place where Asu slept. Her bed is empty now, waiting for a sleeper."

A suspicion flickered on the edge of Lisa's mind. Is that why Santos wanted her to come to Tilcara? Was it her fate to fill an empty space? Is that why Santos used to call her "little sister," to see whether the title fit her? Lisa suddenly remembered the biblical quote, Santos' words when they were lying on the black satin bed in the Botanica. "An eye for an eye," he had said. "A tooth for a tooth." How did it go on? She was afraid it would end: And one woman for another.

"Tell me," she said to Santos. "Why are you taking me to the *chacra*?" She asked the question even though she was not hopeful of receiving an answer.

"To put Tilcara in your soul," he said.

No, his words were no answer. They were a trap. They cast a net over Lisa, entangling her, drawing her deeper into Santos' mysterious quest.

They came to a small village and passed a church. Across the road, weathered men with blankets folded over their shoulders and women, babies strapped to their backs, were climbing into the back of a truck. They stood in the truck bed, crowding together, forming a tightly knit group, cattle about to be driven to the market. Was it a secret code to warn Lisa of a sacrifice, a slaughtering of the innocent, a massacre?

She tried to decipher Santos' profile. There was nothing there to confirm her fears. He looked benign.

On the door of the truck someone had written in white chalk: Jujuy.

"Taking the truck is cheaper than taking the bus," Santos said in a tour guide's voice.

The driver called out *Listo?* to the families huddled in the back, climbed into the cab and pulled out into the road. The passengers swayed and held on to the bar in the centre of the truck bed. A cloud of dust rose up. The women held handkerchiefs over their mouths and noses, passing Lisa ghost-like, veiled.

"I shouldn't have come here," she said. "I don't belong."

"What do you mean?" Santos said, and she winced under the direct light of his eyes. "Everyone is expecting you."

He made it sound like a homecoming.

They slowed at a roadside *tienda* with a gas pump out front. Barefoot children sat against the wall of the store, lined up like birds on a wire. They sat on their haunches, eyed the passing cars curiously and scrambled up when Santos pulled into the gas station.

A woman came out of the store, gave him a smile of recognition, and started pumping gas. Santos stepped forward and took over.

"You need help?" he said. "I'll work for you."

"I don't know," she said. "Ask Jaime Anqua."

"You need his permission?"

She looked him in the face fully. "Will you fight him?" she said quietly.

Santos said nothing in reply.

They got on the road again. Beyond the village, the gravel road turned into a furrowed track.

"Who is Jaime Anqua?" Lisa said.

"He is in charge of the village."

"You don't get along with him?"

Santos shrugged. The land was deserted except for a herd of black cows grazing in the distance. Birds were wheeling high up in the sky, specks against the mountain side.

"Maybe this isn't the right time to visit," Lisa said. "What did the woman at the gas station mean when she said 'will you fight him?' I don't want to get involved in a feud. "

"I tell you how it is," Santos said. "Ten years ago my grandfather, the Saint, was in charge of the village. He made me his heir, but he died too soon. I was a boy when he passed away. So Jaime Anqua took charge. Now it's my turn."

"And he doesn't want to give up his position?"

Santos looked at Lisa darkly. "Jaime wants his son to take over. I asked the Saint: will Simon Anqua succeed his father and take my rightful place? He did not reply. Maybe I'm asking too many questions. Maybe he doesn't hear me because Jaime Anqua is filling his ears with complaints: 'You promised Asu to my son. You promised her to Simon. Instead you sold her to another man. Where is Asu now? Bring her back.'"

Santos sighed. "It is a difficult situation for me. I want to fight Jaime. I want to fight Simon. But the Saint tells me: not yet. Everything has to be in balance first. I cannot go against the Saint. I am constrained to keep the peace."

Until now Tilcara had meant only one thing to Lisa: the abode of the Saint. She thought of it as a white-walled, castellated citadel of the dead, like the cemeteries they had been passing. She thought of Tilcara as a monument to the Saint, but now she realized it was a village populated by a clan at war. She was travelling in a battle zone, caught between the fronts, between Santos and Jaime, between Simon and the promised bride who had gone missing. The Saint wanted a truce, and Santos had brought a peace offering: Lisa.

Santos was hunched over the steering wheel, his eyes fixed on the ruts in the road. Lisa replayed the biblical phrase in her head: "An eye for an eye, a tooth for a tooth." And a woman for a woman. It was the theme song of their journey. Fear settled like dust in the corners of her mind. She had planned an outing for a day. Now it looked like the journey of a lifetime.

A line of tattered trees and tangled brush came into sight, and a hill reaching halfway to the sky. The car slowed down, rattled through a shallow creek, lumbered up the other side and turned into a packed dirt yard. The *chacra,* the kingdom of the Saint: half a dozen mud brick houses, a couple of tin sheds, a gaggle of chicken, a pile of rusting auto parts, and a pickup truck under a lemon tree.

A group of women and children were unloading firewood from the truck. They stopped as the car drove into the yard, turning their faces expectantly. The children broke loose and came running, dancing up to the car, screeching, dropping back stunned when they saw Lisa in the passenger seat. Santos got out, negligently waved to the children, acknowledged the women out of the corner of his eye, and walked up to a wiry old man, standing by the truck cab. They touched hands ceremoniously and spoke in Quechua.

Lisa got out of the car and stood still like a good child, waiting to be spoken to, keeping her eyes on the gaunt, narrow-shouldered man. His lank black hair hung down to his shoulders, his leathery face was ageless, untamed, messianic. It was clear: he was the new Saint of Tilcara, the successor to the throne, Jaime Anqua.

"I bring Lisa," Santos said in Spanish and motioned to her. His words descended on Lisa in a funnel cloud. The voices of the *desaparecidos* were swirling in the air, Asu in her school girl uniform calling Lisa's name, a chorus of missing children crying with high-pitched voices, like bats.

Jaime Anqua stretched out his arms as if to accept a gift, a lamb to be added to the flock. He came and embraced Lisa, held her close, keeping his sinewy arms around her, heavy with approbation. The women and children stood spellbound, observing the ceremony, listening open-mouthed. He began to speak volubly, his hands alive with gestures, Quechua words forming a melodious string of sounds, a vowel-rich flow of words. Lisa hung on his lips, listened to his clucking tongue. He spread his arms as if to say: with me you will enter paradise. Lisa wanted to decipher the saving message of this pagan god, but he stopped the music abruptly and pointed to a cabin.

"*Entra*," he said, switching to Spanish, his fingers on her spine, steering her to the hut. He parted the plastic string curtain that served as a door, and they ducked into the twilight of the cabin. The window was shuttered with wooden *persianas*. Santos stayed back, lingering at the door.

"This is your house," the replacement Saint said, smiling, nodding.

Lisa breathed in the musty smell of long disuse and lack of sunshine. A beetle dropped from the rafters. The cabin was bare, except for a mattress on the tamped earthen floor covered with a woven blanket and, in one corner, a crate holding spools of thread. On the wall, stuck side by side on rusty nails, was a print of Jesus, blond and blue-eyed, and a faded snapshot of a barefoot girl child, looking into the camera stony-faced. Lisa recognized her. She was a blurry miniature version of the school girl who presided over her bedroom in Toronto. She had the same eyes. Lisa was up against a holy trinity: the child in the snapshot, the teenager in the framed photo in Don's apartment, and the young woman at the market stall.

"You like your house?" Jaime said and put his hand on Lisa's bottom firmly, precluding protest. He knew his hand's place at all times: Trust me, daughter. Up close in the duskiness of the cabin, his skin looked oven baked, tanned with the salt of sweat.

"My house?" Lisa said, although there was no longer any question in her mind. She was caught. Asu's home was her home now.

Jaime nodded and smiled broadly, lines seared into the corners of his mouth.

Through the door, Lisa could see the women dragging over two cane chairs and putting them down by the cabin. Jaime accepted the homage and sat in one of them, legs stretched out, inviting Lisa to sit in the other. Santos took up station beside them, hands hanging loose, scanning the crowd like a bodyguard.

"My family," Jaime said, gesturing to the women and children and waving them over. He was the paterfamilias, everyone's *abuelo.*

"Remedios," he said, introducing a solemn olive-skinned beauty. Her black hair was gathered in shiny braids. Two gypsy-eyed women joined the circle: Rosa and Mirella.

Lisa greeted them uneasily.

Jaime gathered the children around and announced their names one after the other, then made them repeat "Lisa" and bring out their store of Spanish, their hellos and how are yous, until they giggled with embarrassment. They were locking their ankles, ducking, looking away, knitting their fingers, but they were not allowed to leave the line-up until they had said: "*Hola*, Lisa". It was like being back in the playground of the nursery school. Lisa stretched out her arms to the replacement tots, but they backed away shyly.

After the performance, Jaime tweaked their cheeks in friendly recognition and dismissed them, making "Off with you" noises, swinging his arms and clapping his hands as if shooing a flock of birds.

Santos seemed to have lost all interest in the proceedings. He was leaning against the wall of the cabin, eyes turned to a distant nowhere.

"Santos," Lisa said, pulling him back into the present. "It's nice meeting your family, but I came here because of the Saint, you know."

He shrugged his shoulders and said something to Jaime. The old man smiled in a cloud of calming words, assuring, appeasing. "You will visit his grave tomorrow," he said. The dusty yard refused to give off any signs.

"I need to go back to Jujuy tomorrow morning," Lisa said to Santos, making a last effort to dodge fate.

"I know," he said vaguely.

Jaime got up with sudden resolve. "Let's eat," he said.

The women had started cooking maize stew over an open fire.

"You sit down," he said, and beckoned Lisa to a trestle table. The women put bowls of stew on the table. Mirella said: "*Locro, muy sabroso,*" touching her fingertips to her mouth and smacking her lips. They went through the dinner in pantomime. Santos kept a moody silence.

"This will make you fatter," Jaime said to Lisa and patted her thighs with proprietary benevolence. Finger language came natural to him, and the women laughed like conspirators, fanning out their skirts on the bench. Santos looked at them with glum, contemplative eyes, and they stopped laughing.

Lisa kept her eyes on the bowl. When she looked up again, she saw the sign. Under the opaque rays of the setting sun, the hills had come alive. Wispy clouds of smoke rose from the ground, creeping slowly upward, expanding sideways, mysteriously spreading, blanketing the ridge. Here and there a low, dancing flame leaped from the ground and glittered below the mesquite brush.

"Fire!" she said.

Yes, Jaime nodded. Fire. The women were smiling at her.

Spontaneous combustion? she wanted to ask. How do you say "spontaneous combustion" in Spanish? The phrase exceeded her second-generation language skills. "Did the fire start by itself?"

"It's a planned burn," Santos said. "The ashes are good for the soil. Afterwards there will be grass for the cattle."

But Lisa knew there was more to it than that. The enchanted village was evaporating before her eyes, leaving behind charred and blackened ground. There was no hope now, and no more answers to her questions. The Saint would stay in his grave. *Alone again naturally.*

She was glad when dinner was over and she was allowed to hide in the soft darkness of her hut, the hut she had inherited from Asu. Mirella came and unfolded the woven blanket for her, putting a fuzzy lamb's wool cover on top. "*Buenas noches,*" she said, wishing Lisa sweet dreams with her eyes.

Lisa lay down on the cot and watched the night sky, as the string curtain danced and turned in the wind. Friday and the promise to phone Jim encroached on her mind and drained away again. It was difficult to think of time in this never land. Catamarca was impossibly far away. The drifting smoke gave a bitter aroma to the air. Lisa could taste it on her tongue. In the hills, the flames melted the mountain side and turned into fiery dreams, a holocaust of fathers flowing like lava, glittering pieces of Soriano-*padre,* Don liquefied, Jorge blowing in the ashes of his accounts.

"THEY'RE AFTER HER."

What was that supposed to mean? Jim thought. Who the hell are "they"? He tried to put a damper on his thoughts. Why bother analyzing the words of a hooker who was resentful because he told her to get lost. Forget the woman. Forget what she said. But Jim couldn't put the words out of his mind. Thoughts of Lisa ran through his brain with an electric sizzle, producing a charged image of Lisa in a dusty village with adobe huts and skinny dogs nosing through garbage – a generic northern village because Jim had no idea what Tilcara looked like. Who was after Lisa?

Back in his flat at the hotel, he kept his ear tuned to the phone. It was Friday night. Lisa had promised to phone. A purry, come-on voice ran amok in Jim's mind. He tried to correct the voice, looking for a fossil imprint of the real Lisa, not the Barbie doll he had conjured up, not the faux Lisa playing in his mind. He was impatient for the phone to ring. He wanted to know that Lisa was alright after the strange warning the hooker had given him. He listened to the sounds of silence in his room, the humming of the bar fridge, the ghost of talk down the hall, the pinging of the elevator. He replayed the ominous words: "They are after her." Kidnappers? Killers? Come off it, he thought. This isn't a film noir. Why was it that every time Lisa's name was mentioned, the irrational part of his brain kicked up and showed him magic lantern pictures?

He poured himself a drink to cancel the dark thoughts, drank too much, drifted off, woke up. It was late, perhaps too late for Lisa to call. He should have arranged a definite time. He should have watched her more closely. He shouldn't have let her go to Tilcara.

He went into the bathroom, splashed cold water on his face to wake up, to make plans what to do next, and decided to walk to the Bar Luna to see whether the hooker was there, hustling for customers. From the way the barman had greeted her, it looked like the Luna was her hang-out.

It was after midnight. The bar was full. There was standing room only at the counter.

"Remember me?" Jim said to the bartender. "I was in here some time ago with a woman." The barista gave Jim a flicker of the eye. He was busy pouring shots. "I think she's a regular here. You know where I can find her?"

"*Momentito*," the barista said. Someone at the other end of the counter had called for a refill. He topped up his glass, wiped the counter, and shimmied back to Jim. "The Quechua you mean? Asu? Not sure how you can get hold of her tonight."

The Quechua. Asu. The words hit Jim like a slapshot. He pushed a roll of bills across the counter. "When she comes in, ask her to phone me," he said to the barista and wrote his number on a coaster.

On the way home, he tried to piece the story together. Asu was the name of the Quechua girl Don had adopted. The name was short for Asuncion. How common was that name? Common enough. But how common was it for a Quechua named Asuncion to speak flawless English? One in a million. It was her alright, Don's adopted daughter. And how did Lisa and Santos enter into the equation? Was Santos the linchpin? Jim put together what Don had told him of Santos, what Lisa had said, what he himself had seen, Santos playing Svengali to Lisa, luring her into his shadow world. He was Quechua, was he not? And if you combined Asu's warning with Lisa's failure to phone, there were enough sinister elements here to make up a plot.

Back at the hotel, Jim waited. He could do nothing else. He nodded off thinking: I'll go to the market tomorrow morning and look for Asu there. I'll ask her what she meant. The ringing of the telephone woke him. He checked his watch: It was two o'clock.

"Hi, lover," Asu said. "What's up?"

"Can I see you?" Jim said. He didn't want to spoil his chances by saying he wanted to talk. The woman wanted action, not talk. She wanted a paying customer.

"Alright," Asu said. "Meet me in half an hour. I'll be at the corner of Banderas and Corrientes."

CORRIENTES WAS ON THE INDUSTRIAL edge of town, a no-man's land of garages and warehouses padlocked for the weekend, silent and black, looking like the detritus of a vanished era. Mounds of discarded tires were piled up against pockmarked brick walls. Mangled fenders and obsolete car parts cluttered the yards. The yellow rings cast by the streetlights were crawling with beetles. It was a delirious landscape.

Jim found Asu sitting on the curb, her skinny legs sticking out into the street. A delicate ankle bracelet made their thinness more pronounced. She looked bedraggled, dazed. He stopped the car and waited in case it was a set-up. The shadowy yards remained still. Asu stood up uneasily and stood illuminated by the headlights of the car. There was dried blood on her cheek. Her left eye was puffy. Jim opened the door for her, and she slumped into the passenger seat. Her blouse was ripped. He could see her small pointy breasts, her bony chest, the accordion contractions when she breathed.

"What happened?" he said.

"Customer roughed me up," she said with a slit-eyed grimace. "Well, never mind. You want it, lover?" The perky edge of her voice was at odds with the distress showing on her pulpy face. She laid an exploring hand into Jim's lap, assessing the contours with her fingertips.

He moved her hand off in spite of his rising excitement, the tremor of an erection springing to life. He was ashamed of hardening under her touch, getting aroused by the wrong woman, a woman whose face was marked with the stigma of violence.

"You don't want it?" she said, her voice shifting to neutral. "Alright. I'm not up to it anyway. Can I ask you a favour instead?"

Jim knew what she was after. Money. This time he was determined to dole out his cash smartly. It's pay per play, girl, he thought. My money for your answers.

But she wanted a different kind of favour. "Can you drive me home?" she said.

Jim put the car into gear. "Where to?" he said, pulling out into the deserted street, eager to leave the industrial desert and return to the populated core of the city.

"I want to go back to my village up north," she said. "It's close to the Bolivian border."

"Tilcara?" he said.

"So you know," she said. "Your girl friend told you?"

"Lisa said she was going to visit Tilcara. Will I find her there?" That's what he had come to ask Asu: where is Lisa?

"I told you to watch out," she said. "I told you they were after her. You didn't take me seriously, did you?"

"They – who?"

"Jaime Anqua and his son, the men in charge of the village."

"What do they want from Lisa?"

"It's a long story. You'll drive me to Tilcara?"

Jim thought he was the paymaster, but Asu had somehow high-jacked the game. He realized how little he had to offer and how much he wanted the information she could give him. Asu had a shrewd sense of its value. She was withholding the goods unless. There were conditions to be met.

"Okay, I'll drive you there," Jim said, but the story still wasn't forthcoming. He didn't want to repeat the question and give Asu an opening to up the ante.

She pulled up her knees, nestled into the curve of the seat with the unhurried grace of a cat, and fell silent. It was hard to tell whether she was asleep or deep in thought. There was something alert about her curled-up body though, as if she could be ready for action at a moment's notice, on the release of a secret spring.

Jim stopped by the hotel, "to pack an overnight bag," he told Asu. But he had another reason to go up to his room. He wanted to take along the stash of dollars he kept for emergencies. There might be a need for ransom money.

He parked the car down the street from the hotel.

"I'll be back in five minutes," he said.

Asu didn't respond. He left her, an amorphous thing in the passenger seat, looking like a forgotten bundle of clothes. When he returned, she was sitting up, looking at him with cool eyes, as if she had woken from a good night's sleep. Jim put his bag into the backseat and handed Asu a wet facecloth. "Here," he said, "wipe the blood off." She put the cool cloth to her cheek and gave him a tiny smile of thanks. "And put this on." He unwrapped a souvenir T-shirt celebrating Argentina's victory in the soccer world cup. He had bought it for his ten-year-old nephew. It looked about the right size for Asu.

She slipped off her torn blouse and fluttered it out the car window as they entered the highway. A passing truck honked.

"*Es un regalo, che!*" Asu shouted, leaning out of the window, cupping her breasts, putting them on display.

"Absolutely free of charge." She laughed a high-pitched laugh, rolled up the window and pulled on the T-shirt. "How did you guess I was a soccer fan?" she said.

They drove north on Route Nine, into the night. Asu's fingers were playing a game of cat's cradle. She was moving to a secret code with infinite suggestiveness, her skinny arms all wrists and elbows.

"You were going to tell me what happened to Lisa," Jim said. He wasn't sure he would get an answer this time.

"Santos took her to the *chacra*," Asu said, speaking from the depth of her seat like an oracle. "The Saint told him to fetch her."

Jim glanced at her sideways. "You believe in this 'Saint'?"

"You think Santos is a charlatan, don't you?" she said. She pronounced the word Spanish style. *Tcharlatan*. "You are wrong. He is a spirit man. He has second sight."

"What's your connection with Santos?"

"He's my brother," she said. "I thought you knew."

The story gelled. It was a vendetta. Maybe Don had lied about buying the girl. Maybe he abducted Asu, and Santos kidnapped Lisa in turn, to get even.

"And how does Lisa come into this?" he asked.

Asu shrugged. "It's my fault, I guess. Santos told me to go back to the *chacra*. I said no, not while Jaime Anqua is in charge there. Jaime pretends to be in touch with the saints, but he's a fraud. My grandfather was a true saint. He slipped into your mind and tugged on your thoughts, softly, softly. You obeyed him in your sleep. When he played his *ocarina*, it was like a resurrection. Every fibre in you wanted to get up and follow him. Santos is like his *abuelo*. He has the *curandero*'s eye. He knows what's ahead. If you don't go back to Tilcara, he said to me, the Saint will make Don pay with his life." Asu sat up. A splinter of unease caught in her throat. "I didn't want to go back, not with Jaime Anqua calling the shots, but it's hard to say no to Santos. His words are like *bolas*. They wrap around your neck, and you are caught. When I refused to go back to Tilcara, Santos took Lisa instead."

So that was the story. Perhaps it was not too late to reverse the deal.

Asu slid closer to him. He could hear her silver earrings jangle. Her words were brushing his cheek. "Is Don very much in love with Lisa?" she asked. "Will it kill him to lose her?"

"Don is in love with you," Jim said. "She's just a substitute."

Asu sighed. "But she doesn't even look like me."

"She has your dark hair," he said. The parallel disturbed him. It made him want to stroke Asu's hair, to find out whether it had the same texture. He suspected it was thicker than Lisa's, coarser to the touch.

"Santos is using her as a decoy to bring me back," she said. "Some *curanderos* use clay figures or cast iron hooks, but the human body is a better magnet." She paused and raised her head as if she was on the lookout and could feel the magic blowing her way. "I think it's working already. Or else I wouldn't be here in the car with you."

The road was deserted except for a few trucks rumbling south in the direction of Buenos Aires. The night had an air of science fiction. The headlights of the oncoming truck blazed up like *Close Encounters of the Third Kind*. There was hardly any traffic going their way. For a while they were stuck behind a semi loaded with pipes. Someone had painted a fancy landscape on the tailgate, in pink and turquoise. The headlights of Jim's Renault nosed ahead and illuminated a hula girl on a beach with palm trees. Above her, the parted clouds revealed a heavenly host of angels. Jim overtook the truck and pulled ahead, outrunning its high beams. They dropped back into darkness.

"Did Don treat you okay when you were living with him?" Jim asked.

Asu did not immediately answer. Her silence was of the dense kind, full of meaning. She was listening to her memories, searching her mind for things half-forgotten, paper-thin memories.

"He treated me okay, except that he was kind of clingy. He is the type who won't leave you alone, as if you owed him something. He had a way of wrinkling his forehead and giving me a starved look. He was starved for love, I guess. He was unhappy."

"What was he unhappy about?"

"Oh, I don't know," she said. "You can't tell with Don. He is a liar. At one point he told me his wife died in an accident. He was all broken up over her death and wanted to kill himself, he said. Later he said his wife divorced him because he couldn't get it up. He did that a lot, changing his stories until you didn't know what to believe."

Jim thought of Don's shapeshifting anecdotes and of the rumours that he had padded his CV.

"Yeah," he said. "His life comes in variants."

"But in the end it was always the same story. Someone hurt Don, and I had to make it up to him."

"I thought he wanted respect," Jim said. "That's what all his stories were leading up to: He had been around. The world owed him respect. He told me he'd been in the diplomatic service."

Asu laughed. "He never told me that."

Jim realized they were off course. He didn't want to talk about Don's foibles. He wanted to talk about Tilcara, the limbo that had swallowed up Lisa. "So Don knew your grandfather in Tilcara?" he said.

Asu settled deeper into her seat, tunnelling back in time. "Don came to the *chacra* when I was ten," she said, panting a little as if the memory excited or scared her. "He offered to take me with him and put me through school. Money changed hands, and the *abuelo* told me to go with Don. We drove off. Before we got to the main road, he stopped the car and said he had a present for me. He handed me a cardboard box tied with pink taffeta ribbons. There was a dress in the box, a fancy thing, I had never seen anything like it before, and white panties, white socks, white sandals, and a baby doll with eyes that closed when you laid her down. I remember thinking: it's too wonderful. It's a tease. I didn't smile. I didn't want Don to see how much I liked his presents. I was afraid he'd take them away again. That's how it goes. If you like something too much, you'll lose it, right?"

The lonely road and the sleepless night were beginning to tell on Jim. Half-way through Asu's story, his mind started to wander, to play tricks on him. He saw Asu in the backseat of Don's car, knees drawn up, counting her toes, refusing to raise her eyes, keeping her happiness to herself. He blinked the mirage away, tried to concentrate on the road, think of another question to ask Asu, to keep her talking, to stay awake. He looked at his watch. It was almost five in the morning.

"And then?" he said.

She cast a languid look at him, and his mind went off into a haze again. He saw Asu casting a languid look at Don, handling the fabric of her new dress gingerly, pretending she wasn't sure she liked it. He heard Don pleading with her for a kind look, a gesture, and Asu withholding heaven. No sweet smile, no sparkling thank-you, no happy look from her still, dark eyes. He saw Don taking her hand, her limp, unresponsive hand. He saw her stripping naked wordlessly, exposing her skinny body to Don's hot and cold looks, slipping on the dress, which turned into a soccer shirt, the soccer shirt Asu was wearing.

Jim came to, brought his mind back to the road and concentrated on the band of asphalt in front of the car.

"Right?" Asu was saying, but Jim had missed her question.

"You aren't much of a talker," she said. "What's eating you, *che*?" There was a skittish breeze in her voice.

"I'm worried about Lisa," Jim said, suddenly awake again. What was Santos' plan? Making Lisa relive his sister's life? Was he preparing a parallel life for her, pandering to Jaime Anqua or selling her off to the highest bidder?

"I need a smoke," Asu said, spilling over to Jim's side, groping for the pack of cigarettes she had spotted in his shirt pocket. "I thought you didn't smoke. That's what you told me at the Luna."

"I tried to quit, but it didn't work." He was back to smoking a pack a day. This time his abstinence had lasted only three weeks. It was hopeless. Argentines were a nation of smokers. There was no getting away from the smell and sight of tobacco.

Asu was trailing her fingers over his chest, stroking him in her feline, half-domesticated way. She was making a play for him. Unknown fibres were tingling under the touch of her fingers, evoking a tactile memory of Lisa. Was that part of Santos' parallel life plan? Jim sensed a remote power, a gossamer net of connections spreading over the highway, growing weblike over himself and Asu, reeling them in, bringing them closer to Tilcara.

"You haven't got any dope on you?" Asu said. "I guess not. I'll get some when we stop for gas. Maybe that's what you need. You're too uptight, you know."

She lit up a cigarette and sucked in the smoke. "Are you getting it on with Lisa?" she said. "What's she like?"

"You've seen her," Jim said.

Asu leaned back, marching her feet up on the dashboard and sliding her naked toes along the windshield. "What's she like in bed, I mean."

Jim dodged her question. He didn't want to feed Asu any more information. He was afraid she would absorb the description and turn into a phantom Lisa. He was afraid of falling under Santos' long distance spell and losing out on the real Lisa.

"Don said she reminded him of you," he said.

"You know, I miss Don," Asu said. Jim was relieved they were off the Lisa topic. Or was he mistaken, and was that Lisa speaking? Was Lisa at this very moment looking at the diamond ring on her finger and saying: I miss Don?

"Don was okay, really," Asu said. "He just talked a lot. Otherwise he was a softie. I didn't appreciate it at the time. He was easy to hold off. It was a game to see how far I would let him go. Everybody plays games, but most of the men I've been with want to be in control. Sometimes they let you win. More often they cash in the chips themselves. No, Don was okay. What got to me were his eyes. He never let me out of his sight. If he wasn't looking at me straight, he was watching me out of the corner of his eyes. He didn't ask me for anything kinky. A little hugging was good enough for him. I bet he got off on me just by looking."

Could the surveillance of eyes stifle ambition? Could dirty looks corrupt and drive a girl to prostitution or did Asu have a natural calling to sabotage herself? Was there a self-destructive germ that Don's eyes brought to fruition?

"Don claimed he adopted you," Jim said. "Or was that just a sexual fantasy of his?"

Asu laughed. "Would it turn you on if I said Daddy molested me?" Her eyes intruded on his mind, bored into him, searching for a cue to his desires. She was willing to put on a sketch of imaginary lust if reality was too dull for him.

"That's not why I asked," Jim said. He had asked on Lisa's behalf. He was afraid Santos would make her suffer whatever Asu had suffered at Don's hands. Perhaps Jaime Anqua had his hands on Lisa already.

"If it feels good, is it still molesting?" Asu said, looking thoughtfully into the smoke curling off her cigarette. "I can't remember. Was it good or bad? Did I love or hate Don? What did I know? I got my knowledge out of *fotonovela*s. Don told me to call him daddy. So I did." She dragged violently on her cigarette as if she had an aching passion in her lungs. "I guess he meant it. He wanted to be my father."

Asu slipped back into the groove of her story. "So he took me to Catamarca. That's where he was living at the time. He introduced me to his housekeeper. She said nothing. Just smirked and put her hands behind her back, afraid of touching me, a filthy little thing. Don told her I was the daughter of a friend. I'd be living with him during the school year. He made it sound respectable, but she kept smirking."

Asu lit another cigarette and breathed throat-catching fumes Jim's way. "The *abuelo* came to visit me once, not long after I left Tilcara," she said. "I was doing schoolwork in my room. I looked up, and there he was standing beside my desk, as if he had come through the wall, but before he could say anything, the housekeeper was at the door. 'Get out of here,' she said to him. 'I am her *abuelo*,' he said. 'You have no business here,' she said. "Get out. *Afuera!*' She shooed him out like a stray dog. I was ashamed of the way he left, without a word. He should have cursed her. When Don came home, the housekeeper told him about my grandfather's visit. 'Better make sure nothing's gone missing,' Don said, as if my grandfather was a thief. I waited for the *abuelo* to take revenge, but nothing happened to the housekeeper or to Don, and I started to have doubts about his power. I should have been more patient."

WHEN LISA WOKE UP, IT was dawn. Grey light was filtering through the string curtain. A car engine sputtered into action. Lisa got up and went to the door. The fire in the hills had burned itself out. The hillside was blackened and bare. In the yard, the women had lit a cooking fire in the *pachamanca* stove and were busy making flatbread. Jaime was sitting at the trestle table, smoking a cigarette. His eyes were following Santos' car bouncing over the dirt track, leaving a plume of dust in its wake.

"Where's he going?" Lisa asked, pointing after the Fiat.

"To find work," Jaime said.

"But I need a ride back to Jujuy."

"*Si, si,*" he said. He ground the butt of the cigarette into the dirt and patted Lisa's arm, smiling: it will all come out alright, just you wait and see. But the future was like the dirt road, meandering out of sight.

Fine white ash was drifting over the bare hills. Lisa wanted to escape like a wisp of smoke, but Tilcara had turned into an open-air prison. She watched her captors going about their work. The women had gone to unload what was left of the firewood. They formed a line to the storage shed, tossing the logs in a rhythmical relay under the old man's supervision. They were oblivious to Lisa. No need to guard her. There was nowhere to go.

"You want to visit the grave of the Saint?" Jaime said. "My son will take you. Simon. He is coming."

"Alright," Lisa said, "but I have to be back in Jujuy tonight."

"What do you want in Jujuy?"

"I have to rejoin the group I'm with," Lisa said.

His face remained blank.

"My friends are waiting there," she said.

He stretched out his hand. "Come here," he said, speaking soft Quechua spells: dear child, in my arms you will find eternal peace.

Lisa shook her head, resisting bondage.

He withdrew his hand, shrugged his shoulders and walked away, leaving her at the table.

After breakfast, Lisa watched the women settling down to their daily chores, sitting cross-legged in front of their looms, weaving blankets, interlacing brown and charcoal grey wool. Their hands passed the shuttle through the warp with practised speed. Mirella glanced in Lisa's direction without stopping her work. She smiled meekly and assured her in broken Spanish that Simon would come soon, very soon, *cada momento.*

At noon a dust cloud appeared where the road met the horizon. It unfurled into a motorcycle, a magical vision, silhouetted against the sky, glinting blue and orange. The lone rider forded the creek with the front wheel lifting, bounded up the hill spraying gravel, and came to a skidding halt in the yard. For a moment he remained still, sitting astride his bike like a victorious general. Lisa expected a cheer to go up from the women and children, a hero's welcome for Simon, but they stared at him tamely, in awe. He dismounted and rolled his shoulders to ease the strain, limbered up his arms and legs, and wiggled his fingers like a strangler yearning to squeeze someone's neck.

Jaime came to greet his son. The two men hugged stiffly, gripping shoulders. They spoke in Quechua. Simon ran his fingers through his short spiky hair, turned and gave Lisa an unhurried, unsmiling appraisal. His neck was a solid column. He had a warrior's chiselled face and determined eyes.

"This is Lisa," the old man said.

"How are you?" Simon said in formal Spanish, keeping his distance. His voice was husky. "My father asks me to take you to the grave of the Saint."

"Thank you," Lisa said. "And afterwards, can you take me back to Jujuy?"

He nodded, but his eyes were opaque with evasion. Jaime took Lisa's arm, pointing her to the truck. "You go with Simon," he said.

Lisa was in a limbo of expectations. "I'll get my bag," she said, to remind the two men: I'm packed, ready to go back to Jujuy.

Jaime smiled indulgently. Such a spoiled child, his eyes said. He spoke softly to the women, and they put a blanket into the truck bed and a basket covered with cloth.

Simon handed Lisa and her bag up into the cab, put the truck into gear and moved out on the gravel road under the midday sun. He drove silently. Lisa kept her head down and did not look back. She was afraid of the powers of Tilcara even as she was leaving it.

"How do you like the *chacra*?" Simon said.

"It's nice," she said.

"It will be nicer when I am in charge," he said. "I work as a mechanic in Salta now, but when I get back I'll take over the gas station on the main road. I will build a new house there, of bricks, with a concrete roof, and open a *taller*. I will make a good life for my family."

"I am sure you will," Lisa said politely.

He looked at her sideways. "You are not enjoying yourself," he said. "You don't look happy."

"I'm nervous," Lisa said. "I don't want to miss my bus in Jujuy. I'm with a group, you know. Santos was supposed to take me, but I don't know if he'll be back in time. Your father says he's gone to look for work."

Simon turned his eyes back to the road.

The black cows were still at pasture, the birds still wheeling above them. They passed all the omens in reverse. The *tienda* appeared in the distance, a hump in the road. They were on the brink of the real world when Simon turned, heading toward the mountains.

"How far is it to the grave of the Saint?" Lisa said sharply.

"Not far," he said casually, but there was a warning at the back of his voice: enough of this. Don't try my patience.

The truck entered an abandoned quarry carved out of a granite cliff, a moonscape, a rocky labyrinth. Far above them was the sky, azure, cloudless. Simon brought the truck to a stop.

"This is the Saint's place," he said and put a hand on Lisa's arm. "It is a very special place. You can relax here."

He reached into the glove compartment and brought out a plastic bag, dipped his hand into it and poured a mound of leaves from his cupped hand into Lisa's: a gift, a bribe to buy her good will.

"Coca," he said and offered her a cake of lime as well. "You chew the leaves together with this and spit them out. The earth will receive the leaves together with your troubles."

Lisa studied the mound of leaves and the cake of lime, considered them, braved the temptation of making a dream escape, opened her hand and scattered the leaves on the floor of the truck.

"No," she said. "I don't want to go all mellow. I told you I have to catch the bus in Jujuy."

He turned away as if to shield his thoughts from her. The muscles in his face were working. He was wrestling with anger. He got down from the truck, went to the back and lifted out the blanket and the basket. He spread the blanket on the ground, uncovered the basket and brought out a bottle and a dozen maize cakes wrapped in leaves and tied with straw. His will to please Lisa had revived. He patted the ground, inviting her to join him for a picnic.

Lisa was reluctant to play along, but she could not afford to lose his good will altogether. She got down from the cab of the truck and sat beside Simon on the blanket, careful not to get too close, to stay on the just visiting side of friendly. She took a sip from the proffered bottle. It burned her throat, gripped her stomach, spreading an electric storm. Did *Dr. Brown's Elixir* have Quechua roots?

"Foul!" she said, grimacing and wiping her mouth.

He laughed, put the bottle to his lips and drank freely with gulping swallows, unwrapped the maize cakes and motioned her to eat. "*Humitas en chala,*" he said. "Mirella made them especially for you."

Lisa took one and ate impatiently. "Look," she said. "It's getting late. Can we go now?"

"You are a hard woman," he said. His voice had gone surprisingly soft as if the contrast could change Lisa's mind, as if it would show her the justice of his complaint. He put the stopper into the bottle and lay back. For a while he looked up into the sky wordlessly, then he turned on his side.

"Why are you in such a hurry to go away?" he said. "This is a beautiful place. You should stay for a while."

"I can't stay," Lisa said.

"You should listen to the Saint," he said. He looked up at the wall of rock. In his eyes was awe for the miraculous. The quarry floor was littered with boulders in curious shapes. He named them to Lisa one by one, like a proud guide: sleeping woman, tortoise, man with two heads. He traced the rock contours in the air, followed with his fingers the curves and humps of their imaginary flanks and monster heads. "You see the man with the two heads?"

Lisa saw nothing because anger bloodied her eyes, or the drink had seared her brain. Her arms were no longer her own. They were electrified. They were conducting a lightning war. A stormy battle was brewing. The sleeping woman stretched and rose. The neck of the two-headed man undulated, an aurora borealis arose behind his head, a fine interplay of mauve and green. Lisa could see his stony heart pumping. The tortoise was breathing, expanding and contracting. The quarry was in motion, and Simon's hands were shrieking, every finger a hissing stab in her ear. He stretched out his wiry arms toward her, encircling her with a deafening grip. His face reared up close, eyes rimmed in black. His breath was on Lisa's face, burning her skin. She was fighting monsters. She screamed, and Simon stopped moving, melted into the rocks and became one of them. Lisa closed her mouth, and the screaming came to a halt. The monsters ducked back into their hides and became ordinary rock again. The tortoise was lying motionless beside the two-headed man, and the woman went back to her granite sleep. Only Simon was left, flesh and blood, as Lisa took her fingers off his throat and marvelled at the stigmata left behind.

He jerked his head back, touched his throat and looked at his blood-stained fingertips with surprise. His pupils melted in disbelief.

Lisa bared her teeth at him, but the beast within her was fading to black. She drew her lips over her teeth and looked with wonder at the bite mark colouring Simon's throat.

"Did I do that?" she said. Her mad fancy dissolved. She could hear the voice coming out of her throat, a small girlish voice saying: "I didn't mean to hurt you. I was frightened."

He got up slowly, keeping his eyes on Lisa. With sudden determination, he snatched up the blanket and basket and threw them into the back of the truck. "You are crazy," he said. "Let's go." He jumped into the cab and started up the engine.

"Go where?" Lisa wailed, scrambling up and climbing into the truck, afraid of being left behind. "To Jujuy?"

He refused to answer her.

"At least drive me out to the road," she pleaded, but he drove back to the *chacra*, cutting across the fields, driving with furious speed. He did not even give her the consolation of seeing civilization from a distance.

In the yard, he came to a screeching halt, opened the door of the truck and pulled her down roughly, tossing her bag on the ground beside her. Jaime had come out of one of the sheds and watched tight-lipped. The women saw his displeasure and lowered their eyes.

Simon spoke angrily to the old man, mounted his bike, hit the starter button, waited for the roar, twisted the throttle, and pulled out of the yard, gathering speed downhill. He ripped through the creek in a misty spray and sped off along the gravel road.

A child set up a wail, as Lisa crouched down in the yard beside her bag under the stormy eye of the old man. She had no pleas left. She was in disgrace. The women went back to work silently. No one paid any more attention to her sitting in the heat of the hazy afternoon sun. She looked down on her hands and saw Don's diamond ring on her finger, a sparkling reminder of the outside world, Don in Mar del Plata waiting for her return, Jim in Catamarca waiting for her phone call. She stared into the labyrinthine depth of the gem like a gypsy into her crystal ball, and saw her future. Simon had given her the clue when he said: "You are crazy." Madness was her calling, her passport to the outer world. What would they do with a madwoman in Tilcara? Get rid of her, that's what. Send her away. They had no use for a crazed woman. Madness was her ticket to freedom.

"Madwoman" Lisa whispered to herself, and decided on the spot to add the role to her repertoire, try it on for size, speak out loud, louder, for all of Tilcara to hear. "I am mad," she shouted. "I am crazy!" The words took hold of her, seeped into her pores and filled her lungs. Her shout drew a curious audience. The children came running and stared at her; Mirella and Remedios left off working to see what was going on. It was as if the curtain had opened on Lisa's show. She rose up screaming and waving her arms, whirled around the yard, chased off the children. Make way for the madwoman, I am fearless now! She gave them a shrieking, reeling performance. They fled. The women retreated, hiding the children in the folds of their skirts, protecting their eyes and ears against the onslaught of Lisa's madness.

The old man stepped in front of her, pinned her arms to her sides and arrested her banshee dance.

"*Basta,*" he shouted. "*Calla la boca.*" His eyes were raging against Lisa. He threw his arms around her neck, corralled her like a stray animal, and dragged her out of the circle of huts, down the slope to the creek that curved around the *chacra* like a moat.

Lisa kicked his shins. "Let go of me," she screamed. If he wanted to get rid of her, there was no need to be brutal. She was perfectly willing to leave.

She squirmed in Jaime's arms, stiffened her legs to impede the march to the creek, but he only tightened his hold. When they reached the edge of the water, Lisa saw what he was up to, what they did with mad-women in Tilcara. They locked them away. There was a wicker cage suspended from an overhanging branch by a chain, a prison for the mad. She started to fight Jaime in earnest then, but his wiry arms allowed no resistance. He dragged her into the water, and the children came dancing after him, Jaime's little helpers. They splashed into the water, grabbed at Lisa's hands and held her legs, as he lifted her into the cage and tied the door shut with a rope. The tree branch sagged under Lisa's weight, the cage touched bottom, water crept up Lisa's ankles. The children jeered, but the old man sent them back up the slope with a gruff command. He glared at Lisa, brandished his arms like knives and spoke to her under his breath, a Quechua curse.

Through the screen of his wheeling arms, Lisa saw Remedios clamber down the slope. She was lugging Lisa's bag. The old man stopped cursing, took the bag out of Remedios' hands and emptied it by the creek, contents spilling. Lisa's passport fluttered open and came to rest in the short grass, beside her wallet. The rest of her possessions formed a trail to the water. A pencil with a broken tip and a sticky candy dropped to the sandy bottom of the creek. A comb floated away, a T-shirt, a bra tangled up with panties drifted in the current, hung up on the roots of a tree, waved for a moment like a glad streamer, and sank waterlogged. Jaime turned the empty bag upside down and tossed it aside. It was a ritual purging of the *chacra:* madwoman Lisa in tote bag effigy, cast out, and spilling her guts.

Jaime spat into the water, a tobacco stained circle of phlegm thinning out, dispersing, disappearing, leaving no trace except in Lisa's mind. Was it a sign foretelling her watery death?

Would her skin dissolve in the creek's water like Jaime's spittle? He climbed up to the yard without looking back, done with the problem of the mad woman, and on to his ordinary chores.

The cage was too narrow for Lisa to crouch down, barely wide enough to bend her knees. She had to contort her body to take off her sandals, rescuing them from the shallow water at least, if she could not rescue herself. She clutched the sandals to her breast and watched the creek etch a glistening, jagged pattern on her dusty shins, felt pebbles shifting under her feet and thought of flash floods. There was something in her guidebook, a warning about sudden downpours in the mountains swelling creeks, carrying a deluge of splintered tree limbs and rolling stones, a flood come and gone within an hour. Was her sentence death by drowning? Lisa tried to remember the season for flash floods, but it was difficult to measure time standing in a creek that flowed ceaselessly, eternally. She looked into the leafy roof of the tree above her and thought of the days that had passed and might pass with the water lapping at her legs, softening her skin, carrying away tiny flakes, invisible to the eye, eroding the top layer, eating down, all the way down to her bones. Yesterday, today, tomorrow – Lisa wondered how they kept track of time in Tilcara. Did they cut notches into tree trunks? She counted the days on her fingers. Three days since her departure from Catamarca, five days since Mar del Plata, twelve days since Toronto. How many days since her last period? Too many. She stood very still, trying to listen to her body. She followed the blood stream to her womb, and sensed a thickening, a second life force within her. Will they take pity on the child in my womb, she thought as she was listening to her body? Will they lay claim to the child? She leaned forward, reached her hands down and trailed her fingertips in the cool water to refresh her memory of time. She touched her face, an anointing, a sacred rite to make the soul rise. A breath of courage stirred. She pushed against the cage, rattled the door, yanked at the rope fastening the door and barring her escape. The distance between the canes was too narrow. She could not get a grip on the knot. Her bitten fingernails slipped off without loosening it. She looked around for a cutting tool, but the only thing within reach that was not soft was Don's ring, and the facets of the diamond were not sharp enough to cut through the fibre.

She caught a movement out of the corner of her eye and looked up. Mirella stood at the top of the slope overlooking the creek. She was shading her eyes and nodding. She's still there, the nod said. She turned and disappeared from sight. A small boy showed up next, fixed his eyes on Lisa, slid down the hill, and stopped at the water's edge, ill at ease. He was holding something, an object half hidden in his fisted hand: a pocket knife.

"What do you want?" Lisa said to him. She spoke sharply. She didn't know: was he friend of foe?

He took a step back, uncertain what to do next, searching his mind for bits of Spanish, chewing his upper lip to soften it and allow the words to pass.

"What do you want from me?" Lisa said again, more softly, afraid of the knife in his hand.

He waded into the water, and stopped short, keeping his distance from her.

"My mother says: this for that," he whispered and pointed first to the knife in his hand, then at Lisa.

"Me? She wants me?"

"No, this!" he said frowning, and Lisa, following his eyes, realized he was pointing at her hand, at Don's ring.

"The ring?" she said, and he nodded eagerly.

It was an offer sent by heaven. "Alright," Lisa said, tugging at the ring, but she could not slip it off her finger. She twisted it, yanked it, skinned her knuckle, frantic with the effort at first, then stalled by the impossibility of budging the ring.

"I can't do it," she said to the boy, sucking at her knuckle, lubricating it with spit, pulling at the ring again. It would not come off.

The boy looked bewildered. He did not know what to do next. He had been given no other lines to speak. His eyes flashed back and forth between Lisa and the ridge of the hill. Mirella appeared and gestured impatiently to him: What are you up to? A purple shade of guilt crossed the boy's face. He dropped the knife, splashed on shore, and scrambled back up the hill. Mirella received him with a slap to his cheek. In a moment, both were gone. The ridge was once more deserted.

The knife glinted in the water, agonizingly close to Lisa's cage. She squeezed her knees against the bars of the cage. The sharp edges of the canes cut into her skin, but she ignored the pain. She slipped her sandals through the bars, extending the reach of her hands, moving the knife a minute distance, imperceptibly closer, and closer again, patiently angling for her prize fish, until the blade lodged against the bars, and she was able to pull it through.

She straightened up and applied the knife to the twisted fibre of the knot, hacked through the rope, one strand at a time, until it frayed and broke with a snap. The door of the cage popped and opened a slit, barred now only by sand and pebbles. Lisa held her breath, her eyes on the ridge, listening to *chacra* noises in the distance. It seemed to her that the snap of the fibre and the popping of the door were loud enough to summon her captors, but no one came. Still, she did not dare to make her move. She waited for the cover of dusk. When the outline of the trees on the ridge was no longer distinct against the sky, she squeezed through the door of the cage and began collecting her possessions, groped for her wallet and her passport in the sand, plucked her bag from the muddy bank, where Jaime had dropped it. She fingered her possessions, one by one, like the beads of a rosary, a prayer of thanks. She felt cured, delivered from paralysis like the cripple in the bible. Something in the core of her brain had loosened up and allowed her to move spontaneously, without mediation. She needed no crutch, no counsellor. She knew her own will. It *was* a miracle.

She waded along the creek until she was out of her captors' sight, then circled back to the gravel road to make her getaway. How long a walk was it out to the main road? An hour? Was there a bus to Jujuy? Maybe a *camion*, an open truck, like the one she had seen on the way in. Lisa walked softly like a thief, because she was taking away something that belonged to Tilcara: a child. *Alone again naturally* was no longer playing in her head.

ON THE OUTSKIRTS OF SALTA, Jim pulled into a gas station. It was getting on to noon. He looked over at Asu. The swelling had gone down, but there were black circles under her eyes that gave her cheekbone a dull bluish tinge. Their eyes met in an accidental collision. Asu's eyes had a liquid sheen. Was she shedding tears for Don? Was Lisa, too, weeping in Tilcara? Jim put his arms around Asu (or did he mean, Lisa?) and pulled her close. He felt her narrow shoulders, felt the bones and muscles working below her skin.

She pulled back. She wasn't Lisa after all. Suddenly prickly, she got out of the car, walked into the shop by the gas pumps and came back with a plastic bag of dope. She rolled herself a cigarette, took a drag and passed it on to Jim.

"Don't worry about Lisa," she said, looking at him like a difficult child entrusted to her care.

The dope made a believer of Jim. His fear lifted.

Asu offered to drive. "I don't have a licence," she said, "but nobody ever checks."

Jim handed over his car keys. He had no arguments left. He put the passenger seat back as far as it would go and stretched out. He needed sleep. The interior of the car turned blue and the roof disappeared into a vacuum. He was content to lie back. The purring of the engine thickened. Asu's voice reached him like a gentle, lulling stream, flowing on, lapping the edges of his ears. She was talking of the nuns, the Sisters of Mercy. Hellfire and damnation. Very strange, he thought, he couldn't make anything of those two words, not after Mercy.

"You get turned on by Catholic private school girls?" Asu said in a clinical way, as if she was conducting a survey to help her improve her professional skills. "Some men do." She talked on, giving him snippets of her life, a directionless story, or did it just seem that way to Jim in his half dream? Did he miss the point?

"Jaime came to Don's house," she was saying. "Santos was with him. The *abuelo* is dead, Jaime said. I'm in charge now. I took Santos' hand. The Saint lives on in his bones, you know. They should have put him in charge of the *chacra*. Jaime talked and talked." The whole car was full of words, Jim thought, full of names bouncing between the car roof and his eyes. "He argued with Don. The *abuelo* had no right to sell me, he said. I was promised to his son. The money Don paid the old man was owing to him, he said. He wanted compensation. To get rid of Jaime, Don paid up."

It was a confusing story of broken promises. Jim slipped into a dream of Jaime. He looked like San Simón the Trickster. He was staring at Don sullenly. No, staring at Jim: he had taken Don's place. Jaime/San Simón was haggling with him. He wasn't willing to let Lisa go without compensation. He wanted Jim to pay up. Twenty dollars, he said and held out his hand. Jim reached into his wallet and slapped a bill into Jaime's palm. The scene went into a loop. Twenty dollars, Jaime said. Jim gave him the money. Jaime left and returned walking backwards. The dialogue started over again, Jim paid up again, faster and faster. What if the images never stopped and he was caught? In a way it was amusing, like a merry-go-round, but the whirring stopped abruptly and Asu's voice faded in.

"Don told him to go away. That's it, he said. You won't get another peso out of me. We'll see about that, Jaime said. That's when the letters started." Asu's words were like a voiceover, coming from a great distance, probably because she was sitting up, and he was lying down. In fact he was stuck under the desk in his office, embarrassed to be listening in on a conversation that was private. Someone was standing in front of the desk. Jim could see only his polished shoes. Don's shoes. Jim looked up at him. From his vantage point under the desk, Don was a tower of a man. He couldn't make out the expression in his eyes, but his jowls looked truculent.

Anqua is a blackmailing bastard, Don said to someone out of Jim's sightline. The girl was desperate to get away, he said, and I felt sorry for her.

Jim couldn't stand it any longer. He crawled out from under the desk and showed himself.

You abducted her, Don, he said.

Don wasn't in the least surprised to see him. He had been talking to Jim all along. There was no one else in the office. I have nothing to hide, he said. I'm fond of Asu, in a fatherly way. I didn't abduct her. I paid for her.

Paying out money was wrong, Jim said, but he was getting confused. Was he talking about the money he paid Asu? It was stupid, he said. I shouldn't have done it. Immediately he felt that he had made a tactical mistake. He shouldn't have admitted anything, he shouldn't have made any concessions to Don, but he had no time to correct himself, because he was returned to himself with a jolt, was back in the car with Asu, and the scene slipped into disarray.

"School was easy," she said, straying into Jim's dream. "I sailed through Grade Twelve. I was bored, until I met Rául. Don totally disapproved of him. He called him a 'Street Arab' – I'd never heard that expression before, but I thought it suited Rául. I started calling him *mi Arabe*."

Jim reached for the lever and moved his seat back into the upright position, back into full view of the road, the real world and Asu's life story. He tried to picture her at seventeen, but all that came to mind was his niece, a fast-food pudgy teenager who lounged in front of the TV like poured wax. Asu hadn't lost her gamine body. She could still pass for seventeen. Asu had stopped talking. She was hunched over the steering wheel.

"I'm getting tired driving," she said to him. "We're past Jujuy, you know."

They stopped at a roadside market and ate empanadas and drank coke.

"Let's go," Jim said when they had finished their meal. It was late in the day, and they still had a distance to go, but Asu was trawling the store, looking at the stuff on the shelves. She picked out a clay flute.

"An *ocarina*," she said, "like the one my grandfather had."

It was a small grey thing lying smoothly in the palm of her hand. She put it to her lips and produced a few reedy notes. A boy came out from behind the counter and said: "*Deje me*." He reached for the instrument and played a haunting tune, like birds singing in a cave.

"*Muy lindo*," Asu said, and paid for the flute.

Outside, she handed Jim the car keys. "Your turn again," she said, and they got back on the road.

"So you ran away with Rául," he said. "Where did you go?" He wanted to know. Every detail counted.

If his parallel-life theory was correct, somebody was going to play Rául to Lisa.

"We didn't go anywhere," Asu said. "We stayed in Catamarca. His sister took us in, but she had three kids to support. The house was crowded. There was a lot of bickering about money. She said we were free-loaders. I was a whore. Rául was a pimp. Maybe he was. Or maybe he just liked watching. Jaime was after me, too. He wanted me to come back to the *chacra*. In the end I broke up with Rául. I was hoping Don would take me back, but he'd quit his job and gone to Canada, and someone else was living in the house on Calle Solís. So I knuckled under to Jaime. I didn't go back to the *chacra*, but I started working at the market and agreed to give him a cut of my earnings."

No happy ending. Is that what was in stock for Lisa?

"Slow down," Asu said. "Turn at the gas station." She pointed to a narrow rutted road going off to the left.

A young Quechua was filling up his motorcycle, a blue and orange BMW 80. He replaced the nozzle and screwed on the tank cap. Turning their way, he gave the Renault a passing glance and got stuck on Asu. Their eyes locked. She rolled down the window and yelled at him: "Hey, strap on your helmet or you'll lose your head!"

He jumped on his bike, made a screeching half turn, almost sideswiping Jim's car. "*Puta*!" he shouted, "they'll put you in the cage like the other one." He pounded his fist on the trunk of the Renault before roaring off, trailing curses.

Jim watched him in the rear view mirror until he was out of sight. "What the hell was that all about?" he said to Asu, who was hooting with derision.

"He's an idiot," Asu said, tucking in her laugh.

"You know him?" Jim said.

"He is from the *chacra*. My fiancé."

"You are engaged to this guy?" Jim said, incredulous.

"Not any more," she said, screaming with laughter. "I've lost him, I think."

"What did he mean: they'll put you in the cage?"

"That's what Jaime used to do to punish us when we were children. He locked us into a cage. It's a plaything actually, a swing, hanging from a tree branch that sticks out over the creek, but he locked us in and scared us with stories of flash floods coming and drowning us. A couple of times someone did get caught and got a soaking." She laughed as if it was a harmless hoax.

"And who is 'the other one'? Does he mean Lisa?"

"Don't worry," she said. "There are no flash floods at this time of the year." She ran her tongue over her lips and gave Jim a teasing smile. "Well, rarely."

Jim turned on to the gravel road, a bone-rattling track. The setting sun was casting a red glow on the withered land. Undulating hills stretched to the horizon, and dust was blowing through the open windows of the car, a gritty breeze. In the distance Jim saw peaked tin roofs rising over the crest of a ridge.

"The *chacra,*" Asu said.

There was a dip in the road ahead and a band of water, glittering in the sun. A barefoot woman was wading through the shallow stream, hugging a tote bag to her chest and a pair of sandals. She stopped when she reached the other side and bent down to put the sandals back on her feet. When she raised her head, Jim recognized her with a pang of joy.

"It's Lisa," he said.

He stopped the car and got out. Lisa put down her tote bag and shaded her eyes against the sun, as if he was far away and hard to discern. He folded her into his arms, but there was no answering embrace, no smile, just stoop-shouldered relief, and a dead zone in her eyes.

"It's you," she said with wonder in her voice, but she wasn't looking at him. She was looking past him at Asu standing by the car.

Jim did not have to introduce them. Lisa already knew who she was. "Don has a framed photo of you in school uniform," she said. "It's on the wall in my bedroom." She kept close to Jim, speaking from the shadow of his body. "I think I'll ask him to take it down when I get back to Toronto." She was hanging on to Jim's arm, in need of protection from Asu.

"Go ahead," Asu said as if she had been asked for permission. "Take it down. Rip it up if you want." She laughed. "Or give it to him," she said, pointing to Jim. It occurred to Jim that she had never once addressed him by name, never admitted him into her life. Listening to Asu's story had given him no privileges. She was about to vanish into the forbidden city, the place populated by saints.

The *chacra* came to life, summoned by the noise of the car engine. A posse of kids came running down the hill, splashing through the creek, hugging Asu, twittering like birds. She joined hands with them, danced them along, allowed them to march her up the hill in a tangled, triumphant parade.

On the crest of the hill, Jim saw a group of women and an old man – the boss? The ruler of Tilcara? He was standing there with his retinue of women, at the border, a line he was unwilling to cross: so far and no further. The women were solemn, as if they couldn't make up their minds whether Asu's return was a good thing, or bad. The old man's eyes were fierce.

"*Vete al Diablo*," he shouted in their direction, waving his arms in a large gesture of sending them all to hell.

"*A tomar por el culo*," Jim shouted back. The site visits had served him well. He knew the language of crude rage.

Lisa pushed into him, nudging close. He felt her trembling fear.

"Don't," she said. "Don't." She was crying.

"It's okay," Jim said. "I'll get you out of here." He opened the car door for Lisa and put her bag into the back seat. He didn't attempt to console her. He needed consoling himself. The exchange had happened too fast. He hadn't considered what it meant, that he had to let go of one love to receive the other.

He started up the car and did a three point turn. In the rear view mirror, he could see Asu standing on the ridge beside the women. She raised both of her arms and wiggled her fingers waving good-bye or just welcoming the sky into her heart. In any case, the decision was made.

"Go, go," Lisa said with a hard sob like someone who had a narrow escape. Jim shifted into drive. "Don't stop."

When they got back to the main road, a semblance of life returned to her eyes. "Thanks," she said, "I'm so glad you – ." She didn't say what she was glad about.

"I'm glad, too," Jim said without conviction.

They were stuck behind a Coca Cola truck grinding along at forty miles an hour, blowing diesel fumes with every change of gears.

"So what happened at the *chacra*?" he said, and reached for Lisa's hand. "I got worried when you didn't phone yesterday."

"They wouldn't let me go, but I – ." She trailed off.

"Didn't let you go? You mean locked you up? Asu said something about a cage."

"But how did you – ," Lisa said, and stopped. She hadn't said a complete sentence since getting into the car. All her sentences ended in mid air. Jim wondered whether she had been reduced to sign language at the *chacra* and was just finding her way back to the spoken word.

He started explaining the Asu connection, but it was hard going. He didn't know how much to admit. Every word felt like a confession, as if he had done something illicit. There was an obstruction in his throat, a hairball of bad conscience. He didn't know why he had scruples: because of the flicker of lust he had felt for Asu? Because of the confusion when Asu and Lisa merged in his imagination? But that was just the dope fogging up his brain, and everything was cleared up now and settled. Asu was back where she belonged, and Lisa was sitting beside him in the car.

He waited for Lisa to tell her story in turn, but it was as if someone had changed the setting on the main valve, choking off her words and keeping the emotions tightly sealed. She said nothing.

"Why were you so scared?" Jim said, prompting her. "Did they give you a hard time at the *chacra*?"

She finally pushed out a complete sentence. "I don't know. I couldn't understand them."

"You don't need to speak Quechua to know when you are being hassled."

"It wasn't a language problem," she said. "In any case, I got away."

"So they did lock you up?"

"I don't want to talk about it."

"And where was Santos when all this happened?"

Lisa answered him with a weary pull of her shoulders. "He drove off and didn't come back."

Jim noticed she kept to the facts, holding back the mood. She had no descriptive adjectives. She didn't explain. Her voice was curiously flat and lacking intonation. It wasn't the voice Jim remembered. The dust of the *chacra* had filled her lungs and clogged her vocal cords. Her kicky animation was gone. No fluttering hands, no crazy highjinks, no hiccupping laugh. The light in Lisa's eyes had gone from crazy mambo to moonlight sonata. Her glitzy smile had diminished to a quiver in the corners of her mouth. And now that Lisa was so quiet, so curiously sane, now that the whole collection of her foibles was gone, Jim realized how much he missed them.

She sighed, and a breath of life stirred in her voice. "If I tell you that they wanted to keep me as a replacement for Asu, you'll think I'm crazy."

"No, I don't think you're crazy," Jim said. On the contrary, he was worried Lisa had lost her knack for craziness.

"It's strange," she said, "Asu showing up at the exact moment when I was leaving the *chacra*. It couldn't have been coincidence. It was a sign. I was no longer needed."

Now that Lisa was talking of signs, Jim knew she was going to be alright. She was a bit stiff from the ordeal, but she was going to bounce back.

Conversations in the car had limits, for Jim at any rate. He had to keep his hands on the steering wheel. He couldn't say what he wanted to say to Lisa just by moving his lips. He had to make an impression on Lisa's arm, on her neck, on her shoulders. He had to feel her flesh, the faint traces of muscle under her skin, to tell her that he was on her side. He needed both hands to make his point, that he was satisfied with the exchange after all. He reached over and squeezed her hand.

"How was your visit with Hetta Soriano?" he said. "Did you find out anything more about your father?"

"Let's not talk about him anymore," she said.

"Come on, Lisa," Jim said. "That's not fair. I want to know how the saga ends. What about the uterine memories?"

"You told me to keep that stuff in, Jim. You said to me: the best place for fantasies is in your head."

"I meant: don't vent indiscriminately. You spilled your whole life story the moment we were introduced. And now that I know you better, now that I am involved in your life, you clamp up."

"I know, Jim, but every time we're together, there is interference, something getting in our way."

"What's in the way now? Tilcara? Santos?"

"No, I'm over that."

"Don?"

She didn't answer.

"What about the new life you were going to start?" he said.

"I can't do it, Jim," she said. "I thought I was through with Don, but something's come up. A complication."

The reward for rescuing Lisa was slipping from Jim's hands. Don, not he, would be joining Lisa on stage – unless of course Tilcara had ruined her dramatic talent for roles requiring passion and flesh-fusing heat, and all performances were cancelled.

He pulled over to the side of the road and took Lisa into his arms. He made a last effort. He was willing to take her as she was, soft and melancholy, but his hand brushed against the hard surface of the diamond on her finger, and he had to let her go.

She looked at him sadly.

"It's not working out," she said.

In her eyes he saw the vertigo of exhaustion.

LISA COULDN'T MOVE HER ARMS. She was sodden with sleep. The blanket was like a straitjacket. The phone kept ringing. It's Jim, she thought. He's calling me from Catamarca, and I can't unearth my arms from under the blanket. When the fuzz in her head cleared, she realized it was the alarm clock ringing. 07:01 was blinking at her, neon lit. She hit the snooze button. The clock rustled faintly as 07:01 turned over to 07:02. She wanted to slip back into the vastness of sleep, but Tilly was already awake. Lisa could see her through the open door, sitting up in her crib, holding on to the railing. Her pyjama pants bunched up around her knees, weighed down by soggy diapers. Yippie the Dog had gone overboard and was lying on the floor spread-eagled. Tilly was looking down on him puzzled. She turned her head, saw Lisa moving and started whining.

"Okay, Tilly," she said, "gimme a minute, sweetheart." She lay back and closed her eyes, trying to dip back into the dream of getting a call from Jim. Where did this dream hope come from? She hadn't heard from Jim in a long time. Perhaps the Catamarca project was finished, and he was back in Toronto, and that's why she felt the pull, why she felt those vibes. Lisa tried to put a Toronto aura around Jim's dream image, remember him as he was on the roof terrace of the Park Plaza, the last time she'd seen him in Toronto, but it was hard to conjure up a summer evening when wet snowflakes were drifting against her bedroom window and getting stuck there in fuzzy white patches. She tried again, putting Jim indoors. He was lying on a bed in a hotel room, wanting her. But it wasn't the Park Plaza. It was the Continental in Catamarca, where they made love the last time, and she was in such a sad passion because everything had gone wrong and she had no hope of ever seeing him again.

She tried to go back to sleep, stay asleep a little longer, avoid the room, the bed containing only one body, her own, imagine the happiness of Jim's body next to hers, but it didn't work because Tilly was spiking her whine with little crying jags.

Lisa wrenched herself out of bed, and Tilly switched to a mewling sound of anticipation when she saw her walk to the kitchen and open a jar of Gerber's fruit. I should feed her more solid stuff, she thought, but to hell with Dr. Spock, Tilly loves fruit. After she had changed her, they went back to bed. Tilly was lying beside her, content, eyes half-closed. Oh, yes, please, Tilly, go back to sleep! I can't face the morning yet. Tilly cuddled up to her, breathed against her arm, and Lisa was thinking of the *chacra*, of the first flurry of Tilly's life, a feathery breathing, a whisper resurrecting her courage. She thought of that surge of energy every time she woke up already exhausted, when it seemed too much to squeeze out toothpaste, to wash her hair, to choose which sweater to put on, when a zombie day was looming. She thought of the sense of mission she felt when she put on her crazy act at the *chacra*. Maybe I should do the banshee dance more often, she thought. The last performance landed her in a cage, but it had been a moment of electric revelation. She had felt of one piece, inside and out, knew what it was all about, who was the enemy, how to defeat him. There was no confusion. Every muscle in her body had been tense with the will to act. That banshee dance she did for the old man at the *chacra* and the moment of discovery when she felt the presence of Tilly for the first time, those were the twin highlights of her journey. That's how she thought of her trip to Tilcara: a magical tour, with Tilly as her bring-home souvenir. The banshee dance was a peak performance, but once she escaped the cage, waded through the creek and came out on the road, once she saw Jim and knew she was safe, the electric charge drained out of her. At least that's how it felt, but perhaps the energy was still inside her, in a secret place, a little wilted perhaps, but revivable, and it was just a matter of coaxing it out and reaching that point again where impulse was inseparable from action. In the meantime it was the Monday to Friday routine at the nursery school that kept Lisa going, and on the weekend it was Tilly with her little clockwork body that needed to be fed, changed, and taken for a walk in the stroller.

The disappointment of discovering that Jim's phone call had been only a dream hit Lisa hard now that the pale wintry light started filtering through the window. Life always presented her with insurmountable difficulties in the early morning when she was trying to connect today with yesterday, but she knew: by the time she got to work and helped the children out of their snowsuits and put their boots away and had them sitting in a circle for a sing-along, she would be over the worst.

Tilly started tugging on the blanket and went body mountaineering, crawling over Lisa's arms and legs. She might as well get up and face the day. She climbed out of bed, chugged to the living room couch with Tilly clamped to her hip, putting on the locomotion for her. They watched Mr. Rogers and the antics of Striped Tiger for a bit and got bored simultaneously. She retrieved Yippie, and Tilly gave her a big smile of thanks, the smile that pressed the on-button for love. Lisa cuddled her and hoped for that surge of power hidden somewhere within and wondered what would have happened if a load of crap hadn't been dumped on her when she arrived at the airport in Buenos Aires. It was enough to put anyone into a muddle. It made her want to crawl back to Dr. Lerner. But then she thought: why go back to her? Therapy did nothing for me. I'll talk it through with Don. Every time Lisa said: "I'll talk to Don," her mother winced, but for a while she let it go.

Lisa was entitled to sympathy and understanding after what happened when she arrived at the Buenos Aires airport. Instead of Don, an officer from the Canadian consulate was waiting for her in the arrival lounge. He had the kind of well-worn face that could adjust to any situation. He stepped forward, keeping a little distance from Lisa, large enough not to intrude on her privacy, close enough to keep their conversation confidential and prepare her for the bad news, that Don had suffered a stroke. He didn't use the word "stroke," not right away. He worked his way up to it, looking into Lisa's face and gauging her distress by the colour of her cheeks. He spoke of a medical emergency at first, gradually filled in the details, put in a calming smile and a promise of support, but his diplomatic skill was lost on Lisa. The moment he said "medical emergency," her thoughts slid down a chute, skidded and bounced against a wide-angle screen: Don, motionless on the sofa of the villa in Mar del Plata, his face turned to the wall, so she could see only the back of his head above the blanket, and a pair of feet in white socks sticking out below. If she had checked on Don before leaving for Catamarca –

The consular officer saw that his supportive voice wasn't enough. Lisa looked at him with fixed attention, but her body was listing, sagging into a faint. He took her arm, and the pressure of his hand shut off the mental screen, put an end to Lisa's what-ifs, and made her sigh. So many misunderstandings, but let it be if that's what the signs of '78 meant, the certificates on Dr. Lerner's walls, the red roses, the promise of prayers being answered, the glittering diamond facets, if that's what they added up to: Don's near-death.

"We've been informed that you and Mr. Baker were travelling together," the officer said and waited, leaving the question of their relationship hanging midair. Was she one of those feminists who kept her own name after marriage, or was she someone Don had picked up for a good time? Lisa saw that it was her turn now. She was expected to carry on the official dialogue. She looked at the diamond ring on her finger for encouragement and said she was Don's fiancée. Really, how could she possibly reject Don's proposal posthumously, or post-stroke, which came out to the same thing? They were supposed to get married in a couple of months, she told the consular officer, making it up on the run.

The expression in his eyes changed minutely, from formal to sympathetic. He was well trained in making these distinctions, in using small muscle movements to replace the gravity of office with something softer now that he understood: Lisa wasn't short-range. She had diamond-ring standing. She was entitled to a due measure of sympathy. His eyes started crinkling at the edges. He told Lisa they had flown Don back to Canada for treatment and gave her the details, the ones reserved for next of kin.

LISA'S MOTHER NEEDED NO DIPLOMATIC training to know what had to be done. She went into a teeth-clenching rage when Lisa told her she was pregnant. But the diamond ring made everything okay. Her rage abated. Her face started matching the tidiness of her living room and the subtle shade of the French Provincial sofa on which she was sitting. She decorously crossed her ankles, switched her body from indignation to sorrow, and put on a prim voice of condolence, urging the guest bedroom on Lisa.

"Why don't you stay with us for a while?" she said, but didn't insist when Lisa shook her head.

Jorge took the news of Lisa's pregnancy in stride, as if she had given him a job he knew he could handle, an untidy account that needed reconciling. It was only a matter of making the receipts match the expenditures. He read both sides of the marriage licence application, noted the missing signature, shoved it across the coffee table and made Lisa sign on the dotted line.

"I'm glad *he* signed," he said, "but it's a sad story. *Pobrecita*, I feel sorry for you."

He came around the table and hugged Lisa with all the warmth of the Irish wool sweater he was wearing. It was a Christmas present from his wife, and he was wearing it under duress. Jorge liked suit jackets. He was comfortable in his accountant's uniform, but Maria made him switch to leisure wear when he got home from work. She didn't want the back of his jacket getting wrinkled when he relaxed on the sofa.

"I'll take care of that for you, Lisa," Jorge said and stowed the application in his wallet.

When Lisa left, her mother walked her to the front door and stood on the threshold, oblivious to the crisp cold blowing into the hallway, waiting politely as if Lisa was a dinner guest taking her leave. She was still standing at the door when Lisa backed the car down the driveway. It was Don's car, a Mercury Marquis. You need a big car in real estate to impress the clients, he told Lisa when he bought it the previous year. It was so large that the hood blocked Lisa's view as she backed down the incline. Her mother, waving adieu, came in sight again when the car reached the level ground at the end of the driveway.

Lisa drove back to Don's apartment. That's how she thought of the flat on Avenue Road, although she was paying the rent now. Or rather Jorge said he would, for the time being. The place looked battened down, waiting to be repossessed by the owner. It was strange to see the easy chair unoccupied, the TV silent, the kitchen still messy the way Lisa had left it after breakfast that morning. She was so used to Don cleaning up after her. That's when it finally sunk in. When she saw the congealed bacon fat on the plate and the left-over crust of toast, that's when she understood that it was her place now, and that she could do as she pleased. What Lisa wanted to do was take down Asu's photo, evict her from the bedroom. Some of the mad energy Lisa had felt at the *chacra* came pulsing back. She was going to take Asu's photo out of the frame, crumple it and put it into the trash. Or do something even more dramatic like burning it or cutting it into little pieces. Asu was occupying more than her bedroom wall. She was squatting in her soul.

Lisa wanted to flick Don's cigarette lighter, hold one corner of the picture over the flame and watch the molten bits of Asu's photo drip into the ashtray on the coffee table, eliminate the competition.

For some reason Lisa thought of Asu as "the competition" although she wasn't sure what prize they were in the running for. Don? Jim? Whatever the prize, Lisa needed to reclaim her space, make that wall her own, change it into a testimony to her own life. She got stuck on that thought, hung up on the phrase "her own life." What life was it going to be? She had so many roles going, she couldn't decide, not until Asu was out of her sight. She took Asu's picture off the hook, but found she couldn't take the next step, burning Asu in effigy and covering up the empty wall space with something matching the colour of her own future, something promising, something exciting to open up the capillaries of joy. But she couldn't move. Her energy was ebbing. She went limp, she couldn't go through with it, not with burning Asu's photo, not with planning the rest of her life. Another time, she thought, and stored the picture in the hall closet, hiding it face-down under Don's hat and gloves. That night she slept soundly, buried in a dreamless, anonymous sleep. It was good to have the bedroom to herself.

Jorge came over the next day. It was a business call. He came in the capacity of Lisa's accountant. He pulled off his tuque and left his boots by the door. He put his briefcase on the coffee table and walked around the apartment in his socks, coat still buttoned up, tuque sticking out of his pocket. He was making it clear that this wasn't his home, and he hadn't decided whether it was a suitable home for his daughter. He was prepared to move Lisa out if necessary. He wouldn't sit down. Not yet.

The light from the window kept moving over his face and forming new angles as he passed from room to room like a man checking out a potential rental. He didn't touch anything. He was careful not to intrude on the owner's private life, just letting his eyes roam. They came to rest for a moment on the wall where Asu's photo had been, stopped perhaps by the nail hole and the faint outline of something missing. Finally he nodded: good enough.

He got out of his coat, sat down on the couch and lit a cigarette. Balancing it on the ashtray, he sprang the catches of his briefcase and took out a folder. He told Lisa he'd taken the day off work to look after her business. He listed his accomplishments:

"First I talked to Don's lawyer. Once you are married, you and the baby will have a claim on Don's assets." There were several properties in Don's name, he said, and a term life insurance that had come due on his 50th birthday. The people at the registry office confirmed that the application for the marriage licence was valid. "I explained the situation at the hospital. They were sympathetic. They said they might be able to arrange a bedside ceremony."

Jorge also talked to Dr. Snell and asked him about Don's prospects of recovery. Don wasn't exactly lucid, but there were flickers of recognition. He might recover some of his functions in the long term, Dr. Snell said, but it was difficult to make a prognosis. In any case, they should look into a nursing home for Don.

Jorge got up and looked out the window as if the traffic on Avenue Road explained the rest. Lisa couldn't read the expression in his eyes when he turned back to her, but she could tell he had come to some sort of decision. About Don? About her? He settled in Don's easy chair, rocked back and forth and said: "Now that you are getting married, maybe it's time to tell you."

"Tell me what?"

"Something I've been meaning to tell you for a long time. It's about your mother and me."

He started telling Lisa the story of their courtship. He met Maria at an office party. She came with Soriano and his wife and daughter. At first Jorge thought she was a relative of theirs; then he found out she was working for them as a nanny. He ended up asking her out on a date.

Lisa had heard the courtship story a hundred times. At this point, her mother usually chimed in and added romantic fluff, sprinkled on the sugar. Love at first sight, and all that. Why was Jorge rehashing the old story now?

"I know," Lisa said to him, and watched him shift a little. The story shifted too, taking a new turn.

"But you don't know everything," he said. "We went out a couple of times. I could tell it wasn't going anywhere. Maria was playing it cool – until I told her I was going to Canada. Then all of a sudden there were tears, no, no, she couldn't let me go. She started making it easy for me." That bit was new. So no love at first sight, or at least not mutual love. Jorge started in again, getting back into the groove. "Next thing I know, Maria is pregnant. So I do the right thing and marry her, but I didn't have the money to pay for a second passage to Canada. I told her she'd have to wait until I got a job and saved enough to bring her over. She didn't want to wait. She said she'd borrow the money from Soriano. I had my doubts about that. Soriano was a businessman. He wasn't a bleeding heart. Well, surprise. She managed to get the money out of him."

Another deviation from the family saga. The standard version read: "He gave us the money as a wedding present." Lisa wanted to stop Jorge and make him go back over that part: was it a loan or a wedding present? Was Hetta's version correct after all? But Jorge put up his hand. No interruptions. Not now. He wanted to finish what he had to say.

"We get to Canada. I land a job. Everything is hanky-dory, except Maria is holding out on me." He put it discreetly, looking at Lisa sideways, checking whether she was following the story. "I thought maybe it was the pregnancy. Then I found a letter from Soriano, nothing improper, but it made me suspicious. We argued. If it was just a greeting, I said, why didn't he address the letter to both of us? She didn't have an answer. Then you were born 'prematurely'." Jorge pulled on his cigarette, exhaling a bitter flag of smoke.

From the way he said "prematurely," with an ironic lift, Lisa saw they were turning another corner in the story, getting closer to the truth, closing the gap between the official version and the version that had been playing in her mind for a long time now, the one with Soriano *padre* in it.

Jorge got up, came over to where Lisa was sitting, and took her hand as if to prepare her for the worst, but she already knew what was coming. "So I arrange for a blood test," he said. "The results come back, and I have it in black and white: I'm not your father. I show the test to Maria. She cries. I tell her I want a divorce, but it's not that easy. We are Catholics, and there is no divorce in Argentine law. In the end I decide to make do with the situation. What can I say? We had some good times and some bad times. *Así es la vida.*"

He squeezed Lisa's hand. She was astonished by the simplicity of it all. There had been no need to go to Catamarca. Jorge could have told her for the asking. She didn't know what to say, and he took her silence for shock.

"But it doesn't make any difference, none whatsoever, *chiquita*," he said, patting Lisa's hand. "I love you just as much." He bear-hugged her.

Lisa hugged him back and said: "I know, Dad." She was surprised how natural it came out: Dad. She told him about her visit with Hetta Soriano.

"I had my suspicions already," she said. "Nothing concrete. Just a feeling. But I didn't get anywhere with my questions."

"You actually talked to Hetta Soriano?" he said.

That look again, Lisa thought sadly. He looks at me the way everyone does when I talk about my feelings, as if I was misbehaving, as if I was wrong. He looks at me like that even though I've been right all along. I don't know why people can't accept feelings as proof.

"I don't know what you expected from her," Jorge said. "Even if Hetta Soriano knew about the affair, she wouldn't have said anything to you. It wouldn't be in her interest. If you can prove that you are Soriano's daughter, you are entitled to a share in the inheritance. I'd say: go ahead and sue her, but I see no hope of winning the case. The legal system in Argentina is a jungle. Besides, Soriano's business was sold years ago. God knows where the money is now – in some tax haven, in Uruguay or Panama. Or she put it into a dollar account in Miami. We'd be in court for years just trying to locate the money."

Lisa told him it was okay. She didn't want to sue Hetta. It wasn't about money. She just wanted to know who her father was.

"Let me tell you another thing, *chiquita*," he said. "The money Soriano loaned your mother to go to Canada? I never paid him back. I wrote him a letter and told him I'd put the money into an account for you, and he was welcome to add to it. He never answered. But the money has accumulated interest nicely."

It was a flat ending to Lisa's glorious quest. Instead of a father: a bank account with accumulated interest.

"I thought I should tell you," Jorge said. "But really, the paternity thing isn't all that important. What matters is love."

The moment he said it, Lisa realized: every single one of his words was a sign. Jorge had planted a row of flashing signs to show her that she was on the right path. She knew the baby she was carrying wasn't Don's child, but that was okay, because the words coming out of Jorge's mouth were all starred, *paternity* *not* *important*. She needed a father for her baby. And there was Don who had handed her a diamond ring and a signed marriage certificate and Jorge who had given her the go-ahead in so many starred words. That's when Lisa shelved the question of paternity for good. Well, maybe not for good because when Tilly was born, Lisa saw that she had Quechua eyes.

"Tilcara!" Lisa's mother said when she was told the baby's name. "I don't understand this mania for giving children names no one's ever heard of."

"What about her middle name?" Jorge said.

"I'll call her Georgina, after you," Lisa said.

His eyes went moist. Her mother said nothing. She knew she had lost that round.

BY THE TIME THE BABYSITTER arrived, Tilly was bouncing happily in the Jolly Jumper. Lisa managed to sneak out of the apartment without her noticing. If she saw Lisa putting on her boots, she set up a howl, but it was all show. She stopped the moment Lisa was out the door.

"I don't understand why you decided to go back to work, Lisa," her mother said. "You could live perfectly well on Don's money." She pushed the guilt button. She heckled Lisa. "You have an obligation toward the child. What's your excuse for leaving her with a babysitter? There is no excuse."

"Mom, I love Tilly, but I need to get out. I need a life of my own."

"A life of your own! Tilly is your life now. When I was young, that was understood. It never occurred to me to go back to work after I had you. I stayed home."

Yes, but her mother was typecast for the stay-at-home role. She had no repertoire. Unlike Lisa who had a large supply of song and dance routines that needed practicing.

When Lisa got into the elevator that morning with Mrs. Dorner who lived next door, she didn't say "Good morning." She had used her polite elevator voice for three days in a row. It was time for a change, for something out of the ordinary, for: *It's a beautiful morning.* Lisa liked the old Rascal tune and sang it with the kids in the playroom, with the lyrics cleaned up, because she didn't want to teach them bad grammar. *It ain't no good when the sun is shining* became "it is no good when the sun is shining" in Lisa's playroom version.

Mrs. Dorner looked startled when Lisa sang *It's a beautiful morning*, but what the hell, Lisa thought, it's crazy Tuesday, the day when I visit Don in the nursing home, when "good morning" isn't good enough. She kept humming *It's a beautiful morning*, all the way to the lobby. She reached under her wraparound scarf and, for good luck, touched the pendant she was wearing. It spelled *LOVE* in a square, *LO* on top, *VE* underneath, her charm for a crazy day.

Her mother kept nagging Lisa. "Why don't you take Tilly along when you visit Don?"

"Because she doesn't like visiting Don."

Lisa took Tilly only once. She held her tight because the white sheets on Don's bed were too wan, too deathly pale, and Tilly cried at the sight of the room, the scrubbed floor, the plastic and metal surfaces, so hard and sterile. Her desperate cries unsettled Don and made him blow bubbles at the mouth. After that, Lisa left Tilly with the babysitter. She wanted to keep her life pink and lacy as long as possible. She wanted to protect Tilly from the wrinkled ugliness of the nursing home. She protected her own soul by wearing a talisman, the *LOVE* pendant. She wore it every Tuesday and Saturday when she went to talk to Don.

For a while her mother put up with the phrase "talking to Don." Then she became edgy.

"I wish you wouldn't use those words, Lisa," she said. "*Talking to Don* sounds crazy. You know perfectly well that you can't have a conversation with him."

"But I do," Lisa said.

"Lisa, I know it hurts, but you have to come to terms with Don's condition," her mother said.

This was the woman who still had a hankering for Miguel Soriano, the woman who had never come to terms with the fact that she was married to Jorge, was Maria Martinez now, not Maria Soriano, who thought she could conceal her disappointment under the plumped-up cushions of the French Provincial sofa in her immaculate living room and hide her sad face under a thick layer of creamy foundation and a painted-on smile. Who was she to say: Come to terms with life?

At first, Don was at St. Michael's, a downtown hospital close to skid row. In the winter the lobby was always full of homeless men looking for shelter from the deep freeze. The hospital was run by an order of nuns. They had to suffer the poor. Religion didn't allow them to kick out the bums. Lisa did her best not to make eye contact with them. The first time she walked through the lobby, one of them let out a racist rant, or maybe it was a sexist ramble. Lisa couldn't make out the words, something about fucking immigrants. He was grinning at any rate and leering at her, and his eyes burned a black tattoo into her neck.

There were two beds in Don's room: the one by the entrance had a heavy white plastic curtain drawn around it. The other bed, by the window, was Don's. He was dressed in a green hospital gown open at the neck. The tube of the IV was taped to his arm with an adhesive patch, dripping a colourless liquid into his veins, as if his blood was too colourful and needed bleaching. Don's salt and pepper hair was plastered against the sides of his head and sticking up on top. His eyes were closed. He looked vulnerable, but his brow was smooth, a sleeper's brow. Lisa wondered, were any thoughts drifting through Don's mind? His hand was twitching on the folds of the blanket. She whispered his name, and his eyes opened. They wandered vaguely in Lisa's direction. They too had been washed of colour. They were round with astonishment, straining to make out who/what was moving there by the bed. They fastened on Lisa at last. Don had spotted her. That's what it looked like at any rate, but Lisa wasn't sure. Maybe he was looking through her.

"Hi, Don," she said. Maybe he was mad at her because she had deserted him, left him on the sofa in Mar del Plata, his brain fuzzy with alcohol poisoning or a stroke. "It's me, Lisa."

His eyes came into focus. The corners of his mouth straightened up. A ghost of a smile appeared on his face. Lisa sat down on his bed, perched on one half of her butt, careful not to edge into the territory occupied by Don's body outline, and he pressed her hand. His mouth started working. A burbling sound came out.

Lisa leaned over him and listened to his strained breathing, a whistling breath. She felt his fingers creeping up on her hand, feeling for something, and realized he was feeling for the ring.

"I'm wearing it," she said. She disengaged her hand and held it up close to his eyes. "See?"

He sank back further into the pillow, exhausted now that he had managed the first task he had set himself: trying to pick up where they had left off in Mar del Plata when she told him she'd give him an answer on her return, at the airport in Buenos Aires where he was supposed to pick her up.

"The answer is yes," Lisa said. She knew she should follow that up with "I love you" but she couldn't. It seemed ungenerous to hold out on Don like that. She had lied for trivial reasons before, so why not lie out of charity? She gathered air in her lungs and made herself say: "I love you." Don didn't react, perhaps because lies didn't carry in the thin atmosphere of a hospital. She was wracking her brains what else she could say to cheer him up. She felt bad that she hadn't brought him flowers. The other guy behind the curtain had flowers arranged in a vase on a side table.

"I tell people that I'm your fiancée. That's what you want me to say, right, Don?"

She asked him to squeeze her hand for yes, if he wasn't up to saying anything, and there was a slight increase in pressure, but she couldn't be sure. He had closed his eyes again. His eyelids were like the curtain around the other man's bed. They protected him from prying minds.

Was she condemned to this nudge-nudge, wink-wink, pressing hands, quirky conversation from now on? Lisa almost succumbed to the tragic atmosphere of the room until she remembered the act she had developed in Tilcara: the madwoman's dance. She got up from Don's bed, turned on the music in her head and began swaying her hips. She leaned over Don's bed, doing a kind of Indian belly dance, gyrating, jiggling her tits and waving her hands, and Don's eyelids fluttered. Or maybe it was just that the jiggles were travelling along the surface of the bed, like the tremor of an earthquake, rocking him. Lisa segued into a twist. *Let's twist again like we did last summer.* She hummed the Chubby Checker tune. It was a hit with the kids at the nursery. She was twisting down to the floor when the nurse came in, a big woman with broad see-saw hips that came to a wobbling halt when she saw the dancing madwoman.

Lisa got up.

"Just trying to make it a bit lively for him," she said apologetically, and the nurse gave her a reassuring smile, but at the back of her eyes Lisa read: "She's nuts, for sure."

"I can't get any reaction out of him," she told the nurse, trying to sound matter of fact to re-establish her credentials as a visitor. "When I first came in, he pressed my hand and tried to speak, but now: nothing."

"If he pressed your hand, that's good, honey," the nurse said. "That's something. He is probably tired now."

"Do you think he'll come around?" Lisa asked. "I mean: will he recover from the stroke?"

The nurse had her professional response pat. "I can't tell you, love," she said. "Ask Dr. Snell. He has the information for you."

She busied herself changing the bottle on the IV line. It was Lisa's chance to slip away. There was really nothing more for her to do except to say good bye and kiss Don on the cheek. Am I doing this for the nurse? she thought. No, a kiss is the ultimate gesture between lovers. Why didn't I think of that before? Instead of bringing out the phony "I love you," I should have kissed Don. A smooch is a smooch. It's something real.

She decided to use more body language once she got Don to a nursing home, once he had settled in.

THEN CAME SUPER TUESDAY, SUPER crazy wedding Tuesday. Lisa could not shake off the one-two zombie mood that had swooped down and seized her brain at the bridal store two weeks earlier, when her mother held up a white and cream-coloured dress and made whining noises. "Isn't this gorgeous?" she said, meaning: *Pull yourself together, Lisa, and try to look like a happy bride.* Lisa's skin turned to plastic. Ruches and ruffles swept through her mind, blocking whole sentences, and leaving her in a pearly stupor. From time to time she managed to say no in response to crystals and rosettes or wave off something satiny, but the zombie rhythm made her head nod one-two, one an ivory dress, two a lacy jacket, and now they were at Don's apartment, waiting for Jorge to pick them up and drive them to the nursing home for the wedding ceremony.

Her mother was pinning a corsage on the lapel of Lisa's jacket and looking at Lisa's waistline, at the bump showing there. She pursed her lips. Lisa expected her to say: *We should have left more slack in the waist*, but instead she said: "So Jorge told you," meaning *now you know that he isn't your father, now you know the whole story.* The zombie weight lifted from Lisa's shoulders, bumped by the half-words only she could hear, the *whole story* her mother had spent a lifetime blocking but couldn't go on blocking. The words were pushing up against the hedge of her teeth, against the barrier of her lips, wanting out. It was a story that took more than a simple one-two step, even if her mother wasn't about to ask anyone's pardon for what she had done, not Lisa's, not Jorge's, even if she crossed her arms and kept her eyes on Lisa's waistline. There were more than one-two words in this labyrinthine story, enough to break Lisa's zombie mood.

"I did what I had to do," her mother said. "But when I got married, I kept my vows." Unlike Jorge, who had affairs, who lied to her, who cheated on her. "I was a good wife." And she reeled off a catalogue of things she had done for Jorge: kept the house dust-free, did the laundry, ironed Jorge's shirts, had dinner on the table every night without fail, packed nutritious lunches. She named each one of her chores, reciting them like poetry. She had given Lisa and Jorge a home to be proud of.

But Lisa caught the whining at the end of her mother's list. She meant to say: *I needed a father for my child.* Lisa understood. She, too, needed a father for her child. She too was getting married to the man at hand. Lisa kept a sympathetic silence, but silence was not good enough. Her mother wanted – what did she want? She stepped up her defence and launched into complaints. It could have been a perfect life, they could have been a perfect family, she said, but the happy picture was marred by a philandering husband and a crazy daughter.

There was no more whining in her voice when she came to the crazy-daughter part. She meant what she said, although, really, Liza thought, what does she know about craziness? She doesn't understand. It's not an unfortunate condition. Craziness can be sweet and comforting, it can be glorious and triumphant.

Perhaps I should put on a banshee dance for her, Lisa thought, like the one I did in Tilcara. Maybe I should let off steam and blow her mind with a glass-shattering, hurricane force scream to teach her a lesson in craziness! But now that the zombie mood had broken, Lisa saw her mother with unexpected clarity and realized, surprise! Her mother was not without dramatic talents after all, had written her own skit and performed on her own stage, a marvellous set built on the ruins of her unrealized past, the romantic Soriano past. She had built herself a new life that was earthquake and hurricane proof. No foot stomping dervish dance, no blasting scream from Lisa could shake her mother's palace of illusions. No crazy act could break down her whining mind speeches, and in any case, a wedding in a nursing home was enough madness for one day. Lisa let her mother have the last word.

"You and George!" she was saying. "Sometimes I think I can't take it any more. But it's God's punishment for my sins. I know."

Maybe Don was paying for his sins as well. The Saint has cast a paralytic spell on him for taking away a soul belonging to Tilcara, Lisa thought. There is a sequence of events, a series of moves to go through, each step adding to the score. Asu's return to the *chacra* and the Saint's revenge: two strikes in favour of Tilcara's home team. Lisa breaking out of the cage and absconding with Tilly hidden inside her: two strikes in favour of the visitors. A perfect balance, an end to the cycle of evil.

JORGE ARRIVED AT THE APARTMENT and chauffeured them to the nursing home. A nursing aide had wrangled Don into a white dress shirt and propped him up on pillows and laid his hands out in front, settled them on the coverlet. The creases in the new shirt, fresh out of the package, and the papery skin of his face gave Don the appearance of a mannequin. The staff had decorated the IV tree and the headboard of Don's bed with white streamers and balloons. Lisa's mother couldn't hide her distaste. The party theme clashed with the fancy bouquets she had set up around the room in large vases. And no one could do anything about the pale turquoise walls and the institutional smell of cleaning fluids and the hectoring voice of the intercom pager in the hall.

The official from the registry office and his assistant were vigorously cheerful. When they first came in, Lisa caught them wavering. Should they put on sorrowful faces in view of the grave situation or keep the wedding-day faces required in their official capacity? They settled for glad-facing. Stan Harrison was there to act as best man. He was a colleague of Don's from the real estate office and had come with a smartly dressed woman friend, Maureen. She stood discreetly against the wall and kept looking at Lisa, as if she couldn't get over her choice of husband and expected her to jilt Don at the last moment.

The registrar shook hands all round and began reading the vows. When Don was required to respond, they all looked at him and waited respectfully, in case by some miracle he would come out of his paralysis and say "I do." He said nothing, and they contented themselves with a nod (or did they just imagine it?). In any case, they agreed to take the straining eyes and the dribble of spit in the corner of Don's mouth for his approval of the proceedings. The woman called Maureen was the only hold-out. She still had that incredulous look in her eyes. Lisa was afraid she would speak up and spoil the illusion, but she kept her mouth shut. Stan Harrison stepped forward and said "I do" on Don's behalf. Lisa signed the forms. Stan stuck a pen into Don's hand and dangled it over the paper. They all watched as the nib left random squiggles on the dotted line.

Lisa's mother had tears in her eyes. She knew the proper thing to do in any situation. When she found herself pregnant, the thing to do was to marry Jorge. Now that Lisa was getting married, the thing to do was to take her daughter's hand in her smooth fingers, smile an intimate smile, and weep tears of joy. After the ceremony she embraced Lisa and mouthed: "I wish you happiness" with a lovely inflection, but Lisa's ear caught the whine. She meant, *but how can you be happy*, and her smile faded into the vagueness of doubt. Jorge hugged Lisa, held her close, and patted her back. He said his *felicidades* in a low voice, looking at the side of her face, avoiding her eyes. No one remained unmoved, not even Don. His body began sagging to the left, and the drooling became pronounced. Lisa asked the nursing aide to help her take off the ridiculous shirt and get Don back into his striped pyjama top.

When everyone was gone, she had a heart-to-heart talk with Don. She stroked his old-man hair and told him that the child wasn't his, but she would make it up to him. "I'll make sure the nurses treat you right," she said. "I'll come in – she hesitated a little – twice a week." She could safely promise that much. She couldn't get herself to be more grateful to Don for the financial support he provided for her and Tilly. She had a hard time not to feel indecently happy at the thought that he would never be able to paw her again or call her "Baby."

IT WAS THE END OF Lisa's work day. The mothers had come to pick up their kids. The room was full of boots, jackets, snowsuits, lunch boxes, crayon-smeared papers and comfy toys, which they were trying to match up with the right arms and legs. When the door had closed on the last mother-child unit, Lisa put away the teaching aids. Sandy who minded the under threes came in for a chat, but Lisa told her she'd have to run.

"Oh yeah," Sandy said. "I forgot: It's Tuesday. Don-day. How's it going?"

No change. No change from last week or last month, but over the months the flickers of recognition had become less frequent. Dr. Snell said there had been a number of mini-strokes. The movement in Don's eyes was involuntary. Still, Lisa talked to Don: it was her crazy hour. The numbness she felt when she was by herself went away. She warmed to the occasion and stretched under the sun of Don's unseeing eyes. She put on the fizz, which she couldn't do when she was on mommy duty because she was afraid of scaring Tilly. Craziness was a calling. Nobody should be exposed to it prematurely. It was like religion, a question of conscience. You had to be old enough to know it was for you, if you wanted to benefit from it and purge your soul.

But lately the crazy show hadn't been going well for Lisa. She still performed for Don twice a week, but it no longer cheered her up. An actress feeds on her audience, and Don wasn't there for her. It was hard to play to an empty house. It killed the music in Lisa's ears, it dulled the stars in her eyes. It could no longer be denied: she was primping for a comatose man.

Once she broke faith and went out to a disco. As soon as she heard the booming base, she started smiling, and the lights came back on in her head. Something in her rippled and glowed. She felt a burst of happiness. The funk was back. She got on the dance floor and started solo bopping. In no time she had a couple of guys snapping their fingers and grinding their hips alongside. But the happiness didn't last. Bad conscience rolled in like a bank of fog. What was she going to tell Don when she saw him next? He might start foaming at the mouth when she told him she'd gone disco-dancing. She had a contract with Don. The signature on the wedding certificate and the diamond ring gave him proprietary rights to Lisa's crazy moves.

The morning of the telephone dream, when she thought of Jim, she realized she had reached the breaking point. She couldn't go on with the show at the nursing home. Bad conscience or not, Lisa needed a change of venue for her mad capers. If she gave a live performance, she deserved a live audience. She got no applause from Don. His eyes no longer tracked. Did that constitute a breach of contract? If he didn't appreciate the entertainment she offered, did he lose the rights to it? Lisa hadn't figured it out yet, but she knew she couldn't go on giving solo performances.

That morning she made up her mind to break with Don. His diamond ring was on her finger, too tight to wrench off at night. It was on her hand permanently, a reminder of Don's pledge to take care of her, and her acceptance of his offer. But that morning in the bathroom, Lisa tried to take it off. The power she had first felt in Tilcara was back, sweeping over her, recalibrating her brain, entering her blood stream, moving the muscles and tendons in her arm. She ran cold water over her left hand, rubbed soap on her finger, wiggled the band of the diamond ring, manoeuvred it carefully over the knuckle, yes, it was moving, coming along, but when the ring was almost ready to slip off her finger, Lisa pushed it back. She was going about it the wrong way, she realized. It was important to do things in the right order. If you messed up the order, fate let you know. First she had to talk to Don and offer him compensation. If she stopped visiting, she owed him something in return. It was a question that had to be settled before she could take off the ring, before she could phone Jim in Catamarca and follow up on his dream call. That was the right order of things. But what could she offer Don in return for her release?

That morning, when she went to work, as she got her coat from the hall closet, she thought of a gift for Don. She dug Asu's photo out from under the pile of scarves and took it with her. All day long the memory of Argentina was with her, Don in Mar del Plata, Jim in Catamarca, her mad dance in Tilcara. The memories orbited her head in a swirling rush that compromised her sight, made it hard to see the children in the playroom, hear their questions, or answer their needs. It was a day of dodging memory missiles.

After work, she drove to the nursing home, practising what she was going to say to Don. She couldn't accept his money any longer. Or drive his Mercury Marquis. Or live in his apartment on Avenue Road. She wasn't sure what to do with his money – give it away to charity? To an agency for unwed mothers? But she had to back out of their contract. She hoped Don would understand.

She parked the car in the visitors' lot, took Asu's photo from the backseat, and pressed it to her chest to avoid looking into her dark, accusing eyes. But she felt her gaze nevertheless, entering her like the point of a knife.

In Don's room, Lisa drew up a chair. She put Asu's photo on the bedside table, face down, and looked around for a sign that this was a propitious day for talking about their contract. Don had lost weight lately. His skin was sagging between the collar bones and had turned mottled brown and purple. His face looked deathly white. His right cheek and even the tip of his nose sagged, following the tilt of his head. But what did it all mean?

"Don," Lisa said softly and put her hand against his cheek.

He pursed his lips and breathed noisily. Bubbles formed at the corners of his mouth. Could he guess what she was going to say? Was he protesting already? It wasn't a good beginning.

The bubbles collapsed, leaving a shiny film on Don's lips. Peace returned to his brow.

Lisa moved up her chair. Maybe this wasn't the day to tell Don about her plan to phone Catamarca, but the moment she thought of Jim, his name leaked out into the thin air of the room and floated toward Don. She couldn't stop it. She had to go ahead.

Don's eyes opened. He was staring at the ceiling, unblinking.

Lisa took Asu's photo and set it up on the bedside table.

"Don," she said, "I've something important to tell you."

She leaned over him and cradled his face in her hands, trying to make him look at her. "I can't come back, Don," she said. "I can't. But I've brought you

Asu. She'll keep you company. You always liked her better than me anyway."

He closed his eyes and expelled a long breath.

"You are tired," Lisa said. "I know. You don't have to say anything now." She squeezed his cheeks affectionately. "I do love you, but I can't stay. You understand that, don't you? I have to make a life for myself."

A thin line of spittle appeared at the corner of Don's mouth. Lisa took out a Kleenex and wiped it off. A shadow swept across his face. There was a stir in the air, a movement, a change of rhythm that knocked Lisa off course. She didn't know how to go on. Don looked relaxed all of a sudden. He looked younger.

The room was silent except for a tinkle from the radiators. The atmosphere was foggy, at least in Lisa's head. Maybe it was the uncertain perspective of the city through the fogged up window. No, that was not it. Maybe it was Asu's photo on the bedside table, her eyes firmly fixed on Lisa's forehead. Those eyes always had a deadening effect on her. Lisa changed the angle of the picture to make her look at Don instead. The atmosphere remained threatening. Something in the room had changed. Then she realized what it was: one of those movements you notice only when they stop. The monitor beside Don's bed had flatlined.

ONCE THE PROJECT ENTERED THE final phase and Jim knew he was leaving, he suddenly felt nostalgic. He felt the need for a retrospective, for visiting all the places that held memories, to take documentary photos and buy commemorative souvenirs. He went to Buenos Aires on the pretext of an appointment with the Minister of Public Works, but the real reason for his trip was the need to rewind his life, back to the first weeks of his assignment, when he was one of the crew being briefed on the project, when Don was a new hire, too, and working on the preliminary contract. Jim did a memorial walk around Recoleta, visited the bars in the Boca, strolled along the Calle Florida like a tourist, stocked up on souvenir maté gourds and bought two pairs of shoes with perforated uppers he knew he would never wear in Canada. His nostalgia was tinged with regret. The thought of Don had prompted thoughts of Lisa, and that spoiled the whole scenario. The past became mixed up with the present, the present with future possibilities, seeing Lisa again – a train of thought that ended in confusion. No, let's not go there again, he told himself.

Back in Catamarca, Jim felt the pressure of last chance encounters: last chance to admire the mahogany and brass lobby of the Continental, last chance to mingle with the people in the street and have the local *lunfardo* tickle his ears, last chance to visit the farmers' market. It was late February. The first rain of the season had blown into town, falling gently at first, then descending in sheets, pooling on the pavement and rushing along the gutters.

Jim was rueful. He had planned on taking photos of the stalls, the blue-sky, tourist-heaven variety of photos. Now every colour had a dull grey wash. The vendors were late setting up their tables in the rain-slicked plaza. Jim stood on the sidewalk, watching them unload crates of fruit and vegetables from their trucks when he spotted Asu. It was like a repeat take: the trestle table with the wooden statues, Asu leaning slightly forward with her palms resting on the tabletop, wearily watchful, her shoulders tense. She turned her head, and their eyes met. Jim walked up to the stall.

"You're back," he said. "You didn't last long in Tilcara."

She lowered her chin in a curt nod, but offered no explanation. "I'm living with my cousin," she said, turning her head slightly in the direction of a stocky woman with shiny black braids, who sat on a stool beside her, sipping maté from a gourd.

There was a pause. Asu was unwilling to say more, but Jim couldn't get himself to move on. A sharp pang of desire struck him the moment he saw Asu. A thrill of memory ran down his spine, the memory of his trek to Tilcara, or a longing for Lisa. He couldn't be sure. The two women had become muddled in his visceral response.

Jim stood in front of the trestle table. He and Asu were caught in a freeze frame, looking at each other wordlessly. Asu could read the craving in his eyes. Unlike Jim, she was certain of the object of his desire. A mischievous smile was playing in the corners of her mouth. But, as soon as she saw that he had caught her out, the smile changed to a flinty challenge.

"You want to get together?" she said.

Jim's eyes flicked to her cousin, who had taken a last energetic suck of maté and was holding the gourd in her lap now. She was watching the shoppers strolling past, oblivious to their conversation which was nothing to her but empty sound.

He felt paralyzed by indecision, but he must have nodded or said yes under his breath because Asu was already giving him directions to her cousin's house.

He had the whole afternoon to change his mind, to forget Asu's directions, but he didn't. It was inexplicable, but in his mind Lisa and Asu had coalesced, become one. It's what Lisa-thoughts did to him: they induced Lisa-craziness; he could no longer think straight. At dusk he drove to the address Asu had given him. It was on the outskirts of Catamarca. The house was one of several small bungalows set along a dusty road in no clear order. In the failing light of the evening he saw a weedy yard, bare except for a stunted lemon tree and rabbit hutches tucked against the wall of a small bungalow. At the other end of the yard was the concrete shed Asu had described to Jim when she said: "I'll meet you at the *casita*."

Jim parked the car and walked to the shed. It was windowless and had a corrugated tin roof. A pink and green plastic strip curtain covered the entrance. He clapped his hands, signalling his arrival in the traditional way, and Asu parted the curtain and motioned him in. He ducked into the cool, sombre interior. The shed had a packed earth floor. There was a bed and a wash stand with an enamelled basin and a mirror. Above the mirror was an iron cross, the kind you would expect at the head of a grave. String bags were hanging on hooks cemented into the wall. The quilt on the bed was strangely luxurious for such a spare room. It had an exuberant pattern of red blossoms, lush and voluptuous like a woman's lips, and bright viridian leaves that seemed to glow in the dark.

Asu lit a kerosene lamp standing on the floor in one corner of the room. Her face, illuminated from below, took on a mauve hue. It was as if she had grown a new layer of skin, a magic skin that allowed her to be anything she wanted, to slip in and out of Lisa's body, flashing overlapping images, layers of Asu/Lisa with blurred edges. Bits of dialogue filled Jim's head, bits of scenes with Lisa that eroded reality with whispered asides. It was difficult to focus on the woman who sat down on the bed in front of him, who pulled him toward her, the woman who spoke with Asu's voice and offered to go down on him. But he couldn't allow that. He had to see her face at all times, to make sure who she was.

"I want you on top of me," he said.

She pouted. "I don't do that kind of stuff," she said, but she relented when Jim insisted. "Okay. But only this once, as a special favour."

She folded back the quilt and made him lie down on the bare mattress. "Don't undress," she said. "Just take it out. We aren't making love, understand?"

Jim understood: he had contracted for an orifice. It was a meeting of needy bodies. She needed money, he needed sex.

"You brought a *goma*?" she said.

Jim was prepared. She watched him roll on the condom. Her sternness didn't put him off. His excitement was rising. She straddled him. Her brown-tipped breasts rose above her low-cut top as she leaned over. Her eyes were on him, abstracted, unfocused, as if she was pursuing a private thought. Jim came in a black-out of desire.

"Wish they were all as fast as you," Asu said and got up.

There was no aftermath, except for cleaning up and paying up. Jim expected nothing more. The price did not include romance. But still: something was missing. Did he think she would miraculously turn into Lisa?

"It didn't work out between you and Lisa?" Asu said. She stood in the light of the kerosene lamp, unruffled, intact as if he had never touched her.

"She went back to Don," Jim said, feeling the quivering of an old wound.

He couldn't read the register of her mood, but he was grateful for her unsentimental voice. He didn't want pity.

"I thought Don was dead," Asu said.

"Dead? What gives you that idea?"

"Santos told me, and he's never wrong about things like that."

"He is wrong this time."

She shrugged her shoulders. "You thought you could attract Lisa by fucking me?" She laughed disdainfully. "You've seen attraction work for Santos, and you thought: why don't I give it a try myself? That's what you thought, right?"

"Maybe you're on to something," Jim said.

"It takes a special kind of man to work that magic," she said. She stood close and peered into Jim's eyes, studying him – gauging his suitability as a worker of magic? "There is something there. Dreams. But dreams aren't good enough. You should ask Santos for help. He'll get Lisa back for you."

She ran her hands down Jim's arms and stopped at his watch. "I tell you what," she said, closing her fingers over his wrist. "Leave me your watch. Santos needs something that has been in contact with Lisa, or at any rate in her presence."

Jim was put off by the crudeness of her attempt to get more out of him than the money he had paid her. "You can have the watch if you want it," he said negligently and took it off.

"It's a good magnet," she said, setting the watch down on the table, "but he'll need something more personal. Hair from your crotch maybe." She stepped back. "Take your pants off."

Was he getting an extra treat in return for the watch? Jim lowered his pants and stood by the bed like a Victorian schoolboy waiting for a spanking. She rummaged in a cloth bag and came up with a pair of nail scissors. She sat down on the bed in front of Jim, made him stand close to her, and started cutting the hair in a square around his penis. A nervous current ran through Jim. He felt endangered under the knife. What if Asu's ironic smile had a tinge of sadism, what if cutting and maiming was a trivial pastime of hers? But Asu snipped with earnest concentration and put the hair away in a plastic bag.

"Don't move," she said when she was done with the clipping. She got up and returned with a shaver, one of those pink plastic ones for women, and began running it over the clipped area. The blade was dull. Jim could feel it tugging on his skin.

"Put soap on it," Jim said to her.

"No, no soap. No aftershave. You'll have to suffer a bit for your Lisa," she said, holding his penis upright, gripping it firmly. "Looks like you want it a second time." Jim doubled over and came into her hand.

She stoically wiped off and put away the shaver and the plastic bag containing the flocks of his pubic hair.

Jim would have liked to lie down on the bed and recover, but she wouldn't allow it. "Time's up," she said and smacked him with the flat of her hand. "I'll give Santos the stuff. We'll see what he can do for you."

WHEN MAUREEN CAME TO CATAMARCA for the winding-up operation, there were no polite kisses on the cheek. They shook hands and acted collegial. They pretended they had never seen each other naked. During the drive out to the site, they kept to business talk, discussed handing over the project to the Argentine authorities, the signing-off ceremony, Jim's return to Toronto in two weeks.

"I read the announcement," Maureen said. "You'll be in charge of Foreign Projects. Congratulations."

"Thanks," Jim said in the same hearty tone. Cheerful certainty was a must among people connected on the company flow chart. In his new job at Head Office, Maureen would be reporting to him. "I think I'm ready to get out of Argentina. Preferably before Maggie Thatcher declares war. You heard about the incident on Georgia Island?"

"It was on the news," Maureen said. "You really think they'll fight over a couple of remote islands with sheep farms? It's absurd."

Three days earlier a band of hired thugs had raised the Argentine flag on one of the Falkland Islands. Jim's colleagues were cynical. Galtieri, the new head of the junta, wanted action to distract people from the economic crisis and get the protest marches off the front page news. In Catamarca Jim had seen a truckful of young men in army fatigues, waving Argentine flags and chanting: *Las Malvinas son Argentinas*. It was considered a provocation now to refer to the islands by their English name as Falklands. The government rag made a great deal of an incident, in which someone had pulled an English atlas from a bin in a second-hand bookstore, crossed out "Falkland Islands" and scrawled "Malvinas" over it. At the hotel, the ex-pats tried to speak Spanish only. At the sound of English, heads turned. An end-of-era feeling had overtaken Jim's nostalgia.

The conversation in the car died. Maureen clammed up. There was nothing more to say about the Falkland crisis. It was a two-hour drive to site, and already they were in danger of running out of casual talk.

"Where are you going to live when you are back in Toronto?" Maureen said, starting up again, moving into the semi-private sphere. "Have you made arrangements yet?"

"The company is going to put me up in a hotel for a couple of weeks. I'll probably rent an apartment. Ultimately I'd like to buy a house."

"Right," Maureen said approvingly. "The thing is to invest in real estate. I've done really well with the house I bought from Don."

"Maybe I should phone him up when I get to Toronto and see what's on the market," Jim said.

"Don?" Maureen said. Something caught in her voice, a breath of embarrassment. "Don passed away last month," she said. "He never recovered from the stroke last year. I thought you knew."

Her words entered Jim's brain like a homing pigeon. He realized that he'd kept a niche for the news of Don's death ever since Asu had declared him dead.

"No, I didn't know," he said. "We weren't that close."

"Stan Harrison – a colleague of Don's, got in touch with me after he had the stroke. He said he was looking after Don's clients, temporarily. As it turned out, permanently. I should give you Stan's business card."

Jim's mind was free-ranging. He had slowed down. Cars were passing him. He forced his eyes back to the tarmac. Keep your eyes on the road, he told himself. He replayed Maureen's words: something about a real estate friend, Stan somebody, whose business card she was offering him.

"Okay," he said, "I'll give him a call," and switched back to the news of Don's death. "I wonder how his girlfriend is taking it." He was afraid of saying Lisa's name in case it induced craziness and made him veer off the road.

"Lisa you mean? They got married. Don was in a nursing home by that time. Stan asked me to go with him to the so-called wedding. He was the best man. It was pathetic. A wedding in a nursing home, can you imagine?"

Imagine? Jim had visions of Gothic darkness, the smell of carbolic acid. Don lying on a bed, sheets pulled up to his chin, only his face is visible, his wasted forehead, his waxy cheeks.

"Not that there was anything wrong with the nursing home," Maureen was saying. "In fact, the lobby looked like a Holiday Inn, soothing pastel art on cream-coloured walls, that sort of thing. But the room was what you'd expect in a nursing home: institutional furniture, medical equipment. Depressing. And Don was a vegetable. The whole ceremony was a farce."

Enter Lisa, wearing a hip-hugging mini and hot pink top, Lisa occupying Jim's brain. She still had the same effect on him, still managed to break through the carapace of his rational mind with her sexy smile and her come-on look. It happened every time Lisa's name came up. Jesus, was he still in love with her? He had no time to answer the question. Maureen broke into the scene playing in his head.

"Apparently they signed all the papers and made all the arrangements before Don had the stroke," Maureen said, and Lisa jumped right back on Jim's stage, in a bridal gown. "Lisa was pregnant, you know, and so they went through with the marriage. She had a baby girl last July."

The scene in Jim's head fractured and broke into a thousand tiny pieces. He had no courage to pick them up. He had nothing to model the new Lisa on. He had no mock-up for a pregnant Lisa, for a Lisa mother. For a moment he thought, is it possible that the child, that I – ? But no, that didn't work out time-wise. He couldn't have fathered the child. Lisa came into view again, Lisa the Widow. Funereal images swamped Jim's mind. A funeral scene was shaping up over Maureen's chatter, superimposing black crepe over bridal bouquets. Curtain. Bring down the curtain on the Lisa scenes!

Jim turned off the highway. The winding road to the dam required his full attention.

"I suppose it was a blessing that he died," Maureen said. "Can you imagine being married to a vegetable? Don was in a coma for months, a year, in fact. Stan and I went to the funeral. There was a service before the cremation. You should have seen Don's wife. Widow, I mean. Lisa. She was wearing this black knit dress, a mini, so tight it left nothing to the imagination. Alright, she's got the figure for it, but at a funeral! And the way she carried on, restless as if she couldn't wait to get out, tossing her hair, looking around. She didn't look grief stricken to me. I guess she'll be on the dating scene in no time. There was this flower arrangement on top of the casket and a black and white photo of a girl in school uniform. Don's daughter, Stan said. She died in an accident when she was seventeen. Apparently Don never got over it. The photo was his prize possession. At the end of the service we all watched the casket roll into the furnace, the retort I mean – the casket including the flower arrangement and the photo of the girl. Rather sinister, like father and daughter going to hell."

"Bizarre," Jim said. Especially the bit about burning Asu in effigy. Was that necessary? He didn't know Lisa had a macabre vein.

The conversation lapsed, and he focused on the road again.

"If you decide to buy a house in Toronto," Maureen said, "you should definitely give Stan a call."

Stan's name was coming up rather frequently in their conversation.

"Are you going out with him?" Jim said, and immediately corrected his lapse into familiarity. "Sorry. I shouldn't have asked. It's none of my business."

A blush appeared on Maureen's ivory skin. "That's alright," she said. "I didn't mean to make a secret of it. But I'm not recommending Stan to you because I'm going out with him. Stan is good at what he is doing. He has his finger on the pulse of real estate. He's made me a bundle selling the house."

What did I ever see in Maureen? Jim thought. She's all facts and figures. She has no sparkle, except for the reflection of her jewellery. Maureen was framed in gold: precious metal around her neck and dripping from her ears.

"By the way," Jim said, "if the site manager suggests going out tonight, my advice is: leave the jewellery at home. There's only one drinking hole, and it's a dive. Maybe he won't suggest it. It's a rough place."

"I can imagine. I've been told there is no hotel near the site. They are setting me up in a trailer for the night."

After the meeting, Brian did suggest going out for a celebratory drink. Maureen heeded Jim's warning, but the Disco Embalse had changed. It was a family restaurant now. The new owner had cut windows into the concrete, put in a patio and renamed the place El Pyramido. He was hoping to attract tourists.

"Nice place," Maureen said to Brian at the end of the evening. They were in the parking lot. Brian was holding the car door for her.

"Glad you liked it," he said.

"Jim told me it was a dive," she said and looked at Jim accusingly as if she had caught him in a lie.

"It was at one point," Brian said, "but it's all a matter of supply and demand."

He shut the door after Maureen and came around to Jim's side, grinning. "The whores have moved on to the next construction site," he said. "*Love pitches his mansion in the place of excrement.*"

JIM WANTED TO GO BACK to Asu and tell her: Santos was right after all. Don is dead. Or maybe he had another motive when he strolled through the aisles of the market, looking for her. He wanted to see Asu one more time before leaving Argentina. Just a chat, he told himself. Just a farewell. But the stall with the wooden statues was gone. In its place stood a table piled with jeans and ponchos. He asked the vendor about the wooden statues. She shrugged. *No lo sé, señor.*

Jim returned to the hotel, feeling cheated. He was restless, his brain addled by the heat of indeterminate longing. Snap out of it, he told himself. What do you want with Asu? There is no need to see her, to tell her about Don. She already knows that he is dead. But his mind did a dance of sideways dodging and came back to the main idea: he had to see Asu. No, he wanted to see Lisa, but Asu was the nearest thing to her. And at the drop of Lisa's name, his mind went into a fantasy loop. The confusion spread, the desire hardened. He decided to look for Asu at her cousin's house.

He got into his car and drove through the rain-slicked streets glistening in the light of the streetlamps. The outskirts of the city were sodden and dead. There was no getting away from the damp, from the exhalations of desire. He could feel the rain on the back of his hands even inside the car. The moist air stuck to his skin.

At last, Asu's *casita* appeared in the comet of the car's headlights. He parked around the corner and picked his way across the yard, unsure of the welcome, ready to retreat if Asu was not alone. He saw the yellow gleam of a kerosene lamp through the strips of the plastic curtain. The main house was dark, shuttered as it had been during his first visit, but he had an uneasy feeling that someone was watching him from behind the slats. His footsteps sounded hollow on the wet, trampled grass. As he came up to the shed, he heard the voices of two men arguing, the rapid-fire exchange of angry words.

"*No te vas a joder.*"

"*No te calentés, che.*"

The second voice sounded familiar. The plastic strips were dancing and turning in the wind. Jim caught a glimpse of a wiry body. Santos. He ducked around the corner, flattened his back against the wall of the shed, and listened to the timbre of the men's voices. The low rasp, that was Santos. The other man's voice was loud and brash: "She was no good, I tell you. A crazy bitch. You tried to palm off a crazy bitch on me. Then your sister comes back with a gringo and insults me in front of everyone. Put on your helmet, she says, or you'll lose your head. I don't want your whore of a sister. *Puta. Hija de puta.*"

"*Andate a la mierda!*" Santos said breathlessly. "Asu is too good for you." His voice was full of boiling, incommunicable pain, cracking with anger. Jim heard a scraping of chairs, the smack of flesh against flesh. The curtain swished. The ends of the plastic strips whipped the corner of the shed as the two men came plunging through the door, grappling each other like passionate lovers. Jim caught sight of their flushed faces, their ferocious bare-toothed grins inviting violence. They fell to the ground wrestling, Santos on top, holding a curly-haired man in a headlock, pinning his shoulder, pounding his body into the dirt. His opponent kicked back, scrambled up, grunted, and burrowed into Santos with a frenzy of flailing limbs.

There was a moment of breathless poise, then Santos fell back and collapsed on the grass. Jim saw a glint of steel – a knife, he realized as it hit the ground with a dull ring. The curly-haired man sprinted across the yard, vaulted the fence and was lost in the darkness of the field beyond. A motorbike roared into action and clattered down the street with an infernal blast. The noise faded to a tunnelling sound, an echoing beat, which Jim traced to his chest and recognized as his own pulse. It was a powerful drum beat that seemed to travel across the yard, reach Santos' body, and wake in him an inarticulate groan. In the light coming from the shed, Jim saw him clutch his stomach and blood pushing up between his fingers, a dark unstaunchable flow. He saw him twist and shift into a different dimension, the cosmos of near-death. A wave of pity ambushed Jim and washed away all caution. He stepped out of the shadows and crouched down beside Santos, but his arms were too stiff to comfort the dying man, and his lips too frozen to call for help. Only his eyes were capable of movement, taking in minute details, the matted and trampled blades of grass beside Santos' body, the curve of his parted lips, the tapering ends of his fingers grasping at his shirt as if to tug it off and expose the knife wound, the russet pattern of the blood stains on the fabric of his shirt, the sleeve pushed back from his wrists, revealing a watch. His own watch, Jim realized, the magic token he had given to Asu.

A rattling sound came from Santos' throat, a venting of inner voices. His eyes fastened on Jim, glazed over, and melted into the darkness of non-existence. Jim kept kneeling beside the body, bent over as if in prayer, in meditation, but it was fear that arched his back, a sense of unspeakable peril. He had never witnessed death before. He wanted to take the watch off Santos' wrist, remove any connection between himself and the dead man, but the thought of touching the body filled him with dread, took root in his veins, made his skin contract and his pores slam shut.

A long time passed, it seemed to Jim, before he was able to move again, to draw a level breath and look back at the shed. The plastic curtain had hung up on the rod and gave him an unobstructed view of the empty room with the grotesque funereal cross on the back wall. He turned and scanned the main house, hoping that Asu would appear at the door and explain the scene away, but the house remained shuttered. He got up on one knee at first, then jerked his body upright with a great effort, and walked stiffly across the yard, making himself walk to his car without looking back, step by step like a mechanical man. He drove to the hotel in a haze that admitted no coherent thought, only an unvaried sequence of images, a replay of the wrestling match and Santos on the ground with the lifeblood draining from his body, seeping into the earth.

Back in his hotel room, Jim checked his hands and his clothes for telltale signs of blood, the stigmata of the death he had witnessed, but the violence had left no mark on him, nothing to confirm that what he had seen was real. He washed up carefully nevertheless. He even scrubbed the soles of his shoes. He took off his clothes and soaked them in the bathtub in case they had been contaminated by the air in the yard where Santos had drawn his last breath.

The next morning and the day after, Jim checked the newspapers, studied the local news, read them line by line. Nothing about a murder. Perhaps a knifing in that dusty part of town was not worth a line in print.

IT WAS JIM'S LAST DAY in town. He woke up, riding the tail end of a cloudy dream, of dead men lying in open caskets, of funerals, magic watches, and Lisa in a tight black dress. The man in the casket was Don, no, Santos, his shirt oozing blood.

Jim opened his eyes and saw his two suitcases sitting on the floor, packed, ready to go. He closed his eyes again, pushed his face down into the pillow, shut out the dead men, and brought Lisa back on his mental screen for a solo performance. Yes, there she was, eyes rimmed with black eyeliner, wearing a mini dress and strappy heels, sitting on a barstool, impatiently crossing and uncrossing her legs, taking Jim's hand, sending a charge through his body, telegraphing memories of a tumbled bed, the musky smell of mingled bodies.

She reaches up and touches Jim's cheek. It's nice of you to come, she says, but you shouldn't talk like that in front of Don. Her lips are dangerously close to his. I said nothing. I didn't even open my mouth, he says. You did. You said that you are still in love with me. He shakes his head. I didn't say a word! You didn't say it out loud, but I heard you anyway, she says. The mental screen goes fuzzy. Jim comes out of the dream, his brain still working on a comeback. Why can I never think of good lines for myself? I need to take lessons from Lisa on how to write dialogue, on how to play head games, he thought, as his dream balloon popped, and he opened his eyes.

He shouldn't have opened his eyes. It was a mistake to let in the light. There was a definite link between night and imagination. Conjuring up Lisa worked better in the dark. Jim was afraid that the daylight would wipe out the last traces of her, that she would disappear from his waking thoughts, that he would never be able to resurrect her. My God, he could barely remember what she looked like. A year was a long time between phone calls, between embraces. No, it was longer than a year. Sixteen months. His night visions of Lisa were caught in a time warp. The Lisa of his dreams looked the way she did when they said goodbye at the airport in Catamarca. Jim couldn't imagine her with a baby girl unless he made her a miniature version of Lisa, and not even then. He couldn't coax Lisa back into a dream. He was inconveniently awake. It was an inconveniently bright day.

Jim got up, showered and dressed, his mind back on track in the real world.

After breakfast he dropped his car off at the leasing company, and then he was at loose ends, impatient to get through the leftover hours, until it was time to go to the airport. He walked back to the hotel. In the lobby, the receptionist waved to him: *Señor!* She had a pink message slip for Jim and a small package. The message read: "Lisa called from Toronto. Would like you to return her call."

Instantly the image of Lisa appeared in the discreet half-light of the lobby – a telepathically fixed outline, hotwired to Jim's brain, sparking Lisa, Lisa. He wanted to call back immediately, but he needed to get a grip on himself first and practise the words he would say, come up with decent lines for once.

In the elevator, on the way up to his room, he was thinking: she's didn't give the receptionist her last name. Is she Lisa Baker now? Or is she still/again Lisa Martinez? He preferred to think of her as Martinez. He didn't want even a shred of Don adhering to Lisa when he called her back.

In his room, he remembered the package the receptionist had given him. He sat down and unwrapped it to keep his fingers busy, to gain time and make up a Jim-Lisa dialogue. A small wooden box emerged from the wrapping paper. Inside the box was Jim's watch, with a note:

"Here is your watch back. Santos is dead. Simon killed him. It was murder, but Jaime Anqua paid the chief of police a *coima* to call it an accidental killing. I feel like someone has been burning my guts. Everything tastes of ashes. Time to get out of Catamarca. – Asu.

"PS: Did the magic work? Are you back with Lisa?"

ABOUT THE AUTHOR

Erika Rummel is the author of more than a dozen non-fiction books (social history, biography, translation) and a novel, *Playing Naomi*, published by Guernica (2009). She divides her time between Toronto and Los Angeles, and has lived in small villages in Argentina, Romania, and Bulgaria. She was awarded the Random House Creative Writing Award in 2011. *Playing Naomi* has been praised as a wry comedy "reminiscent of the corrosive but jovial cynicism of media satires like *The Larry Saunders Show* and *The Newsroom*" (Cynthia Sugars in *University of Toronto Quarterly*).

ABOUT THE BOOK

Argentina, 1979. Life has gone stale for Jim, an expat working in Catamarca. Everything is predictable until he meets Lisa. She has the starry eyes, the sensuous lips, and the tango steps that make all rational assumptions go away. Jim gives her top marks for animation but there is a warning at the end of his tip sheet: Danger. Lisa is a little too intense, a little too crazy, a woman with too many scenes playing in her head. Her antics don't faze Santos, a *curandero* who is looking for a medium to channel the dead and attract his lost sister. He lures Lisa to his compound in northern Argentina, where she becomes a pawn in a deadly family feud. Jim goes in search of Lisa. Tracking her down turns into a double mission – freeing Lisa from her captors and himself from the monotony of his life. It takes a fantastic journey through rugged country for Jim to realize that he loves Lisa just the way she is: unpredictable. The story unfolds against the background of a country under military rule. It is a place where kidnapping, violence, and death no longer make headlines, a place where you learn survival skills.

FSC
www.fsc.org
RECYCLED
Paper made from recycled material
FSC® C100212

Printed in March 2013
by Gauvin Press,
Gatineau, Québec